ACROSS BORDERS

Shuvashree Chowdhury

First published in India in 2013 by S. B. Saikia for Kaziranga Books

This second edition published in India in 2018 by CinnamonTeal Publishing

ISBN 978–93–86301–99–4

BISAC Code: FIC000000/FICTION/General

Typesetting and Cover design: CinnamonTeal Design and Publishing

CinnamonTeal Publishing
an imprint of CinnamonTeal Design and Publishing
Plot No 16, Housing Board Colony
Gogol, Margao
Goa 403601 India
www.cinnamonteal.in

For my parents Nitya and Mahamaya Chowdhury

Contents

Chapter 1

Leaving My Childhood

It was raining even that morning. Funny how at this age, when I tend to forget what happened yesterday, images of childhood come back with such force and clarity, as if illustrations in a book I read every day. I can still hear the rain; it was hammering on the tin roof all morning. Ma stood by the window in silence, gazing at the downpour. Rains are a frequent visitor in Assam, but I had not seen Ma looking out of the window so keenly before. Baba sat talking to Ronjit uncle, his cousin, who had arrived the previous night from Dacca. Leaning back on the chair and smoking a cigarette, Ronjit uncle held forth like a teacher in a classroom, while Baba listened silently. Gandhi, Nehru and Mountbatten - he kept mentioning them. Only eight at the time, I was not sure who they were, but was familiar with these names.

I vividly remember that day of 1948. Rainy days were usually good days; or so it seemed to me until that day. Three of us sisters were dressed and ready as usual, but were not sent to school. At first we thought it was due to the rain. Later we realized we were being readied for the sole purpose of meeting Ronjit uncle - a big man, we were told. Ma and Baba were present when I walked into the living room on the ground floor. I was fresh from bathing with water I had drawn from the well behind our house. Strong for my age, I had lifted the iron bucket with the thick coir rope tied to it. After transferring the water into another bucket, I had carried it into the makeshift bathroom, at a little distance from the house.

My waist-length hair was still damp from the mugs of water I had poured over myself head downwards. I had dried it by wrapping a gamcha - the red and white cotton towel, over my head, on my way back into the house. My damp hair had then been centre-parted and loosely braided in two, the ends tied together in red ribbons, by my sister Kalpana. At sixteen, Kalpana was more a self-designated guardian. She followed me into the living room along with Neelima, our youngest sibling. We stood side by side, awaiting Ronjit uncle. Before getting ready, Kalpana had ensured that Neelima, two years younger than I, was also dressed. Her shoulder-length hair was tied with a red ribbon in a ponytail. Three of us were identically dressed, in starched white shirts, pleated white skirts, with red waist belts and red ribbons in our hair. We would wear white socks and black shoes before we left home.

As we waited, I looked forward to our regular breakfast of chapattis or rice of the night before soaked in milk, topped with generous helpings of milk-cream and sugar. I looked towards Ma, but she studiously avoided my gaze, looking out of the window instead at the rain. She looked very sad and I thought I saw a thin film of tears in her eyes. Though curious, I chose to overlook it, as Ma looked sad more often than not lately. She even cried a lot. I think it began since Kalpana, Neelima and I returned with her from her maternal house. I would catch her flick the edges of her sari under her eyes, wiping the tears that trickled down her nose, as she went about her daily chores.

It was not only Ma's recent tears that were strange; circumstances seemed changed around here since our return. There was a new woman living in our home now. She was very pretty and occupied another wing of the house. I would look at her in awe, usually dressed in red saris and always decked in plenty of jewellery. She seemed like a newly married bride. In spite of my curiosity, I had gathered little as yet on her identity. The reason for her staying in our house was a closely-guarded secret.

"Don't you ever go to that part of the house," Ma had said to us sisters, holding us close and looking into our eyes searchingly. "You mustn't even talk to that woman who lives there."

And so we didn't. I hardly saw Baba much lately. Perhaps he was very busy at his clinic and had his meals and slept there at night, I assumed. After all, he was a respected physician of the locality.

Now I restlessly wished the whole ritual was over, expecting Ronjit uncle to walk in any moment. I looked in Baba's direction;

          Shuvashree Chowdhury

as he sat on his reclining chair, reading a medical journal. I did not have the courage to disturb his reserve, so walked up to Ma squeezing her fingers lightly. Then I tugged at her hand to get her attention.

"Ma, I'm very hungry," I said, when she looked down at me questioningly on my persistent tugging of her hand. "Can't we have breakfast and then meet Uncle? We'll be late for school, won't we?"

Ma nodded in response, briskly looking away. She returned her gaze to the rain outside, as if it were an interesting book. I looked at Baba once again, hoping to draw his attention into saying something, figuring Ma was not going to make a move without his initiation.

"Ronjit uncle will be down shortly," Baba replied crisply. But he hadn't removed his eyes from his reading material. "Your mother will serve food after he is here. We don't want to offend him."

Ronjit uncle walked in through the door, as if on cue. His imposing height and frame suddenly increased the door's diminutiveness. It happened every time Baba crossed it with his head bent. I looked from one man to the other, noticing their close resemblance. With nearly the same height and athletic built, the cousins looked more like brothers, although dressed differently. Baba wore a crisply starched white dhoti kurta, while his cousin wore a white shirt and trousers with a black leather belt. Ronjit uncle's black hair, damp from a bath, was plastered on his swarthy face, emphasizing his prominent features - a large pair of eyes and a big nose. He carried himself with a regal air, quite like Baba, with head held erect over upright back and shoulders. On noticing him, Baba stood up respectfully, taking a step forward to greet him.

"Come, come Ronjit-da, I hope you slept well," he said cheerfully, extending his right hand to take his cousin's. "The girls are all here."

Taking Baba's hand, Uncle glanced at the three of us simultaneously. His gaze appraising our faces for a second each, he gushed, "My pretty, pretty ladies, all so grown up."

His broad smile now softening his otherwise stern expression, he added, "I last saw them only months back during Durga Puja. They seem to have grown since then."

Ma had been standing aloof, her head partially covered with her sari pallu. On seeing Ronjit uncle, she promptly looked downwards, drawing the pallu further down over her forehead. She always did this in the presence of any male other than Baba. Ronjit uncle nodded, acknowledging Ma's presence from a distance. Both cousins sat down on the settee alongside the wall, while we remained standing.

Ronjit uncle looked from one to the other of us sisters, leaning comfortably on the cushioned back-rest of his seat. He asked us which class we were in at school, what our favourite subjects were and enquired about our interest in sports and extra-curricular activities, if we had any. Kalpana looked down shyly, averting his gaze, as she replied in her soft, mellow voice. Neelima barely muttered a few words in her childish lisps - more pronounced now out of nervousness. Always more confident and energetic than my sisters, I looked Uncle in the eye and spoke exaggeratedly as in an elocution competition.

"I am in the third standard. My class teacher is Miss Anuradha Borkotoky. She is Assamese, has small eyes, wavy hair, and is very young and pretty. She teaches us all subjects." Then after a deliberate pause for effect, I added "I am also my class monitor."

Ronjit uncle listened, impressed by my confidence and vivacity.

"Who would like to come with me to Dacca?" Uncle abruptly interrupted my monologue, including all three of us in his gaze. "I just started a school at Mihirpur. It is close to the family house where you visit for Durga Puja. The school is far bigger, with more students than you have at school here." Then fixing his attention on me, as my eyes had widened with excitement, he added, "It is a boarding school where a large number of girls live in two large dormitories. It has a big playing field too, where you can learn a lot of new games. Would you like to come with me?"

"Yes Uncle I want to come," I blurted excitedly. "It sounds like fun!"

Kalpana and Neelima remained silent, looking from Baba to Ma. I was independent and had a mind of my own even at eight. It was only later that I learnt the real reason for Kalpana's silence did not have much to do with her decisiveness or the lack of it. Unlike us, she was aware of circumstances leading to our leaving.

        Shuvashree Chowdhury

Neelima was too young and oblivious to anything amiss, as I was.

"It sure will be fun," Baba agreed, smiling indulgently at me. "You will learn a lot too. Your school here is small and does not have as many good teachers and facilities as Uncle's school. You will also make more friends there." Then turning to Kalpana, he added "Kalpana-ma, you must go too. There will be more choice in subjects for you there, though Neelima will benefit most from starting early."

"Neelima is not going anywhere," Ma sharply interjected, turning around to face the men squarely, finally something having grabbed her attention besides the rain outside. Then abruptly, in a strained voice choking with emotion, as if on the verge of breaking down, she added, "How will I live alone and what do I live for if all the children go away? Moreover, Neelima is still very young and needs her mother."

I was taken aback by Ma's reaction. I looked at her and then Baba and finally Ronjit uncle, to fathom what had brought on this unexpected outburst from Ma. My excitement and eagerness to go with Ronjit uncle notwithstanding, I suddenly felt a twinge of jealousy. Why did Ma only want to keep Neelima with her and not me? But I promptly deduced the reason for that. I was a troublesome, rebellious child, as Ma often mentioned. She would be glad to have me off her hands for a while, I brooded.

Ma always found it difficult to discipline and control me. I thereby took advantage, disobeying her. She would complain to Baba, to get him to discipline me. The reasons that deterred my being Ma's favourite, though she never consciously showed partiality to either of us sisters, made me Baba's. He liked my bold and confident ways, looking upon me more as the son he did not have. I rushed to stand beside him now, holding his hand in an assuring manner and tone.

"Baba you don't worry," I said, "I will be back very soon. I will learn new lessons and games and come and teach my friends here."

Still sitting, Baba put his arm around my waist, looked at Uncle and then nodded. Little did I suspect he did not want any of us to return. Kalpana remained silent, a sad look in her grey-green eyes. She came and took my hand in hers, pressing it reassuringly. Perhaps she was sad the implications of our going away eluded me so completely.

Ma's outburst had the desired effect and Ronjit uncle agreed that Neelima would stay. Baba gave in to the decision of his cousin. Kalpana and my departure reconfirmed, Kalpana followed Ma into the kitchen. Neelima and I stayed on with Baba and Ronjit uncle. Their discussions ranged from events leading to the Independence and Partition of India the year before, to the current socio-economic conditions. I listened intently, simultaneously playing with Neelima and her dolls.

In a while, Kalpana came out to the adjoining room, visible through the open door of the front living room where we sat. She had sitting-mats or ashans in hand, which she arranged neatly on the floor in a row alongside the wall. Then going inside, she briskly returned to place a kasha or bronze plate and glass in front of every mat. Ma followed, carrying two large serving-bowls, one of aloo-dum (spiced-potato) and another of begun-bhaja (fried egg-plant). Placing them in front of the plates, she went inside to return with another bowl of cholar-dal (Bengal gram).

"Everyone, come wash your hands and sit down," Ma called aloud.

The smell of the food was compelling; even though Ma's wavering voice was not.

All of us promptly rose, stepping into the dining room across the high concrete threshold. I was delighted at the sight and smell of the savoury breakfast. In the months since our return from Mihirpur, we had barely eaten anything but the basic. It was prepared today, perhaps for the benefit of Ronjit uncle, I thought. The quality of our eating was another big change, since our return. Whenever I questioned Ma as to why we were not eating like before she would sadly say that we must learn to practice abstinence. After we were seated cross-legged on the floormats, Ma served portions of aloo-dum, cholar-dal and a piece of begun-bhaja. Kalpana, back from another trip to the kitchen, served the white, steaming-hot luchis (refined flour puris) onto every plate.

Before we started to eat, a large hand-wash bowl made of kasha (bronze) was passed around. We washed our hands into it, with water from our respective glasses. I poked a finger into the puffed

    Shuvashree Chowdhury

centre of a luchi, watched the steam escape, before tearing a bite size portion pensively. After the first bite along with a dash of aloo-dum, I devoured it quickly. It was like I had forgotten their taste till now, and was not sure when I would eat it again. Kalpana successively served luchis Ma was frying on the charcoal kiln in the kitchen. Once we had had our fill of them, khejur gurer payesh or date rice pudding was served in completion of the meal.

We all stepped outside to wash our hands by the well. Ma and Kalpana swabbed the floor after clearing the dishes. Then they proceeded to have their meal in the kitchen. If it were not for Ronjit uncle's presence, they would have joined us, after serving us the last helpings. As was the custom in our house and many Bengali households then, the women ate after the men and children; at times in the kitchen when there were male guests. Eating on the floor was common and even well-to-do homes, ours being fairly so, did not always use dining tables. The rain was still pattering on our tin roof, though it had now reduced in intensity. It is due to this incessant rain but more so for the frequent earthquakes that our house, though built of timber, had a tin roof.

Ma, having finished her breakfast, called me to follow her to the bedrooms on the first floor.

"Maya, we have to pack your things and get ready," she said matter-of-factly, as I trailed the iron steps outside of the house following her, "Kalpana and you will leave with Ronjit uncle this evening."

All rooms in the house had easy accessibility to the outside, so at any sign of an earthquake we could evacuate easily. The region was prone to natural disasters - frequent floods and earthquakes. I still recall how at the first decipherable quiver of an earthquake, we would all rush outside and sit on the ground in front of the house. Baba and Ma sometimes even rushed us outside amidst a meal or a nap. At nights we usually realised late, but rushed out as soon as our parents or any of the neighbours felt the first tremor and raised an alarm.

Snakes abounded in and about our house. But we were not afraid of them. Rather we played with those that sneaked into the house, feeding them milk out of small bowls placed outside. Most snakes did not bite, unless threatened. But then perhaps I was just lucky for the eight years I lived there. They added to the cheerful associations of my childhood.

Once upstairs, Ma took out two small tin valises. The larger one in black was for Kalpana and a steel-coloured one for me. Into Kalpana's she briskly placed her few saris, blouses, undergarments and a pair of white open-toed sandals. In mine she packed two of my frocks, two skirts and two shirts along with knickers, petticoats and a covered shoe. Sitting on my haunches on the large four-poster bed, watching Ma pack my box, my eyes shone in excitement. It was the first time I had a separate one for myself. Whenever we went to the family home or to Ma's maternal house, the only places we ever travelled to, my stuff was packed into the large common suitcase.

I glanced at Kalpana sitting beside me, to share my enthusiasm, but to my amazement she looked distraught. I noticed tears streaming down her pale cheeks. I shifted my gaze questioningly towards Ma, but she had an expressionless, taut look on her face.

"Take care of Maya, like she were your daughter," Ma said earnestly, looking into Kalpana's eyes, then turning to face me, her hand stroking my hair she added, "Maya, always listen to your Didi and be good."

Kalpana nodded, simultaneously bursting into a stifled sob, a fresh bout of tears running down her cheeks. She hugged Ma fervently. Even Ma's reserve broke now, as she put her arms around Kalpana. They sat clinging to each other, sobbing as if someone had died. I looked from one to the other in total bewilderment. What was wrong with them and how silly could they be, I thought. We would return shortly from visiting Uncle's school, so why were they crying like this?

Hugging Kalpana and Ma simultaneously, I dismissed them mentally as weepy, sentimental fools. I was not going to let their gloomy mood spoil my optimism and cheer, I decided. I doubted I would have the opportunity to miss home. I did not know then, that I would be proven so right, in assuming I would never miss home. Once aware of the reason for our departure, I shut my home and my childhood in a dark recess of my memory. I would not return, not even mentally, nor miss home and my childhood.

"Don't worry Ma, I will listen to Didi and be good, I promise," I

		Shuvashree Chowdhury

said to pacify Ma. "Please don't cry. We will be back very soon."

Ma pulled me into her arms, then pulling back, tenderly stroked my head with both hands saying, "Now, that's my sona-mei (golden-girl)."

I could not help feeling a little sad as Neelima nestled up to Ma, as she sat down, sinking her face into Ma's lap from one side. Kalpana came and sat next to Ma on the other side, while I remained standing in front. Neelima then looked up sideways at me forlornly. I did not know that this was the last time we sisters would ever be this close together with Ma. Those few brief moments of intimacy between us will always remain indelibly etched in my mind. The bags packed, with Ma's urging we all came downstairs into the living room.

Baba and Ronjit uncle's conversation came to an abrupt halt on seeing us. I think now they were discussing the actual reason for Kalpana and my departure. Ronjit uncle, I learnt later, had tried to dissuade Baba from sending us away, but unsuccessfully.

Ma went into the kitchen to prepare lunch, followed by Kalpana. Neelima and I remained with Baba and Ronjit uncle. This time we were barely able to hear their solemn discussion, which they resumed in hushed tones. Lunch was late that afternoon. It was served in similar manner as breakfast in the adjacent room, only that the kasha plates were larger now. We took our seats on the floor-mats. Each plate was lined with a number of small empty kasha bowls, a slice of lemon, a pinch of salt and a large green chilli. In the centre of the plate was served shukto - mixed vegetables with bittergourd eaten at the start, moonger dal - cooked pulses atop a pile of steaming rice and jhuri aloo bhaja - shredded fried potato. The hand wash bowl was passed around.

Once we started eating, the rest of the dishes were served into the small bowls. Three varieties of fish were served. One was prawn cooked in coconut-milk called chingri maccher malai curry; the second was hilsa in mustard paste or shorshe ilish, as it is better known in Bengali. The third was fish in cumin paste or bualmaccher jeerepaturi followed by kosha mangsho, a deep fried mutton curry. Only Ronjit uncle and Baba were served each of the dishes. Neelima and I were served small portions of rice, with only the dishes we wanted. A tomato-and-date sweet chutney ended the well thought-out meal. Lunch was elaborate not only for the benefit of Uncle, I concluded, but for Kalpana and my departure as well. Ma had made sure to include both our favourite dishes, the prawn and cumin paste fishes were mine and Kalpana's the mutton one.

It would be the last in a really long time that anyone would consciously prepare my favourite dishes. One day my daughters, when grown, would do so, specially on my birthdays. A year ago, they celebrated my seventieth birthday with great aplomb. Ironically, my parents never celebrated my seventh birthday - the last one that I lived with them or any prior to that. After lunch, Baba and Ronjit uncle washed their hands into the hand-wash bowl. Then they left the room.

Neelima and I went outside to wash our hands by the well. It had stopped raining by now. After clearing our soiled dishes, Ma and Kalpana sat down to the meal they had so painstakingly prepared. Neelima and I sat with Ma and Kalpana, while they ate. After they finished, we went upstairs, leaving Baba and Ronjit uncle.

After a nap, Kalpana and I dressed for our journey. Ma came downstairs to the kitchen, to prepare tea. Once Kalpana and I were ready, we brought our valises downstairs to the living room. Baba and Uncle were served tea in steel tumblers. On seeing us, Ma brought us tea, which we drank solemnly. She did not drink tea.

"Are we ready to go ladies?" Ronjit uncle asked, setting his empty tea cup down. "Let's get going, or we'll miss the night train."

We trooped outside; gathering around the olive-green jeep Baba had organised to take us to the railway station. Kalpana and I carried our respective boxes with us. After shaking hands with Baba, Ronjit uncle got into the seat beside the driver, setting his bag on the seat behind. Baba looked sombre shaking Uncle's hand, as though he had just been reprimanded.

Kalpana touched Ma's feet, both their eyes filling up again. Neelima held their hands simultaneously, looking desolate. I noticed that Kalpana did not so much as look at Baba, let alone touch his feet. I touched Baba's feet and he placed his hand on my head. He turned towards me when I looked at him, but without looking me in the eye. I could not decipher his downcast eyes then,

                    Shuvashree Chowdhury

assuming it to be his effort at hiding his sadness at our going. But now I know that it had to have been guilt. I touched Ma's feet.

Then Kalpana and I climbed into the back seat of the jeep, along with our valises. I turned to look at our home for one last time through the jeep's window. Against the darkening sky stood the grey, double-storeyed, tin-roofed house, visible beyond the bamboo-fence and rain-soaked ground in front. The memory stays with me vividly to date.

I saw my childhood home again, only much later during a visit, in my twenty-sixth year. At the time, I would be working in Delhi and Baba would be in his last surviving year. I would then return very briefly, only to ensure Ma receive a share of Baba's house, rightfully also hers. The idea of renewing my bond with the house of my birth or with Baba would not be on my agenda.

I don't know if it is my eight-year memory of my childhood home that would propel me to build my own home one day, or its recollection from my short visit a few months before Baba's death. It would perhaps be the reminiscence of the security and well-being of family and home as a child that would shape my dream of building my own home. But it had to have been the recall of a financially independent woman that would fuel the determination to do so.

I was to live my life, doggedly working towards the ownership of a real home, from which I could never be displaced, as from my childhood home, by my own father. I often wondered afterwards how I didn't read into the tear filled eyes of my mother; or understand Baba's distant and formal demeanour in the days leading to our departure. How did I miss interpreting Baba's absence, or our frugal meals till the last two lavish ones on the day we left? There were all the signs to read and yet I had not comprehended then, the circumstances leading to our going away that day.

As I watch the rain from my study window, writing this chapter today, I can smell the rain-soaked grounds of my childhood home. I would be technically homeless for a long time. It would be much later that I would build a real home, never feeling at home in all the houses I would reside in until then.

That day in 1948, Kalpana and I left to cross over to another life with Ronjit uncle across the Pakistan border. There was no Bangladesh yet and was not going to be for a long time. Mihirpur is a small town near the city of Dacca, in erstwhile East Pakistan, currently Bangladesh. I was about to transcend the border of my childhood.

After the age of eight, I was sucked into adulthood like quicksand. It would only be fifteen years hence, that I would again cross the border back into India. After my graduation in 1964, I would return to work, marry, raise a family and live the rest of my life on the Indian side. A few years later, in 1971, the home that I grew up in was to become a part of Bangladesh, no longer of East Pakistan as when I would leave it. As the country was recontoured into Pakistan, Bangladesh and India ensuing much turmoil, so did my life across its border in developing three distinct identities - childhood, adolescence and adulthood - get chiselled by the rough hands of time and experiences.

Chapter 2

The Two Wives

I left behind my childhood at the age of eight, hauled into adulthood by the follies of my parents. When Ma married Baba, she was only twelve and he twenty six. One would assume their age difference would call for maturity on his part and appointment as her guardian lifelong. But that was far from the reality. Although there was a statute since 1929 to restrain child marriages, its power in controlling this social evil was dismal. Barely stepping into adolescence at the time of her wedding, Ma's marriage was practically over by the time she stepped into adulthood. The initial few genuine years of their marriage, when they lived as man and wife, were effectively utilized in bearing one child after another, to a total of nine. By the time Ma was past the best of her childbearing years, Baba got himself a new bride.

This was before the passing of the Hindu Marriage Act in Parliament in 1955 so his action was irrefutable. A Hindu man could then have as many wives as he pleased. A woman, as unlikely as it may seem in the present, died the wife or widow of her polygamous or even philandering husband. Usually financially dependent, she was lucky if he provided her shelter in his abode till her end. Thus even after her husband's second marriage, Ma continued to live in his house, though as a second-rate resident now. The gates to her parent's house, open for a visit, were no longer open for her to return permanently. She was fortunate, considering she had nowhere else to turn, that Baba allowed her to continue living in his house. After her death, Ma's corpse would leave her husband's dwelling, as was considered auspicious.

Ma now lived in the smaller part of the house, divided into two wings to accommodate both wives. She wondered how all this came about. How did she get relegated to this inferior position?

She had done her best in being the finest wife she had been taught or knew to be, bearing Baba nine children in succession. After everything she had done for him and his family, her amputation from his life, his taking on a much younger wife in her absence, was sudden and crucifying.

It was not as if Ma was not still good-looking either; rather she was an epitome of beauty. She had a honey-coloured radiant complexion, shapely facial features with high cheekbones, a sharp nose and a well-constructed mouth. Her almond shaped luminous eyes ended in slits, giving her a slightly northeastern look and her long black hair accentuated her tall, lean frame.

After all, it was Ma's exquisite looks that had sealed her fate with the tall, swarthy complexioned, handsome young doctor, Baba. He carried his well chiselled face with an arrogant upward tilt, adding to his distinguished personality. After qualifying in medicine from Calcutta, he had at first set up a private practice in his home town, Mihirpur. It was at a short distance from Dacca, then a part of India. Baba is believed to have turned down numerous marriage alliances, as the women were not sufficiently good-looking. His quest for beauty had ended on seeing Ma. He had visited her home with his entourage of five family-members including his parents. Ma had walked into the room with shy, downcast eyes, balancing a tray of sweetmeats. She set it down on a table in front of him, without even noticing him. The sight of Ma's angelic face had brought on Baba's instant approval. The marriage was therein confirmed and very shortly solemnized.

Ma dropped out of school to get married, having passed the sixth standard by then. She was the eldest of six siblings, three girls and two boys following her. Her parents, even though financially sound, were pleased to begin early the process of dispensing their duty of marrying off the girls. In fact, they considered themselves blessed to commence the marriages of their children rather well, having found Ma a qualified, eligible groom.

After the wedding, Ma went to live with Baba's joint family. She was little aware of the intricacies of keeping house at the time. But she picked up the ropes fast, and got absorbed in the net of domesticity. As the eldest girl child in her own family, she had been used to helping her mother with domestic chores, so she

    Shuvashree Chowdhury

easily fit into the role of homemaker. It was in the role of wife that she seemed to be taking baby steps.

Ma was not only beautiful, but of a good temperament, warm, caring and dutiful towards her elders. She was mature for her years, and carried out her domestic responsibilities rather well. Soon she became the favourite of all adults and children in the joint family. A girl like Ma would be the ideal wife any man could dream of having, but Baba was not just another regular small-town man. He was initially as happy with his choice in bride as his family, but soon the differences in their mental wavelength started to surface. Baba concluded that what he wanted was not just a model wife, but an interesting companion, a partner with whom he could communicate at various levels. But their age, educational and intellectual differences came in the way of that. In trying to bridge their mental gap, Baba encouraged Ma to read, even if she was unwilling to continue her formal education. But she was reluctant.

With children coming along, Ma did not find the need for further formal education or reading. What use would it be, she wondered, in dispensing her duties as wife, mother and daughter-in-law? Girls in Ma's time, still common in India, are brought up to consider marriage a bond with a man's entire family, not merely to him. Wasn't she already executing her responsibilities well towards all of them? If his entire family was happy with her, she presumed he must be too. She had given birth to a child almost every alternate year since her marriage, so it was apparent she did not neglect her physical responsibilities to her husband either. Additionally, as part of a joint family, she brought up her children keeping in mind the needs of the entire family.

However to Ma's chagrin, she soon learnt that her husband expected much more from his wife. Perhaps his education, city upbringing and resultant exposure, as compared to other men of their town, made it so. As a village girl, this was beyond Ma's comprehension and thereby abidance. For example, Ma was naturally beautiful, but Baba preferred sophistication. He wanted to groom her in the way he had seen women in the city. Baba would often bring her makeup - lipsticks, kohl, face powder and rouge, in addition to perfumes, expensive saris and jewellery. But Ma had no inclination towards makeup and to his dismay did not use any, not even to please him. She wore the silk saris and jewellery, but that too only on festive occasions. Ma found great comfort in her simplicity; little realizing it might one day cost her so dearly.

The most vital ritual of Ma's beauty regime was the application of a thin layer of coconut oil on her face at night, followed by a finger-massage with light strokes, finally wiping off with a thin muslin cloth. She used mustard-oil as body-oil, instead of the perfumed ones Baba brought her, using soap only on occasion. She wore her sari the traditional Bengali way, not in the sophisticated way of city bred women. Her long hair, always drenched in coconut oil, would be tied in a plain bun behind her head. She never used scented hair oils, or wore fancy hairstyles except for wearing a real gold clip with tiny bells on her bun, when she decked in jewellery on festivals. Ma was the quintessential Bengali housewife and mother, though with her slender physical frame, she looked far from matronly.

There would be little conversation between Ma and Baba from the start, except on the subject of their children, or any incident she needed to have him know of. As far as Ma was aware, like her, most women did not speak much with their husbands; neither did husbands find the need for it. She little imagined then that the lack of communication would gnaw at her marriage, making Baba find communicative companionship elsewhere. In her naivety, she had assumed the thick dash of vermillion she wore on the parting of her hair and the big vermilion bindi she sported high on her forehead would keep her husband safe and away from all evil. After all, were they not visible symbols of her safeguarding her husband's longevity, ensuring he remained bound to her forever?

* * *

It was late one evening. Married for a few years now, Baba was returning home from visiting a patient in the neighbouring village. He was riding his bicycle by the river's edge, about to step onto the boat with it, in order to cross the river. His mind raced ahead, to the steaming hot rice and maccher jhol (fish curry) with accompaniments, that would be placed before him after a quick wash on his arrival home. The acute hunger rumbling of his

    Shuvashree Chowdhury

stomach perhaps made him oblivious to his surroundings, which in any case he was familiar with since childhood. Suddenly he felt the excruciating pain of something hard like a shaft of bamboo hitting the back of his head with brutal force. He toppled off the bicycle, falling sideways on his face, to the ground.

The last thing Baba recalled before he passed out was the sudden numbing of the part of his head that was struck. He had seen his blood gushing onto the grassy ground in front, close to the water's edge. When Baba awoke, to his surprise he was comfortably in his own bed. It was the same one Ma had customarily brought along with the rest of the bedroom furniture, when she first arrived. His head hurt, but slowly acquainting his eyes to the steady late morning sunlight, he opened them wider. Ma was seated at his feet looking worried, chanting something under her breath, possibly prayers. Noticing his eyes were open, she visibly heaved a sigh of relief and then promptly ran out to call the rest of the family. So like Ma not to care for a few moments of privacy with him, Baba thought resignedly.

Baba's father came in looking anxious, followed by his mother, his two brothers and their wives. Baba blinked in the bright sunlight coming through the large window, in an attempt to fix his gaze on them. Though not aware, he had slept through two successive nights, from the heavy medication. With sudden recollection of the night of the attack, thinking it to be just the night before, he sat upright.

"Baba, do you know who attacked me?" Baba asked his father, without prologue, facing him seated at the foot of the bed, "why would someone want to kill me I wonder? I have been away long and I don't know of any enemies I might have here already."

In going over the details of the incident mentally, Baba shuddered to think how lucky he had been, to survive the battering. It had perhaps lost full impact, due to the distance of the attacker from him, seated as he was atop his bicycle at a height. Nonetheless, if he had been left to lie there undetected, he realized, he might have bled to death. He was fortunate to have been found, considering the late hour and the darkness that he had laid enveloped in.

"Yes, we traced the perpetrator of this cowardly act," his father replied sullenly, and then suddenly turning angry he added, "My son, this place is not safe for you to live in anymore. You were lucky to have survived this time, but we cannot afford to take another chance. All sorts of crazy people seem to be on the prowl."

It had been learnt that Baba's assailant, awaiting his return in the dark, was another neighbourhood doctor's aide. The elderly doctor by the name Kailash Bonik was suffering losses after the arrival of another and perhaps better qualified doctor (Baba). He had wanted him killed, or at least frightened off. It was, however, difficult to tell whether it was the doctor's personal idea to kill his junior or the result of a bout of brainstorming by his staff and compounder.

The reason Kailash Bonik had started losing even his regular patients, was more significant than that the villagers were keen to be treated by one recently educated from the city of Calcutta. The new doctor was kind to the poor, often treating them for free, if they could not afford to pay his fees. He supplied medicinal mixtures for common illnesses at affordably low prices. He prepared the concoctions at home, several of which in later years would bear his children's names, for easy recall by the illiterate village people. His potions were becoming as popular as his kindness. Moreover Baba was available on call twenty-four hours. He would rush to a patient at any time of day or night if they were unable to come to his clinic. Baba was passionate about his work, which was much appreciated, resulting in his popularity.

"Baba, I cannot run away in fear," Baba replied forcefully, looking his father in the eye, the jerk making him wince from the shooting pain on his bandaged head, "people here need me. The village needs someone who can save them from that fleecing Doctor Bonik."

The family, extremely worried after the initial shock of the news had settled, insisted that Baba listen to his father. With the combined persistence of his family members, Baba eventually gave in. It was thereby unanimously decided that Baba could not remain in Mihirpur, it no longer being safe for him to do so. Baba's father had immense faith in his son's capability. He knew what Baba lacked for in experience, he compensated for by a strong intuition about the causes of illnesses. His patients had faith on his diagnosis and cure.

    Shuvashree Chowdhury

Baba's father was certain he would restart his practice successfully anywhere, so advised him to go to a distant land. He would rather have him away in safety, than live in constant fear of his son's life. Baba agreed to leave his hometown. He could have gone back to Calcutta, but he preferred to serve the poor, where there was lack of medical aid. The place he chose was one he had learnt of from others in Mihirpur who had their businesses there. It was a small town called Barpeta in Assam in the east of India. This was in pre-independent India and before the existence of Pakistan, much before the conception of Bangladesh. Ma had no say in the matter at all. She merely followed her husband.

* * *

Baba bought a small house with a piece of land in Barpeta, close to the main market. Ma and their only child, a girl, joined him subsequently. The couple started life over. In time they would build themselves a much bigger house. Baba set up his medical practice quite effectively as expected, building his clinic within the extensive house grounds. Due to the rough terrain of his newly acquired domicile, he often visited his patient's houses on horseback, in addition to his bicycle. He had bought himself a horse and a bicycle, which eased his commuting considerably. Soon he was a popular, respected figure in the locality. In addition to selling his medicines from his clinic at home, he hired the services of four men to sell them in the local bazaar. To draw the attention of people to the colourful mixtures in transparent glass vials, the salesmen danced to popular tunes, incorporating in them the names of the medicines.

The medicinal mixture for common cold was bottled in the name of Kalpana, the eldest daughter, for fever and muscular pain it was Maya, the name of their sixth child, and the one for malaria was named Mohini after Ma. There were quite a few more. The palm-sized glass bottles had portion markings pasted on them in white paper, to facilitate consumption of the accurate measure, since spoons were uncommon then. In a short time, Baba's potions became very popular, doing brisk business. The medicines could not all be sold without the physical examination of the patient, leading patients to throng his clinic. Selling the medicines in the bazaar was good advertisement, ensuring he had a steady flow of patients. Baba had good business acumen for a doctor, which was but natural, since he hailed from the Vaidya Saha business community of Bengal.

In spite of his strong business insight, Baba was kind to the poor and needy, and this added to his goodwill. His patients trusted him, knowing he would not sell his medicines or charge fees only to make fast money. As before, he did not charge the poor who he knew could not afford to pay for his services or medicines. At times out of sheer gratitude, they brought him vegetables or fruits grown in the tiny portions of land around their huts, also fish from the ponds or eggs and poultry. He accepted these graciously, handing them over to Ma proudly as his earnings. With the money he saved, Baba soon bought a grocery shop in the bazaar area, selling all essential commodities. He brought his elder brother Gour along with his family from Mihirpur to run the shop, giving him good commission on the sales.

In the meantime, Ma busied herself running the house. She got pregnant almost every alternate year. Between giving birth and raising her children, her time passed fruitfully. If not for the children, it would have been difficult for her to spend the unending days, habituated as she had become to the constant demands of a joint family. Moreover now her parental house was not nearby, so she had no one to really visit. Living with a large joint family in Mihirpur after marriage had prepared Ma for the rigours of managing a household and a family on her own. She had little experience when she first came as a bride, but being a keen learner, by the time they moved and set up house, she was well versed in domestic intricacies, including the raising of children.

Ma turned out to be an excellent cook, taking a great interest in culinary intricacies, even though she did not prepare non-vegetarian dishes other than fish. She was reluctant to cook meat. Baba did not mind, preparing the chicken or mutton dishes himself, when he was in the mood. He had learnt to cook when at medical college in Calcutta, while his mother returned briefly to the family home in Mihirpur. She had accompanied her son to Calcutta, taking an apartment in Nimtala Street with him, from where it was not difficult for him to commute to Medical College on College Street.

     Shuvashree Chowdhury

Having his mother around, Baba could concentrate on his studies, without the need to worry about running a household as well. Baba's father visited them, combining the trips with business.

In all, Ma gave birth to nine children. But only three lived beyond the age of six years. The first two were male children, stillborn at her parent's home. She had gone there well in time for the delivery, as was the common practise for women, staying on for a few months after giving birth. At thirteen years, during the birth of her first child, Ma was physically and emotionally hardly prepared for birth and bringing up of children of her own. She would return to her husband within a month or two of rest after every birth, only to get pregnant again, thereby adding to her weakness. Ma's third offspring, who was the first to see the light of day, was unfortunately female. It was this girl child aged two years, later named Kalpana, who Ma brought with her, to her new life at Barpeta in Assam.

Ma never gave birth to another male child but had six girls in succession. Of the nine children only three made it into adulthood, while the others did not survive beyond infancy and childhood. At the time, epidemics like malaria, typhoid and tuberculosis were rampant, especially in remote areas in Assam. Unlike in the present, these diseases proved fatal, often entire villages perishing due to an outbreak. Ma and Baba's second girl after Kalpana, died aged six, from a sudden bout of high fever and shivering, possibly malaria. The third daughter died from an outbreak of cholera in the village. I was the fourth-born girl. The fifth girl Neelima, younger than me by two years, also lived a full life.

The sixth girl succumbed to a bout of intestinal worms in infancy, even before Baba, injection in hand, could administer it. The seventh, last of Ma's children, died at the age of four, from a fall from the balcony of the first floor at home. She had been the prettiest, with light brown hair, greyish-brown eyes, and a radiant pink complexion. Distraught at the loss of one child after another, Ma wondered whether she was cursed. Why should this be happening to them, she asked God repeatedly, when her husband saved so many lives? Feeling cheated, she cried till she felt she had no more tears left. Then the simple village girl that she was, Ma reconciled to her fate, accepting her losses as the will of God. She counted each loss as revered sacrifices she had made to appease the Almighty, possibly for a grander purpose. With a doctor husband, she had little to blame the children's deaths on, but the mystical.

She knew Baba loved his children, and she believed he had done everything in his power to save their lives. He was after all powerless against God's will. In later years, I often wondered, would Baba have tried harder if there was any male child to save? Would the added effort have saved them? Perhaps so, but Ma never could imagine that the gender of her children might have had anything to do with her husband's inadequate efforts or competence as a doctor. Baba desperately wanted a male child to carry on his lineage, to become a doctor and learn the ropes of the trade from him, to take over his practice one day. In spite of Baba's goodheartedness, added to his education and exposure, he possibly succumbed to the chauvinism of wanting a son. Why could he not consider raising us daughters as sons?

* * *

Only three of us girls, Kalpana, Neelima and I, out of Ma's nine children, would live full lives, going on to marry and have children. Just when Ma thought she had lived her share of losses and suffering, felt insulated to any further emotional upheaval, life struck her the biggest blow. It happened after the death of her last child. She and Baba had gone home to Mihirpur for the festival of Durga Puja with the three of us. It was the only time of year that the entire joint family got together. Ma and Baba were going to be part of the family celebrations after several years. They looked forward to meeting their respective families. Each year one of Baba's uncles, with his wife and children, were assigned to conduct the five day Puja. It included the Sashti Puja on the first day, the next three days of the Puja, till the bisharjan (immersion) on the fifth and final day in the river that ran just behind the family temple.

After the Durga Puja celebrations that year, Baba returned home to Barpeta in Assam. Ma stayed back with us girls for the Lakshmi Puja, which is customarily conducted at the venue of the Durga Puja, a week later. After the immersion of the idol of Lakshmi, along with Ma, we left for her parent's house a few miles away. She intended to stay there till Kali Puja, which is celebrated by Bengalis

Shuvashree Chowdhury

on the day the rest of India celebrates the festival of Diwali. Our school back home would be closed till then.

We were at Ma's parents' house, when one evening, much to her curiosity, a messenger came from Baba's house in Mihirpur. The news he conveyed hit her like shrapnel.

"Boudi, Dada-babu has married again," he said urgently, when Ma met the elderly house-aide across the fence of her parent's home; "we got the news only this morning."

She stared at the man in disbelief, her mind without sensation, as if just blasted. Slowly she regained her composure. Still mentally dumbfounded at the verbal blast, she reconfirmed the implication of the messenger's words, visible in the sympathetic eyes of the aged man. Then Ma bolted inside to tell her parents.

The news of Ma's world collapsing was as crisply delivered to her as the news of death. It was after all the death of her marriage, and superfluities would not tone down the impact of the blow. Ma was not in the know of any other woman in Baba's life. She was neither aware of anything so wrong in their marriage, for Baba to take a drastic step to marry again without informing her. Ma, leaving us with her mother, on her father's advice, rushed with him to her marital home in Barpeta. She could try to salvage any remnants of her marriage, if at all that was possible. It would perhaps be like trying to recover prized belongings from the cinders, after a fire has devoured one's home. On the way, her initial disbelief turned to rage at Baba's impertinence in bringing another woman into their home, that too as his wife.

After the overnight train journey, followed by a tedious bus ride, wherein Ma relived the years of her marriage, she felt ready to confront her husband. On reaching the house, Ma barged inside. She pushed aside the gate of the bamboo fence, heading to the clinic, knowing Baba would be there.

"What is this I hear?" Ma said venomously, seeing Baba seated behind his doctor's desk, "you've married again?"

Seeing the ferocity in her eyes, the stern expression on her face, like he had never seen before, Baba's face lost colour. He looked at her sheepishly, as if caught committing a heinous crime. After a moment of dithering from the suddenness of Ma's barging in and her accusation, Baba decided to confront the issue.

"Please forgive me Mohini," he blurted to Ma's surprise, igniting in her hope that he would reverse the wrongdoing. Then abruptly looking away to avoid confronting her hurt look, in response to what he was just about to say, he whispered softly, "Please leave me, I beg of you."

Ma stared at Baba in astonishment for a few seconds. Her sliver of hope cruelly lambasted on the floor of his cruelty, she slouched on the desk in front, unable to bear his temerity. Her father, who was a step behind and just as shocked, put a hand on her shoulder in a bid to allay her. The candour of Baba's words, their implication of his forsaking her so callously, was as sharp as that of a wasp's sting on her face. She was amazed at his trite attitude, the banishing finality of his words.

Coming from Baba who she had so much respect for, whom she looked upon as a man of character and principles, it was unbelievable. How the emergence of a new woman in his life had changed him, making him unrecognizable, she thought. But Ma was a proud woman, whose self-esteem instinctively usurped the hurt she felt. She composed herself, bracing herself from asking him another word. On the way here, she had felt she had the right to question him, entitled to demand from him an explanation, perhaps even threaten him to send the other woman away. But the firmness and conviction of his decision, the manner of its conveyance, rendered her wretchedly speechless now. Losing loved ones to death like she had the children was painful to say the least, but she had not lost herself then.

The desertion by her husband, the humiliation of his remarrying and then asking her to leave him was devastating. This blow was possibly worse than news of his death might have been. She felt the lump in her throat and the simultaneous constriction in her chest choking her. Even a garbage bag is treated better, the used one first disposed, before a fresh one is installed. Baba had taken on a new wife, without a decent send-off to Ma, least of all any information. Any attempt to speak, she realized, would squeeze her heart, wringing out tears she thought had dried forever. Ma decided she was not going to allow the perpetrator of her emotional fragility see its outpourings. So she picked up her bag, along with the remnants of her dignity, and taking her

   Shuvashree Chowdhury

father's hand walked out the door, shutting it firmly behind her.

Ma, along with her father, took the train back home to Mihirpur, numbed into silence the entire journey. She decided not to tell us girls yet that our father had taken on another wife, that we had been unceremoniously banished from his life. On her return, slowly pushing her hurt aside, she began to worry about how she was going to bring us girls up now. She had no money and we were still very young. Ma knew her parents could not bear her burden, certainly not along with us children. They had as yet to marry off her younger sisters. Baba's parents were not willing to take on our responsibility either. They expected her to accept the veracity of her situation as Baba's first wife and go and live with him. In spite of herself Ma concluded she had little option than to swallow her pride and return to her husband's house after all. Why deny us children a good upbringing, make us grovel in poverty, when we were as much Baba's responsibility as hers?

How dependent she really was as a woman, Ma thought desperately, first as daughter, then wife, now most as mother. In spite of being shunned by her husband, she had to find in herself the humility to return to him for her sustenance. It was going to take her a while to brace herself emotionally, before returning to the scene of her dishonour, which would be constant thereon. Till she could muster the strength to face Baba and his new wife, Ma came to live at Baba's parent's house with us girls. Living with her own parents long would allow room for talk, and could prove detrimental to the marriage prospects of her sisters. Ma was unable to ask her in-laws for money for her personal needs, so she made do with mere food and basics. Baba's cousin Ronjit uncle, elder to him by a few years, enraged at Baba's neglect of his wife and children, took up the responsibility to give Ma some pocket money regularly.

Ronjit uncle had a flourishing business that he started after his return from the First World War. He had been a soldier in the British army and had won awards and recognition at war, including good contacts. Being affluent now, he undertook a lot of philanthropic work for people in his hometown, by founding a school, college, hospital and medical centre. He thought of it as his social and moral obligation. Helping members of his family, including his cousin's wife, was the least he could do. Ma gratefully took his aid out of sheer necessity. But it expedited her decision to return to her husband's house in Assam. After all, it was Baba's responsibility to provide for her and his children. Why should she depend on handouts from his cousin? Even if she had to share it with another woman, her husband's home was still her rightful home, as his first wife. Therefore, she returned with us girls.

Ma assertively walked into Baba's clinic one morning, with us girls in tow, looking at him defiantly. She was not about to plead with him to take her back, she decided, rather was going to exert her right to live here in the house. Why should she beseech and grovel, when he was in the wrong? How did he think he could get away by shirking his responsibility towards the children? He could live with his new wife if he pleased, as long as he provided for her and his children. When Baba saw us girls, and Ma's defiant look, he could not turn us away. Though he had taken on another wife, Baba was not a philanderer. What option did he have, but to allow us shelter in his house. In fact, he was known to be kind hearted and generous. We were given a corner room on the ground floor of the house, where Ma renewed life afresh, living there till her death.

It was nearly three days, before Ma got a first glimpse of the woman who had displaced her in her husband's life. That morning Ma was by the well behind the house, putting the clothes to dry on the line. She saw a face just above the sari she had hung. Ma froze in recognition, a dagger passing through her heart, taking her breath away. Thereafter she felt no pain, no anger, not the slightest twinge of jealousy. Numbness had taken over, rooting her to the ground. This is how she would feel about this woman - anaesthetized, till her dying day. This woman had usurped Ma's position as wife, robbed her of the status of the lady of the house, relegating her to becoming a stranger in her own home. Slowly regaining composure, Ma became acutely selfconscious of still wearing sindur on the parting of her hair, and the shakha, paula and loha around her wrists.

Why was she still adorned in the symbols of marriage of Bengali women, when her marriage was in reality dead, Ma pondered? The shakha (shell bangle) mirrors the qualities of the moon, implying

    Shuvashree Chowdhury

that a woman remains serene and calm; and the paula (coral bangle) is beneficial for health. The loha (iron) signifies that a relationship assumes the qualities of iron - to become tough and enduring, which hers had failed miserably to do. But then, she would continue to wear these visual signs of her extinct marriage till the death of her husband. So what if these symbols had proven ineffective in warding off the biggest threat to her marriage - another woman? Ma now looked closer at Baba's second wife. She was wearing the identical symbols of marriage, except hers shone brighter from newness and perhaps from requited love, unlike hers.

* * *

Baba met Ashalata on a visit to a patient, she being the sister of the man suffering from jaundice. The first time he saw her at the bamboo-fence of her brother's modest single-storied house, he was struck as if by lightning by her beauty. She had large, dark beguiling eyes shielded by her lush eyelashes, comparable to a deep sea. With a luminous heart-shaped face, wavy, black, centre-parted hair, cascading down to the back of her knees, she was like a Lakshmi pratima (idol). But what grabbed his attention away from her face, was the all-white cotton sari she was draped in, with no trace of jewellery or make-up, not even kohl, starkly depicting her widowhood. She carried herself with grace, leading him into the house. Baba was bewildered at the irony of a woman so young and beautiful, destined to lead an existence devoid of colour, severing all ties with humanly pleasure.

As a widow, Ashalata was supposed to stay out of the way of visitors, especially young, male ones like Baba. But she had come to lead the doctor to her brother's bedside. His wife was beside herself with grief and worry, weeping at his bed-ridden feet, after a severe bout of his vomiting. The other inmates of the house - her brother's two sons, were away at school, having delivered the message of their father's state to Baba. After assessing the patient's condition, Baba gave him a bottle of his medicinal-mixture to arrest his nausea and vomiting. He also gave him a bottle of liver tonic, advising him to follow a strict diet. After Baba had completed his medical call, Ashalata led him outside through the low doorway.

"Dactar-da," she said in a soft mellow voice, handing over his bag and fee of Rs. 3 (he charged Rs. 2 at his clinic) at the fence-gate, "thank you so much for coming promptly."

In the course of the next few visits, Baba became a close friend of Ashalata's family. Everyone called him Dactar-dada. It was not long before he learnt the particulars of Ashalata's misfortune. Her husband had died on the night of their marriage, even before it was consummated, of a snake bite not uncommon in those regions. The poisonous snake had crept into a vacant room during the festivities, coiling itself comfortably on the damp floor. The groom walked into the room in the darkness after the wedding, stepping on its tail. The reptile dug its poisonous fangs sharply onto his bare feet, before slithering away. Ashalata walked in on her husband lying on the ground, frothing at the mouth. By the time she could recover from the shock and get help, he breathed his last in front of her. The husband's family, who were due to spend the night in her house, were convinced she was a bad omen.

The next morning, Ashalata's husband's family left the house with his corpse, rather than with the newly married couple, as planned.

"My brother's soul will never rest in peace, if I see your face again," the husband's sister wailed hysterically, on the way out of the house, "you are a witch; you have gobbled up my brother."

Ashalata's planned bidaai (farewell ceremony to the new bride) turned out to be her farewell indeed. Life bid her good-bye that day. In Hindu society then, the death of the husband led to the killing of a woman's soul. She thereafter lived her life as a corpse, shrouded in white, in the confines of her house, at times even a single room. It was as if she lived in a sealed coffin that had been lowered into the earth. Ashalata had barely known the man she married, but was ironically expected to love him in death and remain loyal to his memory. Baba was pained to hear of the cruelty Ashalata had suffered.

A widow should be allowed to lead a happy and complete life, having already suffered the loss of the husband, Baba mentally reasoned. The only way Ashalata could even dream of fulfillment now, he thought, was perhaps through remarriage and motherhood. A Hindu widow could choose to remarry then,

Shuvashree Chowdhury

or remain single, as legalized by the Hindu Widow Remarriage Act of 1856. But Baba doubted her interest in remarrying. She had very apparently chosen a life of widowhood for herself. Those like Ashalata who intended to stay single, dedicated their lives to the upbringing of their family, or lived in the pursuit of spiritual enlightenment. They were respected as brahmacharinis (celibate women dedicated to spiritual pursuits) and lived life as monastic's wearing plain white clothing, as Ashalata did. She ate only vegetarian food with no onion, ginger or garlic, even though some Bengali widows ate fish. Unlike meat and spices, fish was not known to be heating on the body and therefore not a threat to their celibacy. Ashalata cooked her own meal, of a mere fist of rice, boiled with a few pieces of vegetable. She ate once a day, in her room, all by herself.

Widows who chose not to remarry could opt to be initiated by a swami to be a sanyasini and wear yellow or orange saris. Then they did not participate in community functions such as weddings, except to observe or give their blessings. They led prayer groups during holy festivals, gave discourses if qualified to do so and performed pujas on occasions, where there was a gathering of people for spiritual purposes. According to the general guidelines for widows in Hindu culture, widows who intended to remarry could follow the customs of an unmarried girl. She could dress like before marriage, without using red kumkum on her forehead, using the black one instead, signifying she is open to marriage proposals. Ashalata had chosen not to remarry. This was clearly depicted by her plain attire.

Baba was appalled that a woman like Ashalata should become so submissive to the pressures of society, allowing it to dictate how she led her life. But then that is how the social order was, a woman had no identity without a man in her life. Ashalata's situation perhaps, in addition to her youth and beauty, led Baba to fall in love with her, in spite of his much married and parental status. Perhaps her being within her child-bearing years had something to do with it too, raising his hope of bearing male children through her. But Baba knew it was not going to be easy to change Ashalata's dedication to her widowhood. First thing he had to do, Baba realized, was help Ashalata identify a cause. She lacked the will to really live; burning in the cinders of failure destiny had relegated her to.

It was ironic that fate had given Ashalata the good-looks and calibre but not the opportunity to be a wife and mother. Baba, in order to reinstate her interest in life, decided to strike her compassionate chord. He tried to awaken in her the desire to be needed, by making herself useful in society, to the poor and the ailing. He asked her if she would be interested to come to work with him at his clinic. Ashalata seeing a ray of hope and purpose in her dark-cloud filled life could not turn down this proposition. This was possibly what God had planned for her all along, she thought optimistically, to be of service to humanity not just to one man in marriage. Her life took on a new meaning, and colour returned to it, in spite of the white saris she continued to wear. It felt like viewing a rainbow in the sky, at the first rays of the sun after a shower, even amidst a drizzle sometimes.

Ashalata had just decided to take the long walk to Baba's clinic daily, when dark clouds of hesitation suddenly threatened to change her mind. The mental clouds were accompanied by thunder in the form of her brother's vehement protests. But undeterred, she still went. She began to like the work as Baba's assistant - administering injections, draping bandages and checking pulse and body temperature of patients. But it all came to an abrupt halt, when Ashalata was struck as if by lightening, by her brothers nasty insinuations one evening.

"What will people in the locality say?" her brother yelled, as she was just about to leave, "they will think I am a pimp who sends his sister out because he cannot feed her, or worse still, they will say my sister is warming the young doctor's bed."

Ashalata was shocked at the preposterous thought, but more hurt that her own brother should talk of her in such a demeaning way. The tears sprang to her eyes and she ran inside, locking herself in her room. After she had wept her heart inside-out, calmness prevailed. She then realized, that however cruel her brother's words were, they were not far from the truth. The neighbours were bound to speak badly of her. A young widow leaving the shelter of her home, to interact with a man on a regular basis, not to mention her exposure to other male patients as well, was sure to raise eyebrows.

          Shuvashree Chowdhury

They would take it as her attempt at inciting men of the locality. She swiftly cut the wings of her dreams, letting them crash on the hard-ground reality of her widowhood. Reconciling to her fate, she withdrew once again, into the dark world of her loneliness.

When Ashalata did not turn up for two days, Baba was surprised, considering the enthusiasm she had shown in the few days of working. It was when she had not come for another week that he decided to go over to her house. This time he was not met at the fence-door by Ashalata, but by her brother Shib Shankar, now back on his feet though still recuperating. He led Baba inside, but in spite of attempting to put on a welcoming expression, there was a distinct rebellion in his attitude. He was caught between his gratitude for Baba for curing him on the one hand, and resentment on the other for instigating his sister to dream beyond her limitations.

"Ashalata hasn't been coming to the clinic," Baba stated haltingly, once he was seated inside and offered a cup of tea. "Is she at home now?"

"Dactar-babu, Ashalata will not go to the clinic anymore," Shib Shankar replied curtly, his tone bordering on hostility.

"But why?" Baba asked sounding appalled, even though sensing immediately the cause of Shib Shankar's objection to her going, "she will be mentally refreshed, and it will help me too."

"No, Ashalata cannot go. She is a widow," he replied firmly, then closing the door to any further discussion he added, "people will spit on me."

Shib Shankar had made up his mind and trying to convince him otherwise was futile. Moreover knowing the neighbourhood well, Baba knew Shib Shankar was not entirely wrong in his presumption. He finished his cup of tea hurriedly, and just when he was about to get up to leave, Ashalata stepped into the room.

"I'm really sorry, Dactar-da," she said, "for my inability to come to work with you. I would not like to bring any shame on my family."

"In that case, I will have to marry you then," Baba said matter-of-factly, "if that is what will give you back your life."

Shib Shankar's eyes opened wide in shock, from the suddenness of the proposal, as the very consideration. He looked from Baba to his sister and back again. Ashalata gulped in shock, after the implication of Baba's words sank in. She then walked into the inner room rapidly, her head bent down, trying to swallow the idea.

"Did you mean what you said Dactar-babu?" Shib Shankar asked awkwardly, regaining his composure. Then in a voice now turned mellow with a renewed respect and gratefulness, he added, "do you really wish to marry my sister Ashalata?"

Baba nodded, though stupefied at his impulsive marriage proposal.

"It is so kind of you …" Shib Shankar replied, seeing Baba nod in assent, bending with folded hands, "knowing that she is a widow … to take her responsibility for life. It is indeed heroic."

"Yes I will marry your sister, Shib Shankar," Baba replied resolutely, as if to internalize his own impulsive decision, "but it is not out of any kindness or sympathy. Ashalata is a fine young lady."

"It is your magnanimity to think so, Dactar-da" Shib Shankar insisted.

"I hope you are aware, I already have a wife and three daughters," Baba blurted, "but I wish to take on Ashalata's responsibility, if that will give her back her life. More so, because I know she will make me a good companion and a fine mother to our children. Hopefully she will bear me sons to continue my family name, and carry on my practice."

"Ashalata is a very talented girl" Shib Shankar quipped, relieved to have her off his shoulders, "she will make you very happy. I'm certain."

"Should we not take Ashalata's consent, before we finalize the alliance?" Baba asked earnestly, "I don't want her to be forced into something she may not be ready for."

"She will certainly agree to a new lease of life with you. Asha has so much respect for you, that it is her privilege" Shib Shankar replied, then seeing Baba's uncertain look, he added, "but still for your satisfaction, I will ask her." He briskly walked into the inner room and returned beaming broadly, "Ashalata is shy, but has nodded in consent."

Luckily, Ma had not yet returned, Baba recalled. She would remain in Mihirpur till Kali Puja, which was still a week away. Baba

    Shuvashree Chowdhury

asked for the arrangements to be made, for as soon as possible, wanting the wedding over before Ma's return with us sisters. He did not hesitate to add he would take care of the entire financial burden.

"I don't want an elaborate ceremony and am sure neither will Ashalata," Baba said, "but we need to hold a function, to make the marriage socially acceptable and prevent unnecessary gossip later."

The wedding was promptly planned and executed. It was a small private affair in Ashalata's house, attended by a handful of people. When Baba saw Ashalata during the wedding ceremony, he could not believe his eyes. He gaped in awe at the transformation in her, draped in the red silk sari and resplendent in all the jewellery he had bought her for the occasion. She moved into Baba's house right after the wedding, superstitious of spending the night at her brother's house.

After the initial euphoria of his new bride's arrival, Baba began to feel a sense of foreboding. After executing his impulsive decision, guilt stealthily crept into his mind. It would slowly take firm root, becoming a full grown tree one day much later in his life, to die only at his death. Baba had to acknowledge that though Ma was not his idea of a perfect wife, she did the best she could, and was a good person. She certainly did not deserve this treachery, but he had taken a decision and was going to abide by it. He tried to squash the guilt shoots curbing his happiness and optimism. After all, Ma had not borne him a son, he justified. Without a male heir he had no one to inherit his name and medical practise. He tried to convince himself he was right in marrying Ashalata, in giving her a new lease of life.

* * *

The lives of Baba, Ma and Ashalata impacted mine deeply. Neither Baba nor Ma is alive today. Ashalata, who drove a wedge between them, changing the course of my life irrevocably, continues to live in the house of my childhood, with her six sons. While my mother lost her husband to the beauty, freshness and charm of Ashalata, we sisters Kalpana, Neelima and I, lost Baba to his desire for male children. However, not one of his sons would become a doctor, or gain any eminence in society. When we as children had returned home with Ma, after a long stay at Mihirpur, I did not comprehend that the woman who had come to live in our house was already a permanent resident there. Even less did I realize we were going with Ronjit uncle to his school in Mihirpur never to return.

At seven years, I had not understood the real meaning of marriage, even less the implication of Baba living with a woman other than Ma, in the house. Kalpana, at sixteen, had learnt of the circumstances and could share Ma's sorrow. I had not known that the pretty, soft spoken and gentle woman who had moved in while we were away, had encroached on my mother's territory as Baba's wife and mistress of his house. She had claimed what should have rightfully been only Ma's. In later years, I came to realize that Ma's place had not been usurped by Ashalata, but rather unceremoniously taken away from her by Baba. He spent the night as well as had all meals with his new wife, instructing us to call her Choto (younger)-ma. The implication of the word had not registered in my naive mind then.

We hardly saw Choto-ma, so luckily did not have to use the alias. Ashalata lived in the front and much bigger wing of the house, in which Baba's clinic was. Ma saw to it that we hardly went there. Though she had lost all her privileges over her husband, Ma was not going to give up her rights as our mother, to the one who had stolen her husband. I was oblivious then to the acute distress and humiliation Ma was enduring. She was living in the same house as her polygamous husband, dependent on him for all our sustenance, subjected to emotional and physical neglect, passed over for a younger woman. In fact since our return I hardly saw Baba either, except for the few moments just before leaving for school, when I peeped into his clinic to waive goodbye if he was busy, or say a few words if not.

It was much later that I was to become acutely sensitive to how Baba had withdrawn from us since his marriage to Ashalata. His earlier warmth and closeness slowly receded into a mere aching reminiscence in my mind. With the awareness, came the earnest hope that it was his guilt that inhibited him, causing him to drift away. Though I squashed such disarming optimism from deluding

		Shuvashree Chowdhury

my belief that his distancing himself from us was in emotional preparation to welcoming the sons that were to arrive in due time. I found it difficult to accept the brutality of his abandonment, once realizing the real reason for us being sent away to boarding school in Mihirpur with Ronjit uncle. I had been gearing to be the son in his life, oblivious that my acting a son did not amount to his having one.

All through my growing years, Ma's helplessness angered and saddened me simultaneously. It propelled and spurred my ambitions to prove to Baba that I could be more proficient than any son he would ever have. I knew I had to be financially self-reliant, as well as emotionally independent; never allowing anyone to treat me the way my father had my mother. I learnt early on how it feels to be cast off by a husband, forsaken by a father, to become a stranger in one's own home, losing one's identity. I realized there is no individuality more lasting than from one's education, skills and work achievement. The identity provided by birth, marriage, relationships and domicile are easily washed away or transitory. These lessons formed the foundation of my resilience, for my life across borders.

Chapter 3

The Home That Adopted Me

I stood awestruck for a few moments in front of the colossal iron gate flanked by liveried guards. Then stepping onto the well-mowed, infinitely stretching grass-field, bounded by a hedge of multi-coloured flower plants, I excitedly squeezed my sister Kalpana's hand.

"Didi, have you seen this?" I exclaimed, "Isn't it beautiful?"

After briskly looking around, taking in the sight of the enormous white, green and reddish-ochre building that bordered the field at the furthest side, I added, "And look at the big school building Didi! Such a huge playfield, just as Uncle had mentioned."

Kalpana merely nodded, though the admiration in her wide, grey-green eyes was unmistakable. In spite of her melancholy throughout the journey since leaving home in Assam, Kalpana looked enthused now. She had not envisioned something quite as gigantic as this.

"So ladies, I hope you like your new school!" Ronjit uncle exclaimed with distinctive pride in is voice, noticing our awe. Before we could respond, he took a few steps forward, adding "now come with me, I will show you around the premises."

Kalpana and I meekly followed him, as we took a brisk walk around the field. He pointed out the classrooms, dormitories and the staff room, all located in a series of semicircular buildings spread around the playfield. Then returning to the point where we had started, he led us into the single storey office building to the left of the main gate. Inside, sitting behind a large mahogany desk, was Ronjit uncle's younger daughter, Ratna. We had met her during Durga Puja celebrations at our joint-family's home. Having completed her education, graduating from London, she now oversaw the administration of the school.

 Shuvashree Chowdhury

Ratna was a beautiful woman in spite of her short height. She had wide, luminous black eyes and a full mouth, set in a radiant, heart shaped face. Her long black hair held in a chignon and the neatly pleated navy-blue printed georgette sari she wore gave her a look of professional elegance.

"I'm entrusting these two young ladies to your care, Ma," Ronjit uncle said endearingly to Ratna. "Their valises are in the jeep parked outside the gate. Please enrol them into the school, and show them our ways. I am sure they will soon do us proud, setting examples for subsequent batches of students." Then turning towards Kalpana and me, he added, "I hope you are going to have a good time here and will learn well."

We nodded, before Ronjit uncle left. Ratna asked us to get our boxes from the jeep.

Once we returned with our valises, Ratna introduced us to some of the other girl students. They were standing around on the grass lawn in front of her office. She waved to them, signalling them to come over. This was essentially a residential school, so though it was Sunday and school closed, students loitered about. On holidays they had a list of chores to complete in preparation for the week ahead. They washed and ironed their clothes, changed bed linen and thoroughly cleaned and dusted their personal belongings. Having completed all that by midday, they were free to spend the rest of the day as they liked. One of the senior girls helped us fill out the admission forms. Then we were escorted by the girls to the hostel at the farthest end of the playfield, adjacent to the main school building.

Kalpana and I were thus adopted by our new home, and in time inducted to its regulations. Here I was to spend the next decade of my life. Kalpana would only spend the next two years finishing her tenth standard. Our new home was the result of Ronjit uncle's dream to set up an educational institution for women in his hometown. He wanted to provide all young girls here, an education that his own mother and women of her times had not been fortunate to acquire. Ronjit uncle believed the foremost requisite for women to achieve their emancipation and establish their rights was education. This in progression would lay the foundation to a society that empowered and respected its women. He had a clear vision of what the school he founded was to impart to its students, in addition to the core curriculum. It had to inculcate in its students the skills and resilience to be good daughters, wives and mothers.

By the time Kalpana and I enrolled, the rules of the school had already been set by Ratna in concurrence with Ronjit uncle's vision. Since the schools inception, it was compulsory for students to reside in the hostel. Founded a couple of years back, with only eight to ten girls, it had grown to a few dozen students at the time of our joining. In time it would grow to a capacity of twelve hundred seats. The home did not discriminate on the basis of religion, caste, colour or social status. With the prevalent caste differences and religious and regional ones relentlessly brewing, it was a giant stride ahead of the times. The seeds of religious disharmony had already developed into two full-grown trees - Pakistan and India, but here we were covered in a blanket of social unity with Hindus and Muslims cohabitating. We were taught to create a peaceful society, by promoting mutual tolerance and self-sacrifice, with emphasis on discipline.

We girls did regular menial work, so as to acquire mental maturity and a hardworking, honest personality, with a strong sense of responsibility and morality. Starting out at five in the morning to half past ten at night, we followed a pre-set routine without the slightest deviation. We were made to cook our own meals, as well as sweep, swab and dust the entire campus, to prepare ourselves to become respectable and efficient housewives. The premise behind this was that, every woman, however professionally qualified, whether she worked outside the house or not, needs to be able to manage her home well. The mass cooking was done by us in groups of thirty students at a time. These groups were formed from girls of different ages and academic classes. This enabled the young to learn from the older ones, who in turn were encouraged to train the youngsters. The student groups took turns to cook, clean and serve meals and were self-sufficient in keeping the wheels of the home running smoothly.

In addition to academics, physical education and cultural activities also played a very important role in our lives. It served to promote in us physical agility, inspiring cleanliness and self-reliance. Waking at five even on winter mornings, we were on the

          Shuvashree Chowdhury

playfield within half-an-hour for yoga and drills. This discipline was to build my stamina for the rocky race of life ahead. Voluntary service to society was encouraged, so as to uplift the condition of the rural, illiterate people of our neighbourhood, but also to make us more conscientious. My adopted home in a poor and little known village of East Pakistan, with its activities and cultural undertakings, was to lay the foundation to my fortitude and personality. It would also give wings to my dream of being as capable as any son my father could ever aspire to have.

It was here that I discovered in myself an inherent talent for sports, calisthenics and gymnastics. I was an avid cyclist, soon ranking second at the all-Pakistan national level races. Learning to swim in the large water-body outside the school premises, I became an ardent swimmer. I also excelled in dance, drama and elocution. It was little wonder that in a short time I was Ronjit uncle's favourite, even though a mediocre academic student. In me, he perhaps envisioned a third daughter who would carry forward his dreams. The excess mental and physical energy I possessed, at times also propelled tomfoolery and mischief. It led to my climbing trees on the campus to pluck mangoes and guavas, dodging the guards. I rowed the boats that plied the river alongside our school, insisting on taking the oars from the boatmen.

At times, I would take a boat tied to the river's edge stealthily, to cross over to meet relatives and grandparents.

During our vacations, Kalpana and I remained in the hostel, while the other girls went home. There was nowhere we had to go; after all school was now home for us. Here meals and our beds in the large vacant dormitory were assured. However, we visited our extended family across the river. They lived within the walls of a family compound. Four generations of siblings, cousins, parents, grandparents and children, all lived together in a series of small bungalows surrounding the family temple, taking care of each other from birth to death. It was on one such visit, during my first year at school that I learnt of my father's second marriage. I was a pigtailed, skinny, peppy eight-year-old, and a mighty exhibition of charisma and fireworks then. I wore a huge grin with a bright-voiced curiosity on everything. The shock and emotional blow turned me frigid then on.

This was followed by acute denial, wherein I refused to accept the veracity of what I had learnt. I had been looking forward to going back home shortly and to learn that I was never returning was devastating. But slowly the painful comprehension of Baba's new wife - Choto-ma, our banishment from the life which was rightfully ours, established in my impressionable mind. Baba's desertion was excruciating. The sharp stab of Baba's betrayal and his abandonment would remain with me forever, even though camouflaged. The abscess would fester lifelong to a point I would never really trust anyone again. Ma's helplessness in protecting us from its tyranny, least of all herself, made me realize that no one was indispensable. I recognized I was alone in the world to fight for my survival, and battle I would lifelong.

I learnt the valuable lesson of self-reliance very early, perhaps the cause for my turning into a control freak later in life. I would control every situation, to draw from my own strength, to feel a sense of refuge. I would hoard money, clothes, household articles, electronics goods and almost anything, in fear of that familiar sense of vulnerability I had felt in childhood. I would one day repeatedly forbid my daughters from wasting food, particularly to finish food on the plate, reminding them their leftovers could fill a poor person's stomach. I would goad them into a quality education; urge them to work and save half their earnings, so as to never be in a position of financial vulnerability. I would teach them to respect and value the strength and self-emancipation money provides.

My daughters would never relate to my idiosyncrasies, laughing at my desire to stash saris, jewellery, even utensils, rather than use them. It would give me immense pleasure to look at my hoardings. I would derive mental refuge in knowing I could never be lacking in them, as I had while growing up. My husband would in humour refer to my sitting in front of my bedroom wardrobe, viewing my clothes and jewellery with smug satisfaction as 'stock-taking.' He would not understand, never having lived with one or two sets of clothes only, like I did growing up. Neither would he nor my children know the feeling of awkwardness from wearing the handouts from cousins.

I would save my entire salary, in a bid to save a portion of our family income towards building a home from which no one could

     Shuvashree Chowdhury

ever displace me again. I would rather be the butt of jokes of my husband and children, than envisage being in the position I had once been in. I would not justify my behaviour, knowing they could never appreciate the deep-rooted insecurity that caused it. One has to experience desertion, poverty and insecurity first hand to truly feel their essence. All that would be much later. Now I cannot see a future in which I will not depend on Ronjit uncle, after being ceremoniously handed over by his cousin. I would never comprehend why Baba, with his robust medical practice and other businesses, did not take care of both wives and all his children. At the time polygamy was not illegal in Hindu society, rather it was widely acceptable. Hindu men, like Muslims, would take on more than one wife, even if they struggled to cope with the burden. We were after all Baba's responsibility, however disrespectful it might be to the wives to conjugally live in conjunction with their counterparts. Perhaps we were abandoned because we happened to be girls.

But I must admit, if not for a powerful defence mechanism driving me, I might not have achieved much in life. I might have turned out helpless and vulnerable like Ma, washed away in the strong currents that were to threaten to usurp my position in life often. I would see Baba only a few times while in school, till the final time when employed I would visit him before his death. Ma would continue to live in a tiny portion of her husband's house then, at his mercy, along with Neelima our younger sister and her family.

Once Kalpana married and could send her money, Ma would visit us more often. She was to remain an integral part of my life till her death, though more as a guest and spectator, than as guardian. I realized her incapacity, so did not expect more, always loving her simply for being my mother. In fact from the time I got my first salary when employed, till her death, I would support her by sending her some money every month.

In my first years at school, during Durga Puja, Ma and Neelima did come to spend a few weeks at the family home across the river. Since Kalpana was yet not married, I am not sure how Ma got the money. Perhaps Ronjit uncle sent for her. Though banished from her husband's life, Ma was still among the rightful mistresses of the joint-family house. She would join the rest of the women at the family temple. Kalpana and I spent those times with her and Neelima, enthusiastically participating in the celebrations with the rest of our paternal family. Even though Baba, since our leaving Assam, was no longer a part of our lives, he did visit his parents a few times along with his new wife. I saw Choto-ma, a term redundant after our renunciation from Baba's life, on those occasions when she came with him for the Puja celebrations. Ever since I learnt of her significance in my father's life and consequently in ours, I was to hold no grudge or malice towards her - just an absolute disregard.

I never wasted any emotions on my father's second wife, as there was no betrayal I felt from her. In my mind, Baba was the only and real perpetrator of the turn our lives had taken from the normal. I would never allow anyone to share that status or let diffuse my focused antagonism towards him. Though ironically, I was to love and hate Baba in equal measure all my life. Both extreme emotions, but can in circumstances have a thin, invisible, fragile dividing line, like the geographical borders of two countries. One cannot tell where one country converges into the other but for the manually installed barbed wires, as one cannot the abrupt shift of emotions separated by an incident of treachery. A forced crossing over barbed wires can cause pain comparable to the piercing pain one undergoes in paradigm shift between love and hate over unfaithfulness of a loved one.

The fragments of my life across the border of India converged to form my personality, but it was really my love and hate for Baba that formed its emotional make-up. Unrequited, rejected, abandoned love can breed hate, which is essentially just love inverted. When you love dearly, with sufficient provocation the love can swiftly turn to hate, like it happened with me. My feelings for Baba, were like sand passing through the narrow centre of an hourglass, squeezing through my heart in alternating between love and hate – the top and bottom portion of the hourglass. However, unlike the sandglass which when the top is empty can be inverted to begin trickling and timing again, my heart could not be inverted at will, when full of either love or hate for Baba.

Lifelong, my feelings for Baba were affected though

                    Shuvashree Chowdhury

involuntarily, by factors like my current age and circumstances in life. During trials when my neck was squeezed tight, I hated Baba and when the quality of my life was poor I blamed it on him and his betrayal. When life treated me well as it would later in life, I was to find it in my heart to forgive and love him simply for the father I had known in my childhood. The time taken for my love to change to hate and vice-versa may not have been as regulated as in an hourglass. But change it did, when either side was full, to gradually move to the other by its own initiation.

It would not be till my last meeting with Baba, by now employed, married, and with one daughter, that I would express a wee bit of the turmoil and confusion his behaviour had created in my life. I grew up with a sense of neglect by Baba and conversely with an extreme awe-inspired gratitude for Ronjit uncle. Ronjit uncle's personality always reminded me how starkly different Baba's was, making him truly the poor cousin. I was to wonder throughout my life how two people could have such contradictory characters. Whereas Baba neglected his duty towards his family, Ronjit uncle took his cousin's neglected duties as his own. My adulation for Ronjit uncle, who in my opinion was perfect and could do no wrong, was to one day become another cause for great jest by my husband and children.

But then, how could they possibly appreciate the power of gratitude, running parallel to a feeling of rejection by one's own? They would recount Ronjit uncle's flaws only to tease me. But none of it would ever take away the perfection of his military-disciplined, humble lifestyle and philanthropic character from my mind. Neither would it deter from his being the hero of my life, the paradigm of virtues. Perhaps my husband's inability to match Ronjit uncle's magnified stature in my mind is what would propel his teasing me with an underlying sense of jealousy. If not for the positive role model that I found in Ronjit uncle as a child, I might have grown up with utter disrespect, distaste and distrust for men in general after what Baba had done to us.

Through every crisis, however, I was to never lose faith in God. I believed what he took away with one hand, he provided me with the other. He replenished my losses, even if not always adequately. What I needed materially was provided for by my adopted home and Ronjit uncle. All students received similarly, the school being a charitable institution, where education and boarding was free, except for a security fee refunded on leaving. I could however, not help but feel that I was the only recipient of such benevolence. When you get from sources not rightfully yours, in stark contrast to which is duly yours by birth, you are swamped by appreciation. I was to forever feel my life was an outcome of the handouts I received in addition to my own perseverance. I would in return try to give to Ronjit uncle and his family any help or service that I could.

During the years at school, Ronjit uncle's wife Mrinalini often asked me to help her with chores or run some errands. On such occasions, she was very kind and generous. Occasionally she fed me a good meal; at times she gave me sweetmeats and now and then her daughter's clothes. I graciously accepted my cousins' used clothes, as it was not unusual for younger siblings, even cousins in joint families, to wear what the elders had outgrown. Moreover, I was practical not to let my pride come in the way of possessing a few decent, rather fashionable clothes and shoes, mostly purchased in London by Ratna. Ronjit uncle always preferred young women to wear plain-cut, simple, western clothes and I honoured his wishes. He was of the opinion that western clothes made women look smart, were practical in facilitating easy movement and agility and made them conscious of their weight and figure, thereby promoting overall good health.

Ronjit uncle, however, abhorred the use of make-up and propagated simplicity of dressing and lifestyle. He led a simple Spartan life himself to the extent of sometimes sleeping on the floor. I was to lead my life on many of his principles, though preferring to sleep on a bed. The only time I would wear make-up or heavy jewellery would be on my wedding day. However, I would allow myself to be grease-painted when participating in dance-dramas and plays in school or college. Ronjit uncle approved of my clothes, athletic frame, plain scrubbed face, but above all, my bold, confident and decisive ways. All my life I was to subconsciously seek his approval in everything, which would not cease even after I would one day go away without his permission, crossing over to India, to start a new life. In fact, even after his passing.

          Shuvashree Chowdhury

Ronjit uncle's daughters, as well as school going grand daughters, however, did not find it fit to follow his no-makeup, no-fashion rule. In spite of being reprimanded often, they continued to dodge him in decking up and were to do so lifelong, unlike me. Ronjit uncle was, after all, their father and grandfather, not God like he was to me, for them to follow his words like the Gospel. In time I adopted Ronjit uncle's family as my own, as other than my sister Kalpana they were the only family I grew up knowing. Ratna, not married when I joined her father's school, was soon to tie the knot with a doctor employed by her father. Thereafter, the couple resided in the staff quarters outside the school premises and had a son and a daughter. Ratna's elder sister Madhavi was married long before my joining school, to a businessman from a neighbouring town. She spent five to six days of the week overseeing her father's new constructions for his ever growing social welfare initiatives.

I called Madhavi Bor-di or elder sister and she was very fond of me. On my part, I had a special place in my heart for her, somewhere in the league of my own sister Kalpana. She took me on outings, gave me presents and was more a mother-figure than cousin, teaching me her special cooking recipes as well as ways of the refined world. By imbibing her skills, I would one day turn out to be an excellent cook, much to the gratification of my husband and children.

Ronjit uncle's eldest son was a challenged child needing special care. The younger one was sent to college in Europe, to be groomed to take over the reins of his father's heritage. Madhavi's school going children - five girls and a boy, all about my age - studied at convent schools in Darjeeling across the border. When they came home on vacations, Madhavi at times left the youngest in my care. While she went about working, I built lifelong bonds with her children.

Every year during the Durga Puja, Ronjit uncle gave all women of the extended-family a sari each. I wore mine with a flourish, for the anjali or collective offering of flower and prayers conducted by the priest on each of the five days. With my ardour for dancing, I started the dhunuchi dance, in offering to the deity. Taking the earthen pot with burning incense by the handle, I brandished it gracefully. I danced with agility in front of the goddess Durga and her four children - Kartik, Ganesh, Lakshmi and Saraswati, to the beats of the dhak, the traditional drums. My dance recital was well appreciated by all and even today it is customary for the students of the school to perform a collective dhunuchi dance during Durga Puja. The temple where the Puja was conducted was initially built of mud about two hundred years back by our ancestors. It is currently a concrete building in the central porch of the family's homes alongside the river.

One year when I did not show up for the arati on Ashtami, the second and important day of the Durga Puja, Ronjit uncle stormed at his wife Mrinalini, "Where is Maya? Why is she not dancing?"

"She cannot dance today," Mrinalini crisply replied, close to his ears.

"But, why not" Ronjit uncle retorted impatiently, "she is here somewhere, I just saw her. So why can't she dance?"

"Maya is here, but cannot come to the temple," Mrinalini replied firmly looking into her husband's eyes, imploring him to understand. But when there was no sign of his comprehension, she added briskly, "she is menstruating and cannot come into the temple for the Puja."

"What nonsense," Ronjit uncle shot back at his wife, enraged.

"Ma," he said, in reference to Goddess Durga, "is a woman, isn't she? Then why follow these stupid customs restricting her daughters to her presence? You people make a mockery of womanhood and what Ma represents."

I was summoned immediately. Mrinalini knew better than to refute her husband's wishes. In minutes, draped in the silk sari Ronjit uncle had given me, I was at the temple dhunuchi in hand. As I danced to the sounds of the dhaks that evening, I mentally offered my arati to Ronjit uncle, for his broadmindedness and respect for women, for attempting to liberate us from traditions imposed on us down the ages. That morning he possibly also faced the reality that the little girl he had brought with him five years back had come of age and was now a woman. Ronjit uncle celebrated Durga Puja fervently and lavishly, as he was in reality celebrating Womanhood - the source of life, perhaps in memory of his own mother who had died at childbirth. He lived his life trying

    Shuvashree Chowdhury

to fulfil his dream of the emancipation of women, especially rural women, starting at home, with his family.

This forward-thinking by a male was remarkable, considering the position of women then, especially in rural India and Pakistan. This was when a woman after childbirth was kept in an outhouse, unable to participate in any activity in the household. She was not allowed into the kitchen, let alone cook during her menstrual cycle. A woman, according to Ronjit uncle, should not have to feel restricted in any way by her birth. I was to never forget his lessons on the equality of women, without her needing to act like a man to prove it. Not only did I live my own life by these doctrines, I would also bring up my two daughters to think of themselves no less than any son I might have ever had. One day by my own initiation, my daughter would light her father's funeral pyre at a public crematorium. I would not permit my son-in-law to do so, merely for being born male, while my daughters and I stayed home.

Every year at Durga Puja, the new idol was worshipped wearing Ma Durga's personal set of real gold jewellery. She and her children were adorned in them on Shasthi, the first day of the Puja. These were removed and safely put away in a trunk before the immersion on Dashami, the last of the five-day Puja, to be used the following year. Ma Durga was draped in a new, red Benarasi sari every year, which was then given to any woman in the family who was getting married the following year, to wear at her wedding. The new bride wore Ma Durga's sari, like a daughter would wear her mother's on her wedding day. This was in order to invoke the revered mother's blessing to bestow on her strength and good luck. Ronjit uncle had immense faith in the strength of Ma Durga. He wished upon every woman to find that same strength and power within herself, with the belief that all women have an inherent potency, especially in times of crisis. This was the axiom by which I would lead my life.

For us, it was not merely the celebration of Durga Puja and womanhood, but of religious harmony during religious turbulent times. We did not think of the Puja only on religious lines, but as a coming together of all religions and cultures. Many Muslims and Christians, both students and teachers of the school as well as guests, attended the celebrations, even if they did not take part in the prayers and rituals. Everyone who attended was served a meal, which had been consecrated as an offering to the Goddess. Though there were special cooks to prepare the meals on all five days, we students served. It was a fulfilling experience, as we participated wholeheartedly in the festival. It brought everyone together and was an opportunity to connect. In my case also, with my estranged father and his second wife, who came over a few times. Baba even offered to buy me a sari once, wanting to take me to the local market, but I firmly declined. I was not about to let him buy off his guilt on a whim.

Outside the school gate, a short walk down the pathway was the hospital, which I visited often. Founded by Ronjit uncle with only twenty beds to provide medical-aid to villagers, it later scaled up to several hundred beds. He feared they should not die from lack of medical facilities, like his mother had of tetanus at childbirth, when he was only a child. I came here as it gave me a sense of calm to reach out to the sick and needy or perhaps it was the familiar feeling of Baba's clinic in Assam that propelled me. The hospital initially provided absolute free service, but later patients paid for medication though they were not charged for the bed or three meals. At times I accompanied the doctors and nurses who periodically visited the nearby villages, to train rural people on midwifery, family planning, breastfeeding, sanitation, antenatal and general health awareness.

Since my childhood I had an affinity for the medical profession, having watched my father attend to patients. Perhaps it was my rebellion that would prevent me from aiming to follow in his footsteps in becoming a doctor myself. The relationship with my father would continue to influence my decisions subconsciously throughout my life. But it didn't prevent me from learning as much as I could, from the hospital's well managed pre-natal, nutrition monitoring and child-care facility for children up to five years. I learnt of the treatment for common illnesses like diarrhoea, tuberculosis and sexually transmitted or female diseases. I also joined the hospital team in training on motivating fertile village folks to accept family planning measures, as the hospital provided permanent methods like vasectomy, as well as temporary measures.

 Shuvashree Chowdhury

On my visits to the hospital I also trained to assist doctors. I could handle wounds, bandages and other simple procedures easily. I had watched my mother lose one child after another to insufficient medical aid despite being married to a doctor. The trauma of watching my little sisters die after short spans of acute suffering was indelibly printed on my mind. I would through my learning hope never to be in Ma's helpless, ignorant situation. Many doctors along with some good teachers for the school had been brought in from western countries like Germany, Scandinavia and England, in addition to those from Calcutta, by Ronjit uncle. They were to set good practices for the hospital, school, nursing college and other institutions he founded. My keen interaction with them broadened my horizons. It would one day provide a village girl the confidence to head to north India from East Pakistan all by herself.

I would leave Dacca to join a professional institution, merely from seeing an advertisement in a newspaper. Based on my skills and interests, Ronjit uncle had a career path in mind for me. He hoped I would come and work for him after completing my education. But I was not to pursue his plan, rather follow my own calling. In my last years at school, I would lead the march-past band, walking with my head held high, to my own beats on the large drum hung around my neck. A group of six kettle drummers followed me, with the rest of the school following them. I also taught calisthenics and conducted mass drill displays for functions, in collaboration with Ratna. She played a very active role in promoting extra-curricular activities and sports on Ronjit uncle's initiation. All these experiences enhanced my leadership skills, making me proficient as a trainer and coach, enabling me to excel in my chosen vocation later in life.

As for the home that adopted me, making me a strong, confident and self-reliant woman and devoted wife and mother, even today houses over twelve hundred girls. It is still well known for its extra-curricular and cultural activities, most of which were started during my time. I had earnestly followed Ronjit uncle's wishes then, on setting examples for subsequent students. What better way did I have, with no financial resources at my disposal, to show my gratitude and appreciation, repay a little of what he and his family had done for me? Only much later I would discover I had indeed left a mark as a token of my appreciation, at the home that adopted me, when I was technically orphaned. This would be on my visit there with my younger daughter and her husband during Durga Puja one year.

I was to leave East Pakistan for good in 1964, subsequent to the much publicized Hindu-Muslim riots. After this I would visit my school while nearing my seventieth year in 2008. By now my husband would be no more. I would be living alone in Kolkata, though in the safe haven of my own home, my daughters settled in other cities. I would be profoundly touched when the current batch of school students would mention a certain Maya-di who had initiated the dhunuchi dance at the temple. They would tell me of her role in starting the drill and calisthenics' displays too. However, they would not know that the grey-haired, wrinkled, still upright old woman listening to them attentively, viewing their dances with much interest, was the same Maya-di they were referring to. I would not shatter the image the students had of the young, sprightly Maya by telling them she and I were one and the same.

During the arati amid the Durga Puja in the temple, I would be looking unblinkingly in the direction of the current students dancing, wearing elaborate costumes and make-up. I would then actually be looking past them, imagining the schoolgirl Maya dancing alone all those decades back. I would presently be able to visualize her in a red silk sari gifted by Ronjit uncle, draped high over her ankles. With her long hair in a single plait behind her, she wore no make-up or jewellery. Her simplicity of attire would be the same as the one here now, in spite of ample financial resources. The youthful, expressive eyes of the dancing Maya would not have lost their spark, turning into the wrinkled ones even after a lifetime of struggle. Both Mayas would be in tears: one dancing from the fumes of the dhunuchi, while the one watching - from the haze of memories clouding her mind.

     Shuvashree Chowdhury

Chapter 4

My Sister Kalpana

"Take care of Maya like she were your own daughter" Ma had said to Kalpana, when we left home in Assam with Ronjit uncle. To me, she had added, "Maya, always listen to your Didi."

With these words Ma had entrusted me to Kalpana's care when I was eight. Since then, all her life Kalpana was to live up to the promise she made Ma, taking me on as no less than a real daughter. About eight years my elder, she took her role as my guardian pretty earnestly. Like a substitute mother in my life, she was to provide moral, emotional and financial support. She relentlessly goaded or reprimanded me on my setbacks, while encouraging and applauding my achievements. On my part, my love and respect for her was unquestioning, over and above even Ronjit uncle.

Kalpana appeared for her Matriculation exams two years since our admission to Ronjit uncle's school at Mihirpur, but could not qualify for the issuance of the Secondary School Certificate. It was not easy for her to catch up with the entirely different curriculum and style of learning, after our confined schooling in Assam. She tried a second time to clear the exams but unsuccessfully. However even after she stopped attending classes, giving up on further learning, she continued to reside in the school hostel. There was nowhere else she could go, as returning to Assam was not an option. The school was our home, like it was for a few other orphan girls. The existence of our parents did not make us any less orphaned than them. I was to often wonder if losing our parents to death or being born to poor parents unable to raise us might have been less agonizing.

Loss by death initially leaves a throbbing sadness, reducing to a dull ache with time. Poverty one can blame on providence, while striving and praying for it to go away. But rejection by one's parents can cause deep emotional scars from insecurity and a low sense of worth. Sometimes children sent to boarding school at a tender age perceive rejection, but in our case it was real. Thankfully Kalpana and I had each other to sooth the blisters from our scalding abandonment. Kalpana being elder was to look out for me in every way she could. But I was initially not much of a support, as yet fighting to come to terms with Baba's betrayal. Once when I was running a very high temperature, sitting at my bedside all night, Kalpana applied cold swabs to my forehead, desperately praying to God to spare me, having taken the rest of her family away.

Kalpana's formal education ended with her two unsuccessful attempts at passing its gateway, the tenth standard board exams. She now took a detour by practical learning through work. Initiated by Ronjit uncle, she started accompanying him to work at his corporate office in the neighbouring town of Vishnuganj. She would return every evening to the school hostel, whether or not he returned home. Ronjit uncle's office had a residential complex where he sometimes stayed back. In such case Kalpana would go to office herself the next morning. Ronjit uncle was tolerant of Kalpana's inability to study further, attributing it to her mental and emotional faculties. But he would not concede to the cessation of her practical training. In his opinion, education and exposure, whether formal or otherwise, was essential in building a woman's self-reliance. The time Kalpana spent working with him enhanced her overall personality and confidence, developing her business acumen and managerial ability.

Kalpana by now was a striking beauty, with large greyish-green eyes, high cheek bones, a heart shaped face, fair luminous complexion and light brown hair to her knees that she wore in a chignon. This, added to her newly acquired self-assurance and poise, soon caught the fancy of Sudeep Mukherjee. He was the bright and promising young man, recently taken on as executive secretary to Ronjit uncle. After much vetting, he had been selected from a long list of prospective applicants to a newspaper advertisement. Sudeep was tall and near-ivory skinned, with a long hooked nose, grey piercing eyes and fine, light brown hair. He could well pass for a westerner like Ronjit uncle's expatriate

     Shuvashree Chowdhury

employees and a handsome one at that. He spoke in a soft mellow voice and was very charming, with an even temperament. His sharp mind was always ticking, assimilating business data and churning it with analysis into financial advice to Ronjit uncle.

With Sudeep's keen observation and foresight on a prospective resource, whether human or material, he could instantly tell its worth. He then determined whether it was for keeps and therefore worth acquiring. When his sights fell on the beautiful, talented, yet homely and caring Kalpana, deducing from the way she looked out for every need of her uncle, Sudeep knew she would make him the perfect wife. He was also smart to know that trying to woo her who blindly obeyed her uncle, could either be a total waste of time or at the least a time consuming affair. He decided to take the bull by the horns, proposing to her uncle his wish to marry her. To Sudeep's utter delight, Ronjit uncle agreed immediately, as perhaps he had hoped to see this happening. The marriage would take care of his duty to see Kalpana married well, while having the couple by his side forever.

Kalpana, true to Sudeep's observation, did not have a say in a decision made by Ronjit uncle. She silently agreed to the marriage. In any case Sudeep was Godsent for a girl brought up in a charitable home on the compassion of a well meaning and generous uncle. Sudeep was everything Kalpana, or any girl for that matter, could want in a husband. He was intelligent, handsome and earned well, with prospects for doing much better in the near future. His charming ways had not gone unnoticed by Kalpana, though she had least imagined catching his attention as a prospective wife. Kalpana was pleased with her bridegroom and at the sudden turn of events. I was totally unaware of these developments till Ronjit uncle broke the news to me very abruptly one day.

"I'm taking Kalpana-ma to Calcutta to get her married," he said, as though taking her for a regular health check-up or a job interview, "we will be leaving tomorrow morning."

I uncomprehendingly stared at Ronjit uncle, but once the implication of his words registered, my face lit up in ecstasy. However soon gloom overshadowed it, with the realization that I was not going to be any part of it. I had for long dreamt of Kalpana's wedding, visualizing how beautiful she might look, what I might wear, of all the fun and the celebrations. However it had never occurred to me in my naivety to wonder how all this would come about, who would finance it or where the groom would be found. I am not sure why I was not allowed to attend my dearest sister's wedding. Perhaps it would distract me from my studies, is the thought I consoled myself with. In fact, Kalpana was wed in the absence of any immediate family. Baba, I assumed, was not invited for the obvious reason of his having neglected us. Ma's presence was perhaps not considered significant. Whatever his reasons, Ronjit uncle's decisions, as always, were abiding on us all, with an unquestionable finality.

I first met Sudeep Mukherjee after Kalpana and he returned with Ronjit uncle from Calcutta. By then he was my beloved sister's husband. From the instant we were introduced, liking him, I had called him Dada-babu, literally meaning respected elder brother, rather than Jamai-babu, the term used to address ones elder sister's husband in Bengali. Sudeep soon became my guardian, as Kalpana already was, adopting me sincerely as a daughter. If there was anyone I would truly respect and consult with other than Kalpana and Ronjit uncle, it would be Dada-babu. He would be the second father-figure in my life, even though Ronjit uncle would one day cease to be. Sudeep was to guide, support and mentor me lifelong. He was to address my financial needs, compensating my meagre college stipend till I started working and even get me married, as a father should.

Sudeep and Kalpana were allocated a house in Vishnuganj, close to Ronjit uncle's residence-cum-office. Since their moving, I visited them whenever I could get away from my school schedule. I started spending my school and later college vacations there, no longer needing to spend them at the school hostel with other homeless girls. Their house was a two-storey building with wooden staircases and floors, cosy fireplaces in all rooms, modern fittings and fixtures in the kitchen and bathrooms, and large servant's quarters. The house also had a beautiful garden and a well maintained lawn. The overall amenities were like that of a modern house. It was probably built with an expatriate in mind, but allocated to Sudeep due to his work profile and perhaps his being as suave as any in Ronjit uncle's employment then.

     Shuvashree Chowdhury

Sudeep was elder to Kalpana by twelve years and having married late in life could not wait to meet his successor. He worried there might never be one if he waited. Within a year of their marriage, Kalpana became pregnant. She was ecstatic. In addition to it being any woman's inherent desire to experience motherhood, it was the prime reason for women to marry other than financial security. Anxiously awaiting the birth of the child along with Kalpana, I helped her with preparations for welcoming the new member of the family among our midst. I sewed and knitted baby suits, crocheted socks, mittens and baby wraps, as well as stitched hand-made sheets or kathas. Having already missed the most important days in Kalpana's life yet - her wedding, I was not going to let any part of the next, her child's birth, pass me by again.

Ma was not present at Kalpana's childbirth, any more than she was at her daughter's wedding. She was in Assam all that time, perhaps with no financial means at her disposal to come. No one really considered her presence of relevance at her daughter's first childbirth to sponsor the same. It was too early for Kalpana to request her husband to send Ma money and she did not have any savings yet. In later years she would put away some money from what her husband gave her for household expenses. Ma's presence in our lives was to always remain conspicuous by her absence, especially when we needed her the most. However, we knew her limitations and did not blame her. Kalpana gave birth to a baby boy, at Ronjit uncle's hospital, in Mihirpur.

In Ma's absence, I shared Kalpana's hospital room, assisting her, ushering her son's entry into the world. This experience was my literal annunciation into womanhood and motherhood. As I cautiously took the male bundle in my arms for the first time, I fell in love with his tiny pinkish face. I was to be enigmatically bound to the full head of hair, the beady eyes and long chin from then on. It would be much later that I would ostracize his adolescent form, with good reason, from my life. Maybe the fact that I witnessed his entry into the world, present with Kalpana the whole time, bound him to me mysteriously. Would it be on the strength of this bond that I would forgive him late in life for his follies leading to his parent's misery? Or would it be my deep gratitude to his parents, remaining indebted to them lifelong, that would compel my absolution of their wayward son?

All that would be much later. Now I adopted the fair-skinned, brown eyed baby as if he was my own son. I spent every possible moment watching him curiously. The boy was named Swapnil, which in Bengali means seen in a dream. Sudeep was weak in the knees with happiness to hold his own flesh and blood. This weak spot would rule Sudeep then on, to become the cause of his own and Kalpana's grief. Beset by a blind love, he would smother his child, leading him to go astray in spite of all sincere intentions to bring him up as an ideal son. Kalpana, equally inundated by her motherly instincts, would throw away her better sense of disciplining the child in turns with strictness. She would be a ready aide and perpetrator to her husband's leniency in bringing up Swapnil. They lovingly called him Khokhon.

I spent a lot of time playing, bathing and feeding baby Swapnil, besotted by his smiles and gurgles, whenever I could get away from school. Kalpana looked forward to my visits to take a breather, while also relishing my bonding with the apple of her eye. Starting with baby steps, Swapnil was soon a little boy whom I chased about the garden in front of their house. It was not long before I ran behind him gallantly seated on his tricycle. In time I would also follow his bicycle in teaching him to balance. My dates with him were not merely all fun and games; I also taught him his alphabets, numbers, and rhymes. At times I read him stories till he fell asleep and then tucked him into bed before leaving. I played my role as aunt to perfection, he being the son I would never have, with only two daughters one day.

Sudeep, Kalpana and Swapnil lived in Vishnuganj through my school years, till just before I finished college in Dacca. It was a perfect state of affairs for all of us. Sudeep was happy with his work, remuneration, conveniences and specially the house in Ronjit uncle's employment. Kalpana was content to run an efficient household in addition to bringing up her son. They entertained guests often, giving Kalpana ample opportunity to display her culinary and housekeeping skills, both of which by now she was adept at. On my part I was happy to be part of a real family and home, during my vacations. Sudeep and Kalpana had by now completely taken the place of parents in my life. Ma and Neelima we saw more often, now that Kalpana could send them money to travel. Baba stopped visiting Mihirpur, perhaps busy with his expanding family, one child following another, as I heard.

* * *

It was towards the end of 1963, that sporadic clashes broke out in the district of Khulna in East Pakistan. This was preceded by tension between Bengali and non-Bengali workers in the mills and factories. Led by a man from Khulna, these random riots gave rise to communal riots which soon spread to all the industrial areas. With the Biharis taking the lead, the riot spread to the districts of Jessore, Mymensingh, Pabna, Rajshahi and others. The Bengali Muslims came forward to protect the Hindus then, though many lost their lives. In the first week of December 1963, the then former Prime Minister of Pakistan and most prominent leader of the National Democratic Front, Hussein Shaheed Suhrawardy, died in his sleep in Beirut, where he was undergoing treatment. The whole nation mourned his death, with a renewed pledge to carry on the struggle against the military dictatorship of the Ayub Khan regime.

I was in college in Dacca when the government, looking for an opportunity to crush the unity of the people particularly in East Pakistan, soon found one. A hair of the Prophet Mohammad, kept in the Hazrat Bal mosque in Kashmir, got stolen. This incident was used to incite the Muslims and the ruling Pakistan Convention Muslim League declared 'Kashmir Day' on January 3, 1964. In the hostel one morning, I read in The Pakistan Observer that attacks were being made on girls' schools, women's hostels and on passengers in trains and buses. Reading these articles was very unnerving, knowing ours was a ladies hostel and we could well be the next likely target of the frenzied assailants. When trouble actually came knocking at our hostel gate in the form of a frantic mob, we were very lucky to be rescued in time by a police task force and taken to safety.

In spite of the violent situation, I was not going to run away, not before appearing for my examinations which were due in another few months. I had prepared for them in the two year professional course I had enrolled into after completion of my Bachelor in Arts degree. So I was to spend the next three months hiding in a Muslim friend's house, to return for the exams. In a hurry that I was to achieve financial independence and success, I was not about to relinquish the last two years of my learning, to start over again in India or elsewhere. What good would the attendance of an academic course be without the degree? Without relevant degrees requisite for a fine job, what good would a subsistence of restraint be, financially dependent on others for the rest of my life?

My mother's helplessness in the face of father's treachery always came to mind in times of indecisiveness like this. It propelled me to stay on in Dacca, in spite of the arsonist mood I was enveloped in. Though I was to never literally take up arms, I was intrinsically combating with life itself. How then could external forces deter my battle to win a good life, to hoist the flag of my success in front of my father? Therefore education and resultant economic autonomy I chose over the security of life at the time, deciding to leave East Pakistan only on completion of my final examinations. My personal experiences of the riots still give me the shudders. Even now, I wake up from sleep over vivid dreams of the violence, breaking out in a cold sweat as if I were in the midst of it.

At the very outbreak of the riots, Sudeep arranged for Kalpana and Swapnil to leave for Calcutta immediately. He would not take any chances with their security. I was able to convince him telephonically of my need to stay back, promising to leave right after my exams. He himself stayed back in a refugee camp, in wrapping up his business for a few more months. The evacuees from Vishnuganj who took shelter in two mills as reported by The Pakistan Observer were 24000, though the unofficial estimate of the evacuees was 150,000. As I learnt of this in the safety of my Muslim friend's house, knowing that Sudeep was in that count, I fervently prayed for his safety and reunion with his family. I constantly fought my fear of being brutally murdered if detected to be a Hindu. It truly was the acid test of my ability to fight any threat life would pose thereafter.

Ironically, in the massive communal violence against Hindus, the then government arrested Hindu leaders, along with the

 Shuvashree Chowdhury

Bengali Muslims, who were fighting the mutinous mob to protect the Hindus. In Dacca, Vishnuganj and other affected places, loot, arson, rape, and killings were going on unabated. It was a dry run of the 1971 riots and in many ways the beginning, to the Partition of Bengal. The non-Bengali and Muslim League ruffians did not spare anyone in the so-called holy war, not even an American national Father Novak, was spared. He was brutally murdered for going to rescue a Hindu family in distress. After four days, Father Novak's body was found on the riverbank and his personal belongings, including a wristwatch and a bicycle, were recovered from those who had killed him.

While international papers reported that the Dacca riots were the worst in a decade, the local press was ordered not to print anything on the wave of religious violence. Non-Bengali Muslims killed a number of Bengali Muslims during this riot. Massive migration of the Hindus began after the riot of 1964. Bengali nationalism created a united effort for democratic movements among the Hindu-Muslim communities. After neighbouring districts, when even Dacca was affected, a committee was formed to resist the communal riots in the name of "Danga Pratirodh Committee" or the Riot Prevention Committee, and a leaflet was issued under the title "Purba Pakistan Rukhia Darao" (meaning East Pakistan stand up to resist). The Bengali Muslims under the political leadership of Sheikh Mujibur Rahman, Ataur Rahman and others from the National Awami League; students; journalists of the East Pakistan Journalists Union and intellectuals, took out a procession.

The editors of the newspapers Ittefaq, Sangbad and The Pakistan Observer, led the journalists' procession. In bold letters, the front page of the newspaper Ittefaq read: "Sangrami Bangali Rukhiya Daraon - Revolutionary Bengali Rise in Protest." To me personally, it was a call to my soul for liberation from the fear of self-reliance. I was now practically on my own in Dacca and in the world. The paper also reported that at least ninety-five per cent of homes of the minority community in Dacca and Vishnuganj had been affected for three days, from the 14th to the 16th of January, 1964. Amidst the riots, there was no one who tried to check on my existence in the world, not even Ronjit uncle. While East Bengal was to begin its fight for independence into Bangladesh in 1971, I was already fighting for my personal liberation.

In my view, the only way I could achieve independence was through enhancing my educational qualifications, followed by a good job. It was only natural for me to have such an outlook, indoctrinated by Ronjit uncle and his institution as I was. In spite of all the turmoil around me, I tried to focus on preparing for the exams. I had upset Ronjit uncle in taking admission into the Bachelor of Physical Education course here in Dacca on completion of my Bachelor of Arts degree, as he had wanted me to apply to study abroad. So now I had the added pressure of proving myself to him. I had my reasons for defying him though, of which I could not tell him, my pride preventing me. How could I have told him that his daughter Ratna, whom he had asked to help me with the applications to foreign universities, did not make the effort to do so? I was too proud to ask her. Ronjit uncle and his family had been my benefactors for long. It was time I decided, to take charge of my life, instead of remaining a recipient to their charity any longer.

I had earned myself a scholarship to the professional course in Dacca on my own merit. In addition to the study, I would receive a monthly stipend. This was my breaking away from Ronjit uncle to lead my own life, in spite of my immense gratitude towards him. He would never know the real reasons for my taking an independent decision. After everything he and his family had done for me, his anger was probably justified. He had expected me to go to a good university in the West, so as to bring that learning back to his institutes in Mihirpur by working there. But in my view, he could have probed the cause of my sudden defiance, knowing that so far I had abided by every wish of his. This misunderstanding between us became the cause of his writing me off, even when the riots were devouring Dacca and its neighbourhood.

* * *

Leaving Vishnuganj at the onset of the riots, reaching Kolkata (or Calcutta as it was known at the time), Kalpana and Swapnil went to Sudeep's ancestral home. His two elder brothers resided there with their wives and children, the parents having passed

     Shuvashree Chowdhury

away long. The house was Sudeep's legally as theirs, but with him having left on completion of college, Kalpana and Swapnil were more guests than inmates now. However it was not long before Kalpana, impressing everyone with her culinary skills and charming disposition, came to be accepted as one of them. Swapnil, after initially sulking from the lack of undivided attention he was accustomed to in Vishnuganj, started enjoying the company of his cousins, playing with them with zest. He became particularly close to a cousin named Raju, a few years older than him. Raju was one of the few friends Swapnil would take into adolescence with him. This friendship was to cost him and his parents dearly one day.

Kalpana missed her home, along with the refined lifestyle she had become used to in Vishnuganj. But regularly reading about the unrest there, knowing she was away safely with her child, she reconciled to the restrictive life in a joint family. It was after three months of constant prayers for Sudeep's safety and arrival, that Kalpana was blessed with news of his coming. But even after Sudeep joined her she still worried, now for my safety. However, she had confidence in my fighter instincts, knowing in her heart that I would not allow a riot to thwart my chances of showing Baba and the world my mettle. It was her fervent prayers, in addition perhaps to my own grit and resilience that got me safely out of the violence in East Pakistan.

Once Sudeep reached Calcutta, he was able to get a decent job, as accounting head of a medium sized rubber factory. It was a regular job, with no challenges or much use of his qualifications in economics or law. But in the current circumstances, he could not complain, as he was lucky to have a home and means of livelihood. In large numbers, having left their established worlds the other side of the border in East Pakistan, people camped as refugees in Calcutta. Sudeep was not financially dependent on his brothers now. After living a few months in his childhood home, he began to feel stifled within a joint family, after years of living in a nuclear one. On the job front too, he thought it was time for him to start out on his own. He decided to practice Law, become a financial and legal consultant to businesses grovelling under the current socio-economic onslaught.

Sudeep was able to convince his brothers of his moving out,

to get an office-cum-residential complex, allowing him flexibility of time and working. He told them of his intentions of setting up an independent legal practice, though they advised him to exercise caution. Kalpana, on her part, was happy with the idea of setting up an independent household, to bring up her son the way she wanted without interference. In a joint family, a child belongs to the whole family. Decisions regarding him are taken consulting everyone, not only by the parents. Sudeep and Kalpana soon moved to a duplex house on Amherst Street close to College Street, the so called nucleus of education in Calcutta.

In the claret-red house they rented, a ground floor room at the entrance overlooking the street was converted into Sudeep's office. This office would one day create my destiny. Looking out of the window of this office, Kalpana would be shown by a well wisher, a prospective groom for me. The man who would go on to be my husband, lived and worked down the road, passing by often. However that would be much later. Now, having moved in, Sudeep immersed himself in work. He raked up all previous contacts, in a bid to form a robust client list for his practice. Kalpana engaged the services of two maids almost immediately, to help in setting up and keeping her home. Soon it was time for their son Swapnil to begin his schooling. They decided it had to be the best, obviously an English medium convent school.

Swapnil got admission to a good school in central Calcutta. Just about the time he was due to begin classes, he suddenly fell acutely ill. It started with a sore throat, followed by high temperature, accompanied with nausea and vomiting. Soon Swapnil was in considerable discomfort, suffering alternatively from diarrhoea and constipation. Since the symptoms indicated common flu, it was home medication that was administered for the initial days. After a week when there was no improvement to his condition, in spite of the medicines, the neighbourhood general physician was sent for. On examining the now scrawny boy, the doctor recommended consulting a paediatrician at a renowned hospital immediately.

In Sudeep's absence (he was out of town on business), Kalpana, frantic with worry, rushed Swapnil to the paediatrician herself. A battery of tests was conducted. He was diagnosed with polio. The

 Shuvashree Chowdhury

grey-haired doctor, lifting his head from the test reports on his desk, looked disappointedly at Kalpana through his thick myopic glasses.

"How is it that even educated people like you neglect to immunize your children?" he said in a condescending tone, "don't you know there is currently no antiviral medication to treat polio and it can even be fatal?" After a few moments of silence, again leafing through the reports gravely, he added sternly, "There is only a vaccine to prevent it. All children should be given five doses of the polio vaccine to ensure they remain immune to the virus. This vaccine also protects against diphtheria, tetanus and whooping cough. After the final dose, a child remains immune from these diseases for life. Didn't you hear of this?"

Kalpana looked at him desolately, her large eyes brimming with tears. How could she have missed the vaccine, she thought desperately, especially when she had such easy access to the hospital and medical facilities in Mihirpur? She and Sudeep had got so enthralled by Swapnil's birth, tucked away in the cosiness of their life in Vishnuganj, that they had omitted making that trip to the hospital. Then there was the flurry of activities leading to her fleeing with Swapnil to Calcutta, to ensure the security of his life. All this had led to neglecting to vaccinate him against deadly germs that could threaten his very existence. All she could do now was hope it was not the fatal or paralytic type of polio he had contracted. Kalpana brought Swapnil home wrapped in a blanket of prayer, along with the doctor's advice on strict bed rest and a fibre rich diet. He also gave her a prescription for the symptoms, analgesics for the fever and pain, laxatives for the constipation or medicines to stop his diarrhoea.

By this time, I was already in India, pursuing my Master's degree at a college in Gwalior in Madhya Pradesh. When Kalpana telephoned me to break the news of Swapnil's polio attack, I was aghast to learn what I had lately feared. I was angry with myself, for not having ensured Swapnil was vaccinated in Mihirpur, right after his birth. I was angrier at Kalpana, on my recall of her bringing the little boy, who was limping, into her home from the neighbourhood recently. This had been on my last visit, only a few weeks back. I had been staying at their house in Calcutta on my vacations as usual, when Kalpana suddenly came carrying a little scruffy looking boy.

"Maya, this boy cannot walk," she said, thrusting him into my unsuspecting arms, "please do something. I am sure with your physical education training and all that, you can help him."

I looked at the little boy, but even his innocent face could not control the sudden anger I felt at Kalpana's naivety and ignorance.

"How could you bring him home like this Didi?" I snapped at her. "You don't know what may be wrong with him? You have a little boy at home. Swapnil may easily contract whatever disease he has."

Just then Swapnil came running towards me, grabbing my hand to get my attention, on seeing me carrying another child. I promptly put the boy in my arms down on the floor, indicating to Kalpana with the wave of my hand, to take him away immediately. Kalpana gave me a quizzical look at first and then she picked up the boy in her arms, turned around and walked out the door. As I watched her retreating form, trying to control my exasperation, Swapnil came and encircled my legs, looking up at me to carry him.

The following week after I had returned to my college, the boy from the neighbourhood whom Kalpana had brought, was diagnosed with polio. Ever since I heard the news, I had the premonition of some harm coming to Swapnil. But in fear of worrying her, or worse still, actually bringing something bad on, I did not voice it to Kalpana. However, Kalpana had not told me that Swapnil had been having fever for a week accompanied by other symptoms, till her final announcement of his polio attack on the telephone. If she had, I might have asked her to rush him to a doctor earlier, though I am not sure it would have made the situation any different. After learning of Swapnil's polio attack, I could not help feeling let down by God. How could he do this to someone as thoughtful and caring as Kalpana, who in her naivety had sincerely wanted to help her neighbour's child?

In the weeks following Swapnil's diagnosis, Kalpana watched him round-the-clock for signs of any physical deformity. She knew how polio attacked the limbs and often left them incapable, but luckily she didn't detect any irregularity. After a few weeks when

Swapnil recovered from the fever, she and Sudeep were relieved, earnestly thanking God for saving their son. It was only now when Swapnil had begun to walk that Kalpana noticed him dragging his right leg, instead of placing it in sync with the left. He had developed a limp, but so slight, it might go unnoticed as he grew up, she thought. It could pass as a sign of poor walking posture. Though a little distressed, Kalpana and Sudeep were relieved the disease had not left any severe damage in its aftermath, above all that it had spared Swapnil's life.

Swapnil soon joined school, but he was rather aloof from the start as compared to his classmates. His muscles felt tired and heavy from the slightest physical exertion, which was compulsory in school. His teachers noticed he was averse to any physical activity, but goaded him nevertheless. Unable to cope, Swapnil withdrew into a shell. Kalpana and Sudeep were soon summoned by the principal. His teachers complained he lacked concentration and had problems remembering things he just learned. He was incapable of answering the simplest of questions verbally or in writing, making silly mistakes. He dozed off in class sometimes and was very shy and withdrawn when reprimanded. Sudeep was very alarmed that this should be happening with his son. Being academically well qualified, he had big dreams for his only child. That physical and mental lethargy are common symptoms of post-polio-syndrome, neither Swapnil's parents nor teachers were sensitive to.

At the time, the general awareness about such incapacitating diseases like polio was insufficient. Sudeep and Kalpana were oblivious that post-polio syndrome is a complex condition with a wide range of symptoms that can affect multiple aspects of one's life, depending on the severity of the attack. They little knew that his condition would be an ongoing one, requiring a treatment focused on controlling the symptoms and learning new ways to stay active, despite the muscle weakness. The brain communicates with muscles through the nerves, which polio destroys, causing muscles to die. Most polio survivors live in this state of having fewer cells for years and the very young, like Swapnil, grow up thinking the symptoms are normal. Due to ignorance, rather than treating Swapnil for lapses in his health, Kalpana and Sudeep pressed him to bring him on a par with other children his age.

When in the fifth standard, after being summoned a number of times by Swapnil's school authorities, Sudeep was asked to take his son out of school. This was following his inability to clear the year-end exams for two consecutive years. Not only was he lagging behind academically, Swapnil had no interest in sports or extra-curricular activities either. In spite of Kalpana's severe protests, Sudeep decided to send Swapnil to a boarding school in Dehradun in north India. He assumed the discipline inculcated by a boarding school upbringing would make a successful gentleman of his wayward son. But to his horror, it was not long before Sudeep started getting calls from there too, about the lack of progress of his son. However, by now, Swapnil having made two close friends at school was keen to continue his stint there. He managed to stay on by not failing any class consecutively.

With great difficulty, after struggling through classes, Swapnil appeared for his tenth standard board exams. However he could not pass the examinations on the first or even at the second attempt. During these two attempts he spent part of the time at school, but mostly at home. It was while at home preparing for the second attempt, that he resumed his friendship with his cousin Raju. He was the same boy Swapnil had got close to in the initial months at his father's ancestral home on arrival in Calcutta. Sudeep had requested Raju, who had completed his graduation and was a street-smart young man, to tutor Swapnil. It was under Raju's tutelage that Swapnil, having so far led a protected life, turned an eager disciple initiated to smoking, drinking and sexual promiscuity.

Raju was as yet unemployed. With no income, except for the meagre pocket-money which was limited on purpose by their parents, both the cousins had to compromise on the quality of their desires. Neither was given much money, as money might spoil them, or so their parents thought. Little did the parents realize that money or the lack of it is less cause for children going wayward, as compared to supervision or the lack of it. Raju was tall and handsome, with a baritone voice, and disarmingly charming mannerisms - all the makings of a ladies' man. But he did not have girlfriends in college, for he had little money to take them out, after his personal spends. Swapnil had inherited the good looks of his

   Shuvashree Chowdhury

parents, the light complexion and eyes, handsome facial features and a thick crop of black hair.

Raju came to Swapnil's house every evening, to help him with his studies in preparing for the board exams. He brought along with him the cheap cigarettes and alcohol he was used to. On the pretext of teaching his cousin, Raju shut the room door, so they could smoke and drink in privacy. During these escapades, the two young maids of the house stepped in and out of the room a number of times. On Kalpana's instruction they brought snacks like samosas, cutlets and fish fry from the local shop, along with tea. It was customary in the house to serve every guest refreshments, including sweetmeats and this was, after all, tea time. The cousins usually left the teacups untouched, but gorged on the snacks along with their drinks.

Swapnil and Raju used a ground floor room, adjacent to Sudeep's office at the entrance. The room was alongside the kitchen too, allowing easy access to the maids. The two large bedrooms and puja-room where Kalpana performed her elaborate evening puja were on the first floor. Though Sudeep was usually in his office at the time, he was very busy with his clients. Moreover, he knew Swapnil was under the observation of his cousin Raju whom he trusted, to study. One evening after a few drinks, by now certain his uncle or aunt would not step into their room, Raju started flirting with one of the maids. He looked into her eyes and whispered sweet nothings with sexual overtones. Apparently pleased with the attention, she flirted back with exaggerated, bashful, feminine gesticulations.

Swapnil watched in awe, the ease at which Raju, from smiling to teasing, took the girl's hand in his, as she giggled with her back turned to him seductively. In her early twenties, she was attractive with a dusky complexion, large kohl-lined eyes, and long black frizzy hair now in a neat bun. As Swapnil gaped in total rapture, her hair suddenly dropped open from her nape, slowly unfurling to her waist, emphasizing her full hips. With a light tug at the girl's hand, Raju turned her around to face him. For the first time since seeing her, Swapnil noticed her eyes, the eyelashes fluttering provocatively now, before he let his gaze travel downward. Her sari had fallen off her shoulder, drawing his attention to her dramatically heaving bosom and much exposed cleavage, through a low-necked red blouse.

Swapnil could not take his eyes off her, alternating his sight between her ample bosom and her luscious lips in red lipstick, with which she smiled in mock shyness. While he stared on, hooked to her guiles, Raju slowly undraped her yellow and red nylon sari, dropping it to the floor. Then he gently peeled off her blouse after she helped him with its front hooks. Swapnil visibly gasped at her shapely breasts, the tips firm and erect, just when the other maid entered the room. On seeing the proceedings, she looked down shyly for a few seconds and then locked the door behind her, before proceeding towards Swapnil. As she walked, she undraped her sari in slow deliberate movements, peeling off the blouse. When in front of him, she took both of Swapnil's hands and placed them on her now bare breasts, urging him to fondle them.

Swapnil did not look at the face of the woman who was initiating him into his first sexual encounter so deftly. It was the other woman with the large eyes and pretty face who Raju was now passionately kissing, that was fuelling his lust mentally. The one in front was catapulting it with her adroit manoeuvres. She unbuttoned his shirt and peeled it off, followed by the trousers and underwear. By the time Swapnil was struggling to return both physically and emotionally to the ground, from the jet ride he had undertaken lying face up, the two women were dressed and ready to take the empty plates out of the door, smiling mischievously at him. Raju grinned at Swapnil, as much from his own lusty release, as having freed his cousin from the bondage of childhood, initiating him into the throes of manhood.

Once tried and tested, this orgy in the guise of academic lessons continued for the next two months, till it was time for Swapnil to go for his exams. When he returned after the exams a month later, the elder maid, his partner, suddenly appeared much healthier than when he had left. He did not find anything strange about her having gained weight, as most did in a few months of their being employed in his house. His mother was kind and fed them as good as the family. Happy to see Swapnil, she smiled coyly at him, as she went about her work. She had been awaiting his return, to break the good news, which ironically was about to shatter his life

     Shuvashree Chowdhury

for ever. Raju came the day after Swapnil's return, presumably to resume the good times. That evening the maids were in the room as usual. The evening tea was untouched, but served nonetheless in case Kalpana should ask, along with telebhaja or deep fried snacks and jhalmuri (spiced puffed rice).

"There is something we need to tell you," the younger maid, Raju's partner, started, and then looking towards the other added sombrely, "we have a huge problem at hand."

Raju and Swapnil looked from one to the other woman, then at each other. Raju's expression suddenly grew dismal, quickly turning to alarm, while Swapnil looked puzzled.

"What is the matter?" Raju asked sharply, "come out with it promptly, instead of beating about the bush."

"Didi is with child," the younger woman said emphatically, then turning towards the elder woman, she asked, "Must be about two months, isn't it Didi?"

At first Raju was visibly relieved it was not his partner who was pregnant. He then looked at Swapnil, with his forehead furrowed deep with worry. Swapnil looked back at him enquiringly, the gravity of the situation not having registered in his naive mind yet.

"So what do you want us to do now"? Raju asked sternly, turning towards the pregnant woman, "you want money for the abortion, is it?" Then after a little thought, recalling they had no money, in a desperate attempt to escape the situation he abruptly added, "but how do we know whose child it actually is?"

The pregnant woman started crying, while the other turned ferociously at Raju, "What do you mean by whose? Has there been anyone else here, other than you two? It is obviously Swapnil-da's."

"What, my child, how can that be, are you sure?" Swapnil blurted, snapping to attention as if thrashed with a broom by a God-man to come out of his oblivious trance.

"Yes, obviously yours, who else's?" the wailing woman snapped. "Am I a whore, to be confused about the identity of my child's father?"

Swapnil looked at her in shock, fighting to come to terms with the situation at hand. When he realized his parents would soon come to know of his rendezvous with the maid, his expression changed to alarm, followed by scorn at the mother of his unborn child. He glared at her in anger and through his fury he really noticed her for the first time. She was old and rather ugly, he thought, with a long dark face scarred with small-pox marks, beady eyes, a hawkish nose and a broad mouth with bulbous lips slightly ajar, possibly unable to shut over the set of large protruding teeth. How was he ever going to explain this situation to his parents? What explanation did he have anyway for his predicament, considering she was far from attractive? His mother was going to be devastated, Swapnil concluded.

Raju remained silent, desperately trying to figure out how he was ever going to explain this state of affairs to his uncle and aunt. They had trusted him after all, and his parents would also learn of it from them soon. He knew women like the two maids were not going to give up easily on the situation of a lifetime. How could he have been so stupid as to allow Swapnil to have sex without protection, that too the first time? He obviously could not be expected to be adept like himself at natural birth-control tactics. These women had either planned this, Raju realized, and if not, were going to take full advantage of a situation that had fallen into their arms like a garland from the heavens. Raju knew his uncle was reasonably rich and Swapnil being his only child would naturally inherit everything.

"I better be going now, it's quite late already," Raju said rising abruptly, then turning towards Swapnil he added, "Don't worry Bhai; we will sort this out soon. Give me some time to think."

He walked out of the room, leaving Swapnil with the two women. It was the last time Raju was seen in that house, abruptly bringing to a halt the camaraderie between the two cousins, never to be renewed. When he had not come for a few days, Swapnil went to Raju's house in desperation, to seek his advice. Raju was out of the house or so Swapnil was told the first time, as well as each time that he went in search of him thereafter. It was best to stay away, Raju thought, why would he want to be a part of the mess his foolish cousin had got himself into? So what if he had personally initiated him into it?

A month passed, with both maids threatening Swapnil to tell

 Shuvashree Chowdhury

his parents if he did not find a solution soon. The pregnant woman by now had become visibly so, and she had even begun flaunting it. One morning still in bed, when Kalpana noticed her protruding tummy while she was sweeping the room, startled she sat upright on the bed.

"Are you pregnant or what Meena?" she asked in a firm voice, her tone commanding the woman to look at her, to answer at once.

Meena turned to look at Kalpana promptly, as if waiting to be asked about her condition. Her sari had been uncovering her stomach conspicuously, to gain Kalpana's attention. She burst into tears with her face contorting, eyes turned downward, but remained silent.

"What is the matter, you are? Aren't you?" Kalpana stated, sounding aghast. After a brief pause, to let the implications of an unmarried woman being pregnant sink in, she crisply asked, "Who is the father?"

This was the question Meena had been waiting for, ever since she learnt of her pregnancy. Now was the opportune time to create an impact on Kalpana, projecting her case in a positive, effective manner for maximum effect. The idea was to create much sympathy, so that Kalpana, being the righteous woman she was known to be, would not allow her weakness for her son overpower her choice of the right thing to do in the circumstance. Still looking downward, Meena allowed the tears to flow, her body shuddering with silent sobs that slowly built to a frenzied rock. As Kalpana continued to watch curiously, Meena went down on her haunches, lowering her head till it touched the ground. She began beating her forehead to the ground with firm strokes. As expected, Meena's theatrics had the desired effect in spurring Kalpana's protective streak.

Kalpana promptly got off the bed, blurting "The boy who did this will have to marry you Meena, just you see." Then bending to lift Meena, she added firmly, "Don't worry, I will see to it that he does."

Suddenly bursting into loud sobs, abruptly stopping, then sighing exaggeratedly, Meena replied, "But that is just not possible Ma, as he is not working yet. He cannot marry me." Looking forlornly into Kalpana's eyes, she added, "What am I to do now, Ma?"

"What do you mean by he won't marry you?" Kalpana snapped. "He has to. You just tell me who he is and I will deal with him."

Meena remained silent. Kalpana impatiently repeated, more as a command now. "Tell me who is he and where does he live?" She recalled that Meena went out every evening that too, all decked up.

"I don't know how to tell you this, Ma," Meena blurted. The strain of the act beginning to overwhelm her now, and wanting it over soon she added, "I wish I had somewhere to go, so as to never show you my face again, but I cannot even go home in this condition. It is Swapnil-da."

"What do you mean by it is Swapnil-da?" Kalpana quizzically retorted, the insinuation not remotely registering. As her eyes bore questioningly into Meena who looked back defiantly, the implication of Meena's words presently dawned on her. She realized that Meena meant every word she just said. Kalpana's fair skinned face turned red, the apples of her cheeks and the tip of her sharp nose in particular. The emotions flitting through her ranging from shock to anger, then denial, she whispered, "But he is still only a child, Meena." With the full impact of the situation sinking in, completely washed out and defeated, fury no longer her aide, Kalpana added desperately, "But Meena are you sure he is the father?"

"I knew you will not believe me Ma, no one will, but it is the truth" Meena stated, then meeting Kalpana's gaze, a large pool of worry on which distrust floated like a lotus, she added, "You can ask Raju-da."

Kalpana did not need to ask anyone, she believed Meena, but also understood that her son had been manipulated into the situation. He was merely an adolescent, while Meena, even though still unmarried, was nearing her thirtieth year. Her son had been conned by a devious woman, Kalpana concluded, but it was not going to help matters to antagonize her. Kalpana knew she had to cautiously plan her next move, or Meena could get more scheming. After she discussed the matter with Sudeep, they decided that the only way out was to offer Meena a large sum of money with other

    Shuvashree Chowdhury

material benefits, in lieu of her having an abortion and leaving their home and lives for good.

By this time, I was married, living and working in Calcutta. I was the only person Kalpana and Sudeep could consult on the issue of the adolescent fatherhood. When I heard of the incident I was appalled. Their attitude, their blaming Meena while their son was not attributed any of the culpability, infuriated me. Swapnil was no longer a child, though in my opinion, they as parents were most to blame for their negligence. The incident had taken place in the house. I made it a point to strongly convey my views to them.

"Didi, several times I told you not to keep female maids when you have an adolescent boy at home," I said to Kalpana. Then, on the face of her silence like a child who had failed her exams, I added, "You need to sort out Swapnil, before proceeding to help him sort out this mess. Only then will he ever learn some hard lessons from his mistakes."

Then turning towards Sudeep, I continued offhandedly, "and you, Dada-babu, have allowed Swapnil and Raju this regular evening tryst with the maids. You were here in the adjacent room, but chose to turn a blind eye, thereby perpetrating their misdeeds. I even told you on a visit that I saw the two boys' cosy and giggling with the maids. I had suggested you break up the gathering immediately and tell them off, but you paid no heed. Now see what has happened."

Sudeep didn't reply either. Their silence infuriating me, I faced Kalpana squarely, attacking her mercilessly.

"Didi, you dropped out of school yourself," I said in exasperation. "The lack of education and exposure made you ignorant, you brought a polio-infected boy into your house, infecting your son, whom you negligently didn't inoculate, mentally crippling him for life. You remain so focused on your puja and rituals, neglecting your responsibilities towards home and family, handing over its reins to a bunch of devious maids, who turn your home into a whorehouse."

My tirade came to an abrupt halt, with my husband, sitting next to me in Sudeep's office, putting his hand on my shoulder, in a gesture to calm me down. Kalpana had been detected with extremely high blood sugar, leading to her lack of concentration lately. This condition would eventually lead to her partial amnesia and wandering away from home at times. It would not be good for her to take on any more stress than she had been taking since learning of this. As for me, I loved Swapnil no less than a son, but I was not unmindful to his mistakes, as I would never be to my own daughters. Good parenting is about balancing love and affection with good potions of discipline. Sudeep and Kalpana besieged in weakness for their only son did not so much as reprimand him then or ever, truly crippling him for life.

I took upon myself the task of reproaching Swapnil, hoping to make him take onus for his misdemeanour.

"Swapnil you are no longer a child" I rebuked, "your parents are aging and your mother is very unwell. You have to take responsibility now."

"Don't interfere in my business, Mashi (Aunty)," Swapnil flared, looking at me defiantly, his body language very aggressive, like he would hit me.

He obviously took offence to my chiding him, when his own parents said nothing. I came down very strongly on him following his defiant manner, thereby finally ending the close bond that had existed between us since his childhood. Our relationship had already worn thin over the last few years, when I had tried to guide and counsel him about his studies. It would only be after his parent's passing, haunted by problems that he would come seeking my help and advice one day, in claiming his financial inheritances.

Soon the negative results of Swapnil's second attempt at clearing his matriculation exams were declared. I learnt of it from Sudeep over a telephone call I had made to check on their situation. I promptly suggested to him to send Swapnil over to my husband's office, to learn some practical work from him. He ran his own business and so could take on a trainee at will. Coming to terms with Swapnil's mental deficiency was very hard on Sudeep, but I was able to convince him. Luckily, Swapnil did not dislike his Mesho (Uncle), contrary to his extreme aversion for me by now. He agreed and started reporting to him daily. But Swapnil was not an amicable team player and rubbed other workers the wrong way,

    Shuvashree Chowdhury

getting into altercations. When they complained and my husband reprimanded him, he abruptly stopped coming for work. Then on, he whiled away his days at home.

The turning point in Swapnil's life was Meena's refusal to an abortion and money his parents offered her. She insisted on giving birth and continued to live in the house. Swapnil resumed his relationship with Meena and it was not long before Meena was able to monopolize his affections. Swapnil had no friends and soon the only people he interacted with were Meena and her friends and family. They began to drop in and it was as if the house belonged to Meena and her co-conspirators. Sudeep and Kalpana were by now as if guests in their own house. Too weak, they helplessly turned a blind eye to the course of their beloved son's life. Their resignation led to Swapnil marrying Meena the housemaid, even before he turned seventeen. It enraged and pained me, but he was not my son, so there was little I could do in the circumstances but remain a mute spectator to his "suicide".

When Swapnil married Meena, there was no elaborate wedding ceremony. The prospective groom by now completely enmeshed by Meena, was escorted or rather marched to the nearby temple for the nuptials by her aides. The wedding was solemnized by the temple priest, who made the necessary arrangements, supervised by Meena's partner in crime, the maid Swapnil had been initially attracted to. It was during the wedding that Meena's brother came out of the backdrop of the well-rehearsed play, never to leave his sisters side, moving in to her home along with his family. Raju, the man responsible for the turn of events in Swapnil's life, was called upon to be best man to the teenaged groom.

Raju obliged, for was it not the least he could do for his cousin under the circumstances? It was after all a small price to pay to assuage his guilt. It was Meena's idea for Raju to be present, for if ever a point in question rose on the legitimacy of her marriage, he could validate it. It was by now a month since my angry outburst at Kalpana and Sudeep. Feeling guilty and concerned yet hesitant to encounter Swapnil, I finally resolved to visit them. I was seated in Sudeep's office flipping the pages of the Illustrated Weekly magazine, when I suddenly noticed the golden zari border of a sari. It fell over a pair of bare feet thickly bordered with alta, the red liquid used by Bengali women. I instantly looked up, expecting to see Kalpana, since recognizing the sari as one I had given her a few months back. To my horror it was not her but Meena wearing it, who came in carrying a loaded tea-tray.

After the initial shock of seeing Meena in Kalpana's sari, that too one given by me, I appraised her newly married attire in disgust. She looked horrendous I thought, in the red sari, her dark, scarred gawky face over the huge pregnant frame. My revulsion was propelled more by the fleeting thought of how beautiful Kalpana had looked in the same sari. Meena's audacity in wearing Kalpana's sari, flaunting it when it had been a gift from me, had about sufficiently enraged me, when I took a closer look to find her wearing Kalpana's jewellery as well. The Sitahaar - a long gold necklace and two balas - the thick bangles, around her dark arms with the unkempt hands, looked too familiar. I presently took in the thick smear of vermillion at the centre parting of her oiled and sari-hooded hair, the large red bindi on her forehead and the gold wired shakha and paula, the symbols of marriage on her wrists, all belonging to Kalpana. It made me furious.

After placing the tray she was carrying on the table in front, Meena abruptly stooped to touch my feet. I glared at her with all the hatred I could summon from deep within my gut.

"How are you, Aunty?" She quipped, and then with her right hand on my feet, trying to meet my gaze, she added," give us your blessings."

I stepped backward involuntarily, jerking away from her resting hand. Then I noticed Swapnil standing at the doorway, with a smug look on his face, tilted upward in a gesture of defiance.

"Meet my wife," he said grinning, "now the bride of this house."

It was a fight for me to control the strong urge I had to slap his face, but all I did was look at Sudeep and mumble, "Dada-babu, how could you let this happen?"

Sudeep looked downwards, his shoulders drooping in a gesture of helplessness and defeat. I noticed how old and worn out he looked. I stood up brusquely, walking out of the room in disgust.

 Shuvashree Chowdhury

I was headed to the staircase at the back of the house on my way to see Kalpana, knowing she would be in her room upstairs. As I walked out, I noticed Meena bending to touch my husband's feet which remained rooted to the floor, his face expressionless, not knowing how to react. He had grown very fond of Swapnil over the years when he had gone to fetch or leave him at his school in Dehradun. Sudeep often could not travel due to business engagements. After briskly climbing the stairs, Kalpana's room as I stepped inside, was partially illuminated by a dim blue night-light. She lay awake in bed, staring at the ceiling. It was only about 7 pm and too early for her usual bed time.

I turned on a white lamp and walked towards her, sitting down beside her on the bed. I slowly took her hand in mine. She turned to look at me woodenly, with not the slightest trace of recognition, or seeming as if she did not care for my presence. Seeing her demeanour, I decided not to broach the obvious topic. I had had the time to gulp it down like a cup of bitter medicine on my way up, so was able to check my raging emotions much easier now. The situation was at its worst already, so the only thing to do now was reconcile to it and move on.

"How are you Didi?" I asked tenderly, "Have you had dinner?"

She did not respond. I frantically searched for something appropriate to say, to take away or at least assuage her suffering, but nothing came to mind. In any case, no words I realized desperately would make any difference to her losing her adolescent son in marriage to the domestic maid.

I squeezed Kalpana's hand, as I often did as a child, in coping with emotions varying from fear to excitement, sadness to happiness. Now I was hoping to impress upon her my presence, as well as infuse some of my emotional and physical strength into her. I felt immensely sorry for my harsh words to her on my previous visit, however true they rang. Everything that was dear to Kalpana had been usurped by Meena. She had taken advantage of Kalpana's illness and resultant mental state, Sudeep's age and indifferent disposition, but above all Swapnil's adolescent naivety. I noticed the fine line of tears roll down Kalpana's left eye, while the other shone a brilliant green through the film of tears. I bent down and took her frail wooden frame in my arms, holding her close for a few moments. Then unable to control the tirade of emotions choking me, threatening to usurp the calm I had cloaked myself in on my way up, I set her down gently.

I did not say another word, the silence more powerful, as I slowly got up from her bedside. I walked out of the room turning out the bright light. As I looked back at Kalpana one last time from the door, I found her glassy gaze had followed my retreating form. I did not know at the time that it would be the last time I would ever see my beloved sister. After Sudeep's retirement from active work, the family including Meena and her brother's family moved to a sprawling two storey home in the outskirts of Calcutta. Kalpana had put all her time and effort of the past few years into it, including travelling an hour to and fro daily to supervise its construction, till it was ready. She had even got erected a shed on the huge property, for the two pet cows she had acquired during the time. Well cared for, the cows had been milked regularly, and the fresh milk brought to her in the city every evening.

Kalpana's new home was intended to give a rustic feel, while being close to the city. She had perhaps wanted her new home to have a feel of our childhood home in Assam. Like me, having her own home had been the single-point driving force in Kalpana's life. She had bought the land shortly after moving to Calcutta. After my last visit when I learnt of Swapnil's wedding, the next was a year after at the new house, just before Durga Puja. Like every year, I customarily took gifts of clothes for Sudeep, Kalpana and Swapnil. At the iron-gate leading into the property, my husband and I were met by Swapnil. He was very rude and refused to let us in or even open the gate just to talk. Through the grille gate at a distance, I saw Meena carrying a little girl in her arms.

"I'm here to meet my sister, not any of you" I said firmly to Swapnil, "to give her the new clothes for Durga Puja as usual."

"Here, give it to me then," Swapnil replied brusquely, extending his hand after opening the gate slightly. Barely had I handed the bag to him, preferring it to returning with the gifts, when he flung the cloth bag to the ground in front, adding tartly, "we don't need your gifts."

I was horrified; it took a few seconds for the impact of his actions to register. I looked at my husband standing behind me.

    Shuvashree Chowdhury

He decided to remain silent, perhaps finding it useless to argue with an imbecile.

"Is this the way you behave with your elders?" I said menacingly, turning back to face Swapnil, as he stood glaring at me.

"You insulted my wife the last time, you remember?" he nearly spat at me bitterly, "so now you are not allowed into our house, ever."

His behaviour was perhaps tutored by his wife and her brother. It was pointless arguing with a stupid man. It was not going to make him see any more sense. With a heavy heart at not meeting Kalpana, having to retreat right from her doorstep, I turned around to leave. My misery was compounded with the realization that the dim-witted demon compelling me to do so was her only child whom I had once loved dearly.

In a month from this trip, Ma visited Calcutta. She had continued to live in Baba's house in Assam, though by this time he was no more. Luckily she was allowed into Kalpana's house, even permitted to stay. But barely after a few days, unable to bear Kalpana's state of health, added to her being under Meena's control, Ma returned to my house very distressed.

"Those cannibals, they are going to eat my daughter alive," she wailed. "It is all Sudeep's fault you know, Maya. He ruined my daughter's life, now even his son has turned out to be a womanizer like he was."

It was an appalling revelation to me, what Ma said about Sudeep. Perhaps I had been more absent than not in their lives I thought, to not have realized Kalpana's silent woes. The tremendous respect I had for Sudeep, his having been my guardian, mentor and guide had also presumably blinded me from this aspect of his character. It was only lately, that I had become acutely aware of the inherent weakness of his personality, from his dealing with the issues concerning his son. It was from Ma that I learnt of Kalpana being totally bedridden now.

Sudeep had developed a great difficulty in walking. He had fallen in the bathroom of the earlier house, injuring his hip bone, followed by an extensive hip replacement surgery. Kalpana and Sudeep, elder to her by twelve years and over seventy now, were both at the mercy of Meena and like prisoners in their own home. Kalpana was fed large portions of rice at every meal, just as Meena and her rice-planter family were used to. Her sugar and sweet intake were not curtailed either, though rice and sugar were as good as poison for one suffering from acute diabetes as she was. All this in addition to unregulated medicine and insulin intake, in her delicate mental condition, expedited her ill health. Kalpana was far from the fair-complexioned, green-eyed, beautiful woman Ma had in mind when she visited her daughter.

Constantly in bed now, added to the unhygienic conditions from physical neglect, Kalpana had been reduced to a bundle of shrivelled, rotting flesh from bed sores. I decided to go and get Kalpana to keep her at home with me, so as to take good care of her. I mentally prepared to give Swapnil and Meena the battle of their lives, if that is what it would take for them to hand Kalpana over to me. But sadly the opportunity did not present itself, for when I again found myself standing at their gate, it was to learn that Kalpana had passed away a week back. Swapnil had honoured his mother in death, as he had not in her lifetime, by lighting her pyre and tonsuring his head as is customary for a son.

I was beside myself with anger, before grief could find its way into my heart. The anger was directed mostly at God, for not allowing me the opportunity to take care of Kalpana, as she had watched out for me all of her life. This time, however, I was allowed into the house by Swapnil. I passed him sitting woodenly on the porch stairs, seemingly in shock. Meena looked at me with indifference, as I crossed her at the doorway. Inside I found Sudeep sitting on a chair, staring blankly out of the window. He turned to face me for a moment, but on seeing the accusingly angry look in my eyes, he looked away dejectedly.

"Kalpana was my sister, long before she was your wife and Swapnil's mother," I said to him sharply. Then on seeing the piteous look in Sudeep's eyes, my voice mellowing, I added "Dada-babu, couldn't you have informed me of her death, at least?"

Sudeep remained silent for a few brief moments, before he whispered in response, "Sorry, Maya I just could not. I'm the one who killed her."

          Shuvashree Chowdhury

I looked hard at him. Seeing the guilt, repentance and sorrow, all written large on his wrinkled face, I did not have the heart to press further.

I crisply asked, "When is her shradh ceremony?"

After learning that the final rites would be performed a week later, on the thirteenth day after her death, I left Kalpana's house with a boulder in my chest. The weight of it pressing into my guts was so severe it would not allow the tears to trickle out of my parched eyes. My husband was very saddened to hear the news of Kalpana's death. He had shared a special bond with Kalpana from the start and, along with our daughters, was expecting me to bring her to live with us.

The following Sunday, I attended Kalpana's final rites, with my husband and two school-going daughters. Kalpana had loved my family no less than her own. Swapnil had organized lunch for everyone, after the rituals and puja. In spite of not having the heart to eat a morsel along with the perpetrators of my dearest sister's death, I could not refuse the meal in her memory. I had already turned down the invitation for the customary non-vegetarian meal, in breaking the thirteen day abstinences, the next day.

At lunch I could barely swallow the rice served, knowing it had expedited Kalpana's death. The mouthfuls I stuffed choked me from the recurring thoughts of the piteous manner of her death. But I gulped down my anguish and the rice, along with glasses of water, in tribute to the biggest loss of my life yet.

Chapter 5

The Transition to Womanhood

I passed my Matriculation exams from Ronjit uncle's school in the year 1956. Though I learnt English as an additional language, Bengali being the medium of instruction, I was far from proficient at the Queen's language. Ronjit uncle in foresight knew I would not fare well in life unless I was adept in the usage of English. Therefore, I was sent to a convent boarding school for girls, along with seven others, all of us sponsored by Ronjit uncle, to learn English. It was part of his social welfare initiatives in sequence to his providing free education for women, for those with potential for a bright future. We were to be admitted to the ninth standard, to attend classes over again, with English as the medium of instruction. Here I was to spend two years in trying to think in English, rather than having to translate from Bengali, when speaking or writing English, as I did before.

This school was in Darjeeling in the state of West Bengal in India, even then. All of Ronjit uncle's female children and grandchildren were alumnae here. In fact, two of his granddaughters were still in school when I joined, in junior classes. The eight of us sponsored by Ronjit uncle had travelled by road from East Pakistan, crossing the border with our Pakistani passports. We had travelled unaccompanied, in a jeep, with only an introductory letter to the Mother Superior from Ronjit uncle. He knew her well. After handing over the letter to the bearer on arrival, we waited in the parlour. Soon we were led into Mother Superior's office and she welcomed us warmly. We then introduced ourselves to her individually. On completing admission formalities, another Sister led us on a tour of the rest of the premises, starting with the chapel, ending at the dormitory where we were to stay.

Shuvashree Chowdhury

At the senior girls' dormitory, we were introduced to other girls of the ninth and tenth standard. In time, I would make friends with some girls from Sikkim, Tibet, Nepal and Bhutan. Most students here came from Calcutta, but many were from the neighbouring east Indian states as well. On our first night we retired after the regular 7.30 pm supper at the refectory, served by a number of male Nepali bearers. They had also cooked the meal under supervision of the chief cook, a heavily built, tall, African man. Things around here were very different, we soon learnt, as compared to Ronjit uncle's school in Mihirpur. We would not be required to do any of the regular house-keeping chores like, cooking, cleaning, and washing. We had to only concentrate on our academic lessons, extra-curricular activities and sports, including basketball, volleyball and hockey.

Starting the next morning, our regular day began at 5.30 am when still dark, woken by the ringing of a brass bell. A Sister walked our dormitory on the first floor, overlooking the playfield, ringing it. Darjeeling being a hill-station, it was cold here year-round. We had joined in January, when it was coldest, so we got used to it soon. After morning prayers which we all said aloud, kneeling by our bedside, we got ready in the dressing-room on the ground floor. Thankfully we did not have to rush for outdoor activities thereafter in the cold, but had a study-hour supervised by a teacher in the large study-hall. This was followed by breakfast, then another hour of study, before we joined the day-scholars at the auditorium for the morning assembly before classes commenced. We returned to the refectory for lunch and classes ended by 3.30 pm. After high tea we had an hour of compulsory sports, followed by another study hour, a half hour of collective prayers for non-Catholics and rosary for Catholics. After supper at 7.30 pm there was another hour of supervised study, before we retired for the night after group prayer, kneeling by our bedsides.

I felt truly obliged to Ronjit uncle for giving me this experience of a premium-school education. In return, I wanted to make him and my teachers truly proud of me. It was not long before the Sisters at the school became fond of me. I was after all more respectful and obedient of them than the girls they had brought up since childhood. These girls perhaps did not appreciate the humility that gratitude brings, taking what they got as their birthright, for granted. It was one morning at breakfast in the refectory, that all the girls refused to eat the bread served, claiming it was stale. After a ruckus, everyone walked out defiantly. I remained sitting, eating what was on my plate as usual, refusing to join the others, not afraid to be an outcast. I knew by now not to take things for granted, least of all food. I was never sure from where or by whose grace the next meal would be available.

In fact unlike others, I did not complain about routine, as is common among boarders. They would be unhappy about the early rising and lights out time; the fixed bathing, games and outing time; hating that we led our lives literally by the ringing of a bell every hour. I also did not fuss over the bland food that was served, but ate it with thankfulness. One among the eight of us sponsored by Ronjit uncle, who was a Muslim, constantly teased me after Sunday lunches. She was convinced the meat served was beef, that I was breaking my religious restrictions as a Hindu. I tried to ignore her jibes, though it upset me to think that I indeed was. However I would not ever complain of it, eating perfunctorily. One day I got my revenge when she had sausages for breakfast, not knowing it was of pork. I sadistically minced "you're having pork" into her ears, once she had swallowed the last bite. She ran into the washroom, shoving a finger down her throat to throw it up, in order to retain her religious sanctity.

At the end of two years, fortified with my fluency in English, I was ready for the world and admission to an American missionary college, back in Dacca, in East Pakistan. The same group of eight of us sent to learn English were also sponsored by Ronjit uncle to this institute. He probably had our admissions to this college in mind when he sent us to learn English. The medium of instruction here was only English, without sufficient knowledge of which we could not get admission here, let alone pass our courses. On the first day of our college term, Mother Augustine Mary, the Mother Superior, met us after we had settled into our allocated rooms, just before supper at the dining hall. She was tall and slender, with a fair and flawless complexion. In her blue habit, with soft facial features and a pair of blue eyes peering through metal-rimmed

 Shuvashree Chowdhury

glasses, she was the picture of warmth and strictness combined. I took to her, as well as to college, spontaneously.

After leaving my childhood home in Assam, I am not sure at which point adolescence creeping upon me stealthily, passed me by. I had registered some significant gashes to my conscious memory in transcending my childhood, in spite of every effort to clear my mind, rather shut things out thereafter. It was these harsh emotional chips by the chisel bearing hands of my traumatic early life that sculpted my psyche. My adolescence in Mihirpur, Darjeeling and Dacca did not leave any deep emotional impact, but was a perfect prefatory to haul me into womanhood, so I could start realizing my dreams. My transition to womanhood was discernible by my completing college in Dacca and subsequent forced emancipation from Ronjit uncle's guardianship, in becoming the sole custodian of my life and decisions.

The four years I spent in college, two for the Intermediate and two more for the Bachelor of Arts course, transformed me from a gawky teenager into a refined woman. The nuns at the college, all Americans and women of immense poise and grace, ensured that in addition to academics, we were compulsorily exposed to varied extra-curricular activities like dramatics, elocution, debates, art, music and sports. Since I excelled in athletics and sports, I was an active member of the Sports Club. I also took a keen interest in dance, drama and music that had started from my schooldays. My part as Shylock in the Shakespearean play The Merchant of Venice and as Abdullah the servant in Ali Baba and the Forty Thieves got me a lot of acclaim, even when performed at venues outside the college.

Our college published a quarterly-magazine, which encouraged us students to develop our writing skills. I wrote a number of poems, both in Bengali and English, pondering over the cycle of life, death, rebirth, destiny and God, which were published in the magazine. In the last two years while in my Bachelor of Art course, I was also a member of the editorial board of the magazine, as the Bengali editor. It is during this time that I met and became close to Zaina, a luminous complexioned Muslim girl, with waist length hair, large brown eyes and an exquisite smile, better known to most by her pet-name Lovely. She was two batches my junior, admired my involvement in varied activities and liked my poetry in particular. I grew immensely fond of her sprightly, charismatic and friendly nature. Little was I to know then, that one day she and her family would take me into their home during the subsequent riots in the year 1964, thereby saving my life.

While in college, I did not have money to spend like most other girls. So I did not usually go out in the evenings, but spent the time either reading or writing on the lush-green college lawns. All I had as pocket-money was the Rupees 30 a month I still received from Ronjit uncle's school in Mihirpur, for teaching and helping out during my vacations. Zaina often joined me after classes and we either discussed books we were reading, or poems I had written. On some weekends my sister Kalpana came to visit me from Vishnuganj, which was over an hour's drive from Dacca. She brought home-cooked food in a basket at times and at others gave me money from what she had put away after her household expenses. We spent a couple of hours sitting on a bench on the college lawn, catching up on our respective lives. It is through her visits and updates that I remained connected to Ronjit uncle's world.

Madhavi, Ronjit uncle's elder daughter, came to Dacca when she could make time from overseeing the ongoing constructions at Mihirpur and as superintendent of the school. On such occasions she dropped by my college to see me, before returning to Mihirpur. Sometimes she also took me on outings; it is with her that I first visited a restaurant and had a meal, a Chinese one at that. Though I had little money, Ronjit uncle's younger daughter Ratna's clothes I received as handouts, ensured I was always well turned out. Farida, my roommate, loved watching films at the local cinema hall, but rarely found anyone to go along with her. We often discussed films late into the night, so she knew of my love for the cinema, though I could not afford the cost of tickets.

Farida was very kind in asking me to go along with her for films, insisting on paying for my tickets, making it appear that she needed a companion. It is due to her that I had the opportunity of watching a number of good English, Hindi and Bengali films,

                    Shuvashree Chowdhury

both current and old. In addition to the varied books that I read from the well-stocked college library, the films increased my exposure and awareness to various facets of life. Being a keen observer, I also imbibed the style and fashion of the times, through watching the actors in current films. However, keeping in mind Ronjit uncle's abhorrence of makeup, I was never even tempted to try. Instead I developed a love for perfumes, having received an occasional one from Ratna on her return from trips abroad. I used them sparingly while dressing, wearing different hairdos with my long hair.

I did not have much to call my own, ever since Baba abandoned us, but God ensured I was sufficiently provided for by Ronjit uncle and well meaning friends and relatives. In addition to the valuable lessons of gratitude and humility, I learnt to value financial independence over everything, so as to never depend on anyone later in life. The insecurity of not knowing my next benefactor, for every small aspect of life, would make me strive to build my own home and fortunes one day. I had to ensure I would never encounter this diffidence again. It is one thing to be an orphan, quite another to have parents - in our case a father who didn't care. It is one thing to live in hunger and poverty never knowing of the good things of life, quite another growing up on handouts from generous family and friends, after squashing one's self-esteem, under their luxurious carpets.

* * *

One Sunday, in my final year at college, when Kalpana came to visit me, she brought with her news of the sudden demise of Madhavi's husband, Satyendra. It came as a rude shock to me. I had been very fond of him, calling him Jamai-babu or brother-in-law, and he had doted on me. He was one of the nicest, kindest men I have known, simple and humble. His was my first encounter with the death of a loved one. It made me very sad, but more so for Madhavi widowed at a young age and for her six children, losing the husband and father who adored them. The incident made me reflect on how I might feel if I heard news of my father's death. Would it bother me, considering I had little connection left with him over the years? I realized all I would feel was a dull ache in recollection of the acute pain in losing him as a child, after his withdrawal from our lives.

When a loved one has died long, what remains is the residue of the love and loss. Love then glows soft as the flickering light of an oil lamp, making visible in its light the scar of the loss time has healed. In my case as in Kalpana's the lesions, however, still ran deep, due to Baba's existence - a strong reminder of our loss, even though of long ago. The love perhaps still glowed in us, but the scar of his desertion we hid from the world. We projected an air of indifference towards Baba till his end. To prove his nonexistence in our lives, he was not invited to either of our weddings, as we as brides were given away by uncles. Jamai-babu's untimely death, unlike Baba's forsaking us, was destiny wrenching him away as if in a hurricane, leaving us to pick up our lives and move on in its aftermath.

Of her six children, Madhavi's two elder daughters, who had been studying in London at the time of their father's death, came for a short visit, but returned shortly. The third daughter, Ruma, was in my college, a batch junior. Piya the fourth, closest to her mother, joined college when I was in my fourth and last year. The youngest, a boy named Sujit and a girl Usha, were still in school. I had become close to Piya since the days when her mother had left her and Sujit at the school hostel in Mihirpur, for me to watch over them, while she attended to her work. The three of us Piya, Sujit and I, had some good times together then. We would swim in the adjacent lake or ride bicycles around it, led and coached by me of course, a tomboy then. Though Madhavi's children were five or six years younger than me, they all called me mashi or aunty in Bengali. Sujit went away to college in the US shortly, followed by the youngest girl Usha, and would settle there eventually.

After her husband's death, with the children grown and gone away for their education, Madhavi began to get very lonely. Though she was technically no more on her own now than before; as she had always lived away from Satyendra through the week in Mihirpur, to take care of her father's institutions. The children had been away at boarding school in Darjeeling since long. Even now Madhavi had her parents and sister Ratna (since her return from college in London), for company. Additionally

                    Shuvashree Chowdhury

as superintendent of the school hostel she was amidst the girls always. But being alone and being lonely, are not necessarily auxiliary like mind and emotions are to each other. One can be lonely even in a crowd and yet not lonely when alone, especially if one has an emotional anchor. When her husband was alive, Madhavi though living away, had him to return home to.

It was during this lonely phase of her life that Madhavi met Riyaz, the son of a close friend of her father's. Their families had known each other long and he had just returned from London after completing his Bar in Law. Riyaz had always nurtured a keen interest in the prettier younger sister Ratna, even in wanting to marry her. The alliance was however not to be, since Ratna met, dated and married a doctor in her father's employment. Riyaz's being a Muslim might have had something to do with the improbability of the alliance from Ratna's side, knowing her father would never approve. However his practising a different religion did not prevent Madhavi's befriending him now, as friendship with a Muslim man was legitimate, not marriage. Finding solace in Riyaz's company, Madhavi spent a lot of time with him.

A couple of years younger to Madhavi, Riyaz made her laugh, humouring and cheering her. They went on long drives between Dacca where he resided and Mihirpur where she lived, and to nearby towns and villages. Going on river cruises was another pursuit that took their fancy. They enjoyed taking a steamer exclusively, for privacy. Madhavi's father owning a number of large ones for his businesses, they were not difficult to get. Riyaz's father a reputed barrister had a roaring practice, so it would not be difficult for Riyaz to establish himself soon. Since inheriting his father's professional goodwill and reputation, he did not have to throw himself into long hours of work just yet. The new constructions at her father's charitable works that Madhavi oversaw were complete by now, while the school hostel's operations had fallen into a pattern. So both Madhavi and Riyaz now had enough time for themselves as well as for each other.

In being the dutiful and responsible daughter, Madhavi's other roles - even as wife and mother had paled into insignificance. Since her marriage to Satyendra at the age of sixteen, she had spent only weekends with him. Even then, their six children who came in quick succession had kept her busy. Her children had been looked after by her mother during the week, before they were sent to boarding school. Madhavi had gone about being the son in her father's life, to the extent of donning men's trousers to ease her work overlooking construction labourers. Women wearing trousers at the time was uncommon to say the least, so rather than get one stitched for herself, she had made do with her husband's. Her younger brother Rahul, the actual successor to Ronjit uncle's businesses, was still only in school then. Ratna, who would join her father shortly, to hold significant positions due to her superior qualifications, was away at college in London. Madhavi had not had the opportunity for education similar to her siblings, starting to work with her father very early.

Sometimes loneliness acts as the calm before the tempest of love in a person's life, as it was in Madhavi's. Love can grab one when least expecting, shaking them to the very core; the overwhelming intoxication leaving no room for the functioning of the mind, the heart totally taking over. Riyaz made Madhavi feel truly special as a woman, like she had never felt before, sweeping her off her feet. On his part, he counted on Madhavi's maturity and caring. With companionship and laughter coming into Madhavi's life, could love be far behind? In the aftermath of the draught of widowhood and loneliness, love took her by storm, flooding her, washing away her sense of unconditional responsibility towards her father and children completely. She threw caution to the winds now, sucked into the whirlpool of a torrid affair.

Riyaz did not stop short of sweeping Madhavi off her feet. At the time when she should have been finding suitable grooms for her five daughters, all of marriageable ages by now, Madhavi found a groom, a Muslim man at that, and eloped with him. Riyaz had nothing to lose, either in way of respect of family, children and society like her, or even professionally.

When Ronjit uncle heard of Madhavi's elopement and subsequent nikah, the Muslim marriage, he was getting off a ferry boat, having just crossed the river between home and his institutions. He nearly fainted in shock and had to be physically escorted, leaning heavily on the news-breaker, a relative, on the brief walk home. He was flabbergasted, and then shattered, that

          Shuvashree Chowdhury

his dutiful daughter could dishonour his name so, disregarding his goodwill and family name, ignoring the repercussions on the lives of her children.

When Madhavi's children heard of their mother's marriage, to someone they referred to as uncle so far, they maintained a cold composure. They stayed away, burying themselves in their studies and their lives. Love is an all compelling, powerful force, but did Madhavi have to elope and get married, rather than wait for her children to settle down first? I was let down by her behaviour, for I looked upon her as a role model. Could she not have contained her love responsibly for a while, for the good of her children if not her father? Eloping with a Muslim man was bad enough, added to her being a widow and the mother of six adult children. Her behaviour tarnished not only her own and her father's reputation, but perhaps reduced the scope of her daughters to get good grooms from respectable families.

Madhavi's act was cowardly and self-centric, as with committing suicide, when a person is so compelled by his own circumstances, to spare a thought to what will happen to his loved ones after him. I was happy for Madhavi, that she had found love and happiness, even had the guts to follow her heart. But what I could not assimilate was her acting upon it so promptly and in the drastic manner that she had. My love for her made me blame her rashness on Riyaz, who I thought should have waited to marry her, after she had discharged her duties as a mother. They could have waited for her children to marry, I thought, as they were all over the age of twenty one by then. Madhavi's children however, being strong and independent, with boarding school upbringings, luckily also all fine-looking, found their partners on their own, even if not all to their status or standing.

A few months after Madhavi's marriage, one evening to my surprise she came to meet me in college. She looked radiant in the richness of her attire, resplendent with heavy jewellery. She was obviously coming from Riyaz's house and would have had to dress commensurate to her status as the new bride, of a well-to-do Muslim household. Looking at her, as she walked up the pathway leading to the hostel's parlour, I noticed the apprehension on her face. She was perhaps uptight from anticipating my reaction towards her. I promptly rearranged my view of her in my mind, placing the positive thoughts of how happy I was for her happiness on top, shoving the negative ones of her rashness down under, as I smiled warmly at her.

"You're looking beautiful, Didi" I said, stepping forward to hug her, noticing her hesitation dissolve, as she hugged me in return.

I was the first person in the family Madhavi contacted since eloping, even though two of her daughters were in my college. She probably needed to feel the pulse of her immediate family before approaching them. She knew it would be easier to pave her way back to them through me, after learning of their personal reactions and the stir her behaviour had caused at home. On her first visit, I gave her a brief on what had happened since her leaving and Ronjit uncle's reaction. After that, she came to see me a few times and invited me to spend a weekend at her place. Though I was not keen to meet Riyaz, let alone stay at his place, knowing Ronjit uncle would be very angry with me for doing so, I could not refuse Madhavi. She had always been kind and a pillar of support in my life, in addition to Kalpana.

Therefore one Friday evening, as decided, Madhavi came to pick me up after college. I had not mentioned to anyone, not even to her daughters in college, that I had been meeting their mother, so there was no question of mentioning I was going to stay at her place. On previous visits she had remained in the car, while sending word to me through the driver, after which we would drive to a nearby restaurant for tea. This time, she had asked me to wait at the gate at 5pm. When her car pulled up in front of where I stood at the gate, I was surprised to find someone other than the driver, on the driver's seat.

"Maya, this is Riyaz-bhai," Madhavi said, through the window, turning to unlock the back door of the car, for me to get in.

"Salaam alaikum, Riyaz-bhai" I said politely, in greeting.

"Wa alaikum as salaam," he promptly replied, with a grin.

After I settled into the rear seat of the car, Riyaz revved the accelerator. Soon we were on the dusty road, swarmed by cycle-rickshaws and pedestrians, and then followed a long stretch of free road. I was seated diagonally behind Riyaz, so I got a good view of him sideways, as he looked ahead concentrating on the

                    Shuvashree Chowdhury

road. I could not help noting how average looking he was, having imagined all along it was a really handsome man who had swept Madhavi off her feet.

I had got a glimpse of his stubby features when he turned to greet me initially. His bushy eyebrows, near balding head and dark complexion, quite disappointed me, in sharp contrast to Madhavi's handsome first husband Satyendra. However Riyaz's baritone, the way he held his head over his firm shoulders now, lent his looks an eminence.

Riyaz's home was in the heart of town, in a crowded market place. It was a hefty three-storey house, spread over a large area, with not much space for garden or lawn. It was his joint-family home, but now divided, so each of Riyaz's uncles and brothers had a separate section. On the ground floor of the house was the office, with law books arranged neatly from wall to wall, as well as floor to ceiling, in glass cases, where Riyaz and his father met with their clients. I was made comfortable on the terrace room adjacent to Riyaz and Madhavi's room above the second floor. Sitting on my bed with the door open, I could see the vast star-studded sky, the breeze making the floral white curtains fly, casting shadows in the dim light. After a quick shower and a change of clothes, I met the family downstairs. Dinner was served in the ornate dining room on the second floor.

At the head of the table sat Riyaz's father, flanked by his three sons, their wives and two grandchildren by the eldest son. I was seated at the opposite end to Riyaz's father, in clear view of everyone at the table. Over a traditional full course Muslim meal, with a variety of meats, biryani and desserts, the discussion at the table ranged from the weather, current happenings, to music and art. In the course of the conversations initiated mainly by Riyaz, I was asked about my college, subjects I took, the teachers, as well as my opinion on current topics and politics. I noted with awe Riyaz's sharp wit and intelligent humour, from his views and comments. The way he kept teasing me and Madhavi alternatively made everyone laugh, though he retained a solemn face himself. Madhavi draped in a red Benarasi sari, blushed from his teasing, loving his attention.

Lying on my bed that night, I went over the events of the

evening, since getting into the car at the college gate. It was evident that Madhavi and Riyaz were much in love. They had no qualms of displaying their affections either, even calling each other endearing names in the presence of others. I was genuinely happy for Madhavi; glad she had chosen her own happiness over that of everyone else's after a lifetime of giving herself completely. I concluded she had fallen in love not with Riyaz's looks, personality, money or his being a barrister, but by the way he treated her, how he made her feel good about herself. With his spontaneous sense of humour, he made her laugh till there were tears in her eyes sometimes. I could see why she had bartered a life with him, for respectability, duty and social acceptance. I admired her courage in giving up all for love, for herself.

The next morning, woken by a knock on the door, I found a maid standing at the door with a loaded tea-tray. After I let her in, she set it down on the table in front of the sofa and left. I poured myself a cup of tea, then wrapping my nightgown tightly, stepped onto the terrace, tea cup in hand, to enjoy it with the early rays of the sun. After a few leisurely sips, I glanced towards Madhavi's room, to find it ajar. She was sitting at the dressing table, her back to the door, combing her hair. Riyaz had apparently gone downstairs, perhaps for his morning walk. I strolled into the room and stood behind Madhavi. She looked up at me through the mirror, smiling broadly, bringing her comb-held-hand down to her lap. With my face atop hers in the mirror reflection, I noted the startling similarity of our appearances - the dusky complexions, the shapely noses, the large somewhat oriental eyes and chiselled jaw lines, behind which our thick black, wavy hair cascaded to our waists.

Our resemblances did not stop merely with our looks, I thought wistfully. It had trickled over to our lives lately. We had both recently transited into womanhood, in spite of the over two decades of age difference between us. Mine was the natural transition from adolescence to womanhood, fully aware now of being an attractive woman, from the male attention I received lately. While Madhavi had transcended from being a dutiful daughter, wife, mother, working woman, to being a woman who is loved and cherished not merely for the roles she plays in the lives of those she pays allegiance to. Perhaps it was Madhavi's defiance that gave wings to

     Shuvashree Chowdhury

my desire of becoming the master of my own existence. After my graduation in a few months, I moved out of my cocoon from under Ronjit uncle's protective umbrella, to join a professional course, without so much as consulting him, much to his consternation and his cutting me off from his life.

Chapter 6

The Riots

Itry to climb onto the truck but it is too high. Behind me are a group of girls waiting to follow, watching how I navigate the elevation without a staircase. There is no time for stairs or gear, as surrounded by armed soldiers we prepare to scamper up the dropped back railing of an army truck. Mentally searching for the precise place to grip the wooden frame in order to haul myself up, I am surprised to see a pair of entwined hands placed exactly below my right foot, which is off the ground in readiness for the lug, after my hands have found a spot to clench. Instantly looking down, I see the hands belong to one of the uniformed male students of my class. He nods at me encouragingly, as I place my feet one at a time as in a callisthenics position on his strong hands and jump onto the truck. As students of a physical education college, even dressed the part, it is a simple feat for us.

I turn to look at my rescuer, smiling gratefully, relegating his handsome face to memory. The next girl follows, with another of the seventy-five male students of our class offering his hand this time. In this manner, twenty-two of us girls in sky-blue kurtas, navy-blue cardigans, starched white salwars and dupattas, are loaded onto the truck. Six of the armed men follow us, locking the back railing after them. They encircle us, with guns pointing outside ready to go off at the first sign of trouble. We sit down on the wooden base of the open-air truck, so as to be least visible from the exterior. As the truck pulls out of the iron gate of our college premises, I whisper a silent prayer to God in gratitude, for delivering us from this fortress of death, knowing that we now have a new lease of life.

After the outbreak of the riots and attacks on a number of girl's schools and hostels, it is difficult to pre-empt what may

                    Shuvashree Chowdhury

happen next, so all of us girls have vacated the hostel. However, of the twenty-two of us, only four of us who are Hindus, are in actual danger of our lives, if detected. As our truck rolls out into the neighbourhood, we can hear agonizing screams, as people are running crazily pushing one another, overturning wheelbarrows of fruits and vegetables, trampling over the crushed as well as fresh ones they might have just bargained hard for. There are small to large fires everywhere, with a putrid burning smell mixed with that of blood, sweat and fear. People are running arbitrarily - not sure in which direction. They are unsure of who is killing whom, not even aware if the man running alongside is a potential slayer, to escape the vandalism that has erupted on the streets.

There are lungi clad men on the trot, with lathis, daggers, spears and burning torches, against the fading light of the setting sun. All shutters of shops are either closed or are being frantically pulled down, as those late to react will be looted and ransacked, lucky if they can manage to save their lives. People are making a dash for shops or godowns still open, in a bid to hide, not sure if they should stop to pick up a wailing child separated from the mother in the frenzy. There are partially burnt hulks of cars, serrated holes in place of their windows and windshields, dotting the city like campfires in a National Scout Jamboree amidst pitched tents, silent witnesses to the mass destruction and massacre. Thick smoke is wafting about, heavy with the stench of burning flesh, tyres and charred cars, buses and rickshaws.

There are pools of blood on the pavement, where a man might have been beheaded with one flash of a machete. The body, its skin ashen in death, has perhaps been removed by relatives or shop assistants after the rioters have moved ahead. Ambulances and police jeeps are rushing past, their blaring alarms merging jarringly, the red lights blinking furiously. Hospitals are thronged with the dead and the wounded; their mortuaries being combed in search of loved ones, in earnest prayer that they are not found, giving hope a chance to linger. Photos of missing people have been taped on walls of markets and stores. By now, trips to newspaper offices clutching photos taken at weddings - whether the missing person's own or attending that of loved ones, is forming queues.

Sitting in the military truck securely cordoned, taking in the sights and smell of evil, I look at each of the faces of the girls in our group. There is much animosity around, people killing in the name of religion and ethnicity, but four of us Hindu girls are fleeing under the cover provided by eighteen of our Muslim classmates. They do not see us as different, even ready to jeopardise their personal safety on our account. That we Hindus are a minority has made no difference in the respect of our religious practices at the hostel, by the majority who are Muslim. Beef is not allowed in the kitchen, just as pork is barred. Religion and ethnicity are often politicized, so the ruler or government feels safe, if the common man is divided and killing each other. What better way to divide people, than to exhilarate already existing regional groups into communal disharmony? These riots were spearheaded by non-Bengali Muslims, while the Bengalis are fighting them, to defend their Hindu brothers and sisters.

This morning we had been on the playfield for our regular activity classes, when through the iron gate of the college premises, we heard a man calling out to the kitchen staff at the hostel repeatedly. He was tall, dark and burly, and carried a cane basket on his head supposedly with the beef he was hawking.

"Will you take beef?" he bellowed.

He caught our attention due to his loud incessant calls and knowing the kitchen did not buy or cook beef, we became apprehensive.

"No, we don't need it," Sushil a Hindu kitchen staff, replied firmly.

The man turned around and promptly disappeared from the gate. By now distracted from our class, we concluded this was a ploy to figure if there were any Hindus in the hostel. We knew that a riot had broken in Palpara-Raibagan, the locality adjacent to our Physical Education College in Mohammadpur Dacca. The fires had been visible from our hostel windows.

Around six o'clock this evening, a mob carrying burning torches had come charging to our college's main gate. We could see the blazing fires from our rooms, over the sea of heads, amid the thick black smoke emitted by the torches. The crowd charged towards the heavy iron-gate, through whose grille the young hostel assistant saw the mob approaching. Luckily, a military

                    Shuvashree Chowdhury

sergeant by the name of Nobi Chowdhury, who was posted in the neighbourhood, had been on his rounds nearby. He briskly walked up towards the gate.

"Sir, sir the crowd is approaching" the boy called out to him loudly, waiving his hand frantically, "with torches in hand."

Nobi rushed in front of the gate, pistol upraised in a gesture to fire randomly at the crowds, if they came any closer. His face blazed in anger, reflected by the light from the torches. The crowd immediately stopped short in their tracks, seeing the pistol aimed at them, but more from the expression Nobi wore on his face, implying he would not hesitate to shoot randomly, even at short range.

After the crowd was compelled to retreat, Nobi Chowdhury had rushed inside, to the hostel gate on the first floor.

"Ladies, please open the door," he hollered, through the wooden door, "don't worry, you are safe. I'm an army officer."

No one dared open the door, without making sure who was outside. One of the girls, Shamsur Nahar, climbed two chairs placed one atop the other, with two girls holding her for balance, to peep through the ventilator. Seeing the uniformed athletic torso and the short crop of hair, she was relieved. When the door was opened, I had been kneeling on the floor, praying desperately for God to save us, after having spotted the approaching mob from the window. I did not want to die at the hands of a frenzied mob; it would be such a wasted death. I needed to prove my mettle yet to my father, the world, and to Ronjit uncle who had disowned me after I joined this course on completion of my graduation, without consulting him.

When finally the hostel gate was opened, the girls in fear and frenzy rushed upon Nobi Chowdhury, grabbing him by his hands and shoulders, shaking him hard. It was a spontaneous burst of emotions, as much from the relief and gratitude, as the query on where he was during all those minutes that we lived in acute fear. But over and above, it was a desperate plea to him to take instant action to save us. Flabbergasted by the passionate outburst of so many women, he immediately called for an army truck to evacuate us girls from the hostel. There was every possibility of the mob coming back, so there was no time to waste, no time for us to pack and take our belongings. We had trooped out of the hostel as we were, in uniform. The truck was now taking us to the Dacca University women's hall, called the Chameli Hall. We would be safe there.

We reach our destination after a bumpy ride, through a maze of fires everywhere, lucky to be unscathed. As we go inside, we are warmly welcomed by a hefty lady, perhaps the superintendent, smiling at us sympathetically on seeing our dazed looks. A brief wait later we are served dinner, which we gratefully and hungrily devour. Our last meal has long been put to utmost use by the fear and stress of the day, followed by the long open-air truck ride. The university is not equipped to play host to so many, thus we have to make do with mere usage of the premises, not envisage a fancy bed-and-breakfast accommodation. We retire for the night on the carpeted ground of the hall. Lying close together, we are oblivious to the world in a few seconds, from the heavy meal, the tiredness setting in at the end of the long gruesome day.

Lucky to be alive with our dignity intact, after the threat of the mob-attack wherein we could have been stripped, raped, possibly burnt by fire or acid or at best stabbed, the hall floor is a haven. I wake up in the morning to find our group of twenty-two has shrunk, as many who live nearby have gone home. Our college, essentially residential to enforce the dedicated concentration of students, paying us a monthly stipend of Rs. 50 each to guarantee it, also accommodates students from neighbouring areas. But I have nowhere to go now, no one to even enquire about my survival, leave alone whereabouts. The only ones who care for my existence, my sister Kalpana and her husband Sudeep are unable to come and fetch me or even ask me to come home. Kalpana by now is in Calcutta. Sudeep is in a detention camp near Vishnuganj, since after the riots broke, where he will remain for another few months.

I firmly believe in God. He has presented himself to me in various guises, whenever I needed him most. After my real father denounced me, he appeared in the form of Ronjit uncle to take his place. When Ronjit uncle's place in my life disappeared, God presented himself to me yet again. This time it was in the guise of the father of my close friend Zaina, from my previous college,

	Shuvashree Chowdhury

where I completed my graduation in Arts. I had barely stepped out of the women's hall to clear my head and decide what my next course of action should be, when I noticed a man striding towards me. I recognize him as Farouk Ahmed, the Director of Public Instruction of East Pakistan. I have visited his house often with my friend, his daughter Zaina, and thereby grown close to his family. I feel overwhelmed with emotion on seeing him now, in anticipation of his being my saviour. Seeing him standing in front of me, feels like viewing a helicopter before being air-lifted from a capsized ship at sea.

Farouk uncle is a tall man, athletic and dignified. He wears a rimless pair of spectacles on his sharp nose, covering a pair of deep set, intelligent and kind eyes. His salt-and-pepper hair is neatly brushed back, still damp form the morning shower.

"How are you Ma?" he asks endearingly, and then looking at me tenderly, placing one hand on my head, he adds softly, "come home."

I look at him, smiling, nodding gratefully, knowing he is Godsent, that he truly lives up to his name - he who knows right from wrong. Shamsur Nahar, my roommate, goes with Farouk uncle in his official car, back to the college hostel, to fetch our belongings. I now have a father and a home, when just minutes back no one cared whether I was dead or alive. When all doors close, an unknown one opens as the doors to the Ahmed home does now.

As soon as Farouk uncle returns with my meagre belongings, having dropped my roommate home on the way, I get into the car beside him at the wheel. The roads are now deserted, but the tell-tale signs of the carnage and loot of the past days are there. But sitting safely inside the car now, I view the world and my surroundings differently. I say my prayers to God, snug in the belief he is right beside me in the form of Uncle. Yesterday I was alone in the world, but today I have the protective sheath of a father and a family. Zaina's mother Taahira, an advocate practising at the High Court, opens the door to her home and heart on my arrival. She is waiting at the open door, her long damp hair flying lose in the chilly January breeze, even before we have made it to the front of their two-storey house, on hearing us drive up the pathway.

Taahira aunty is of medium height, reaching much below her husband's shoulder, and an epitome of beauty and grace. Her kohl-lined large eyes stand out on her fair, now finely lined face, with broad cheek bones and shapely slender mouth. Tucking her long black strands behind her ears, she hugs me warmly, welcoming me into her family, adding to her four daughters and two sons. I will be living with them for the next three months, not as a guest but as one of them. No one, not even visitors to the house will know I am not one of their real daughters. This keeps me safe through the time I am with them, as well as ensures their safety in sheltering a Hindu from the riots. I am very lucky to be living with a Muslim family gracious to adopt me with my different religious practices, treating me as their own, in the face of danger to themselves.

"She is our eldest daughter," is how aunty and uncle proudly introduce me to everyone, taking me along everywhere, even when visiting relatives and friends. As one of the family, I help with all household chores and have my meals together with them. On rare occasions when the rest of the family ladle servings of beef onto their plates, they ensure there is a helping of lamb or mutton for me. The stoppage of beef coming into the house could raise suspicion and so is continued; moreover it is not fair that the rest of the family sacrifice their beef treats because of me. Though I don't eat beef if I have a choice, I am not a fanatic about it, having eaten at boarding school. I certainly have no qualms of it being served on the plate next to mine, when compensated by the love, respect, security and gratitude I feel in this safe haven.

Every morning uncle goes for a walk up to the airport, as they live close by on Post Office Road. On waking, I make tea for the two of us and accompany him on his walks, while Aunty ensures the younger children are ready and off to school in the meantime. After breakfast, both Uncle and Aunty depart for their respective work, leaving Zaina and me at home. Farouk uncle has a really big library that awes me. I spend most of my day there, going through his collection of books, as well as arranging and dusting them. I also spend sufficient time with my own study books, of the course I have fled from. I am going back for the final examination and will have to clear it before I can leave East Pakistan for good, having spent two years on the course already. I have decided to go

    Shuvashree Chowdhury

to India, possibly to join Kalpana and Sudeep, for what is left for me here once they are gone?

* * *

Soon it is time for Ramadan. In 1964, the first day of Ramadan of the year 1383 AH, is the 16th of January. It has been over ten days that I am living in Zaina's house. It is here and now that I gain understanding about the actual significance of Ramadan. Muslims around the world anticipate the arrival of this holiest month of the year and unite in a period of community-wide fasting and spiritual reflection. The annual fast of Ramadan is considered one of the five "pillars" of Islam and all Muslims who are physically able, are required to fast each day of the entire month, from sunrise to sunset. The evenings are spent enjoying family and community meals; engaging in prayer and spiritual reflection; and reading from the Quran. The fast of Ramadan has both spiritual significance and physical benefits.

However, in spite of being part of a Muslim household, since I am a Hindu, I have religious independence and am not expected to observe the fast like everyone else. The children and I are exempted from the fast, but I participate in other activities with the rest of the family. Particularly during this time, as well as other times of the year, Muslims are encouraged to read and reflect on God's guidance. The first verses of the Quran had been revealed during the month of Ramadan and the very first word was: "Read." I spend considerable time trying to understand the learning's of the Quran from Uncle and Aunty. I sit with the family when they have their meal at 4am. Though they do not eat anything till sunset, the children and I have our breakfast and midday meals as usual, prepared by the cook.

I look forward to Iftar with the family. Iftar is the evening meal when Muslims break their fast during the holy month of Ramadan. It is often a community affair, with people gathering to break their fast together. Iftar is done right after sunset, by traditionally consuming a date first, when the fast is to be broken, followed by a large meal. I love eating out of the common large platter of Iftar food items, like piyaju and beguni (batter-fried onions and eggplant); jilapi (batterfried sweetmeat dipped in sugar-syrup);

jhalmuri (puffed crunchy rice spiced with onion, chilli and ginger); haleem (a type of stew made into a thick paste from pounded wheat and mutton or beef); khejur (dates); dal puri (a spiced-lentil stuffed pastry) with chola (spiced, cooked chickpeas); fish kebab; Mughlai paratha (paratha with egg-filling); pitha (pounded-rice based sweets) and seasonal fruits and drinks such as Rooh Afza (a rose flavoured drink) and lemon sharbat.

During the month of Ramadan, Muslims, in addition to observing a strict fast, participate in pious activities, charity and peace-making. Many believe that Iftar as a form of charity is very rewarding and that it was practised by Prophet Muhammad. This is also the time of intense spiritual renewal. I am certain God will reward Farouk uncle and his family for their benevolence in hosting me, feeding me and keeping me under-cover all through Ramadan. I am overwhelmed with gratitude for this family, for hosting me during the sacred month, especially when other Muslims are out there killing Hindus in the riot. There cannot be a better form of charity than protecting and feeding the child of perhaps another God. Allah chose this family to give me a new lease of life, but more, to teach me to respect and love people of all religious faiths.

I will later learn of the killings of a number of my close kin by Muslims in the current riot and the subsequent ones leading to the formation of Bangladesh in 1971. But my private experience of living amidst a Muslim family, who adopted me in turbulent times when not even those close cared to find out whether I was still alive, will always spearhead my reverence for the faith. This incident will never allow me to hate Muslims like most Bengali Hindus of my times, who in addition to their own hatred, will leave behind gory tales to feed the hatred of subsequent generations to come. Their hatred is perhaps justified, stemming from Muslims killing their loved ones, wiping out entire families, usurping their land and property, chasing them away from their homes and plentiful lives in East Bengal, to an existence of bare minimum and struggle, in starting life afresh in West Bengal.

At the end of the month of Ramadan, Muslims throughout the world observe a joyous three-day celebration called Eidul-Fitr (the festival of fast-breaking). The aim of this festival is to promote

		Shuvashree Chowdhury

peace, strengthen the feeling of brotherhood and bring oneself back to the normal course of life, after a month long period of self-denial and religious devotion. Muslims are also encouraged on these days to forgive and forget any differences or past animosities that may have occurred with others during the year. Possibly due to these tenets, by now the riots have petered out, from gradually running out of heat since Ramadan started, to being reduced to cinders at its end. I would like to believe its end was hastened by Muslims recalling the teachings of the Quran, making amends to their mistakes, retracting from instigating innocent people to rise in arms against fellow humans; not merely due to the fasting period sapping out the energy of those murderous amongst them.

On the day of Eid, as is customary, Farouk uncle and the family go for the morning sermon and congregational prayers at the nearby mosque. After they return, I join them in visiting friends and relatives, exchanging gifts and greetings, feasting, celebrating the completion of a month of blessings and joy. Shortly after Eid, Taahira auntie's younger brother is getting married at Dhanmundi, a place little distant from where we live. I attend all the ceremonies along with the family and am given a new blouse-piece to stitch into a blouse, to match a sari I own. It is given to me as a token, in living up to the custom of every family member wearing new clothes to the wedding. With all the expenditure incurred lately, since building their house, it is what Uncle and Aunty can afford now. But I sincerely appreciate their magnanimous gesture in considering me a part of the family and in demonstrating so.

* * *

"Come to Calcutta Maya, the riots are over," Kalpana tells me, when I call her one morning, "It is better to get out now. I am so worried for you and your Dada-babu. He has left the detention camp."

"Don't worry about us Didi; we are fine" I reply in a placating tone, and then continue firmly, "I cannot come now, not without appearing for my exams. I have spent good time attending the course, as well as preparing for the exams. Moreover, I fell out with Ronjit uncle over joining this course without his permission, so I cannot drop out now. I have to clear the exams at any cost. The degree will help in my career, in joining a course for higher studies in India."

Kalpana gives in, unable to stand up to my vehement rationalization on my need to stay on in East Pakistan, in spite of the turbulence. In a few days, I return to my college hostel, in spite of Farouk uncle, Aunty and Zaina urging me to wait, as it may not be safe to return yet.

It is ten days since I am back in the hostel, when one morning after breakfast, I am told I have a visitor at the college's main gate. Walking amidst the line of trees on either side of the pathway to the college building, I see from afar a boy in navy-blue shorts, his light-blue shirt hanging loose from his slender shoulders. I instantly recognize him as Bhola, Zaina's younger brother. On seeing me, his light brown eyes light up with joy, but his face, unable to catch up with the rapid change in emotion as his eyes, is still contorted in worry.

"Apa (elder sister)" he blurts elatedly, and then with an urgent tone he adds, "come with me now. I've come to take you home."

"But why, is something wrong, Bhola?" I ask flabbergasted, trying to read his expression in anticipation of bad news.

"Yes Apa, there is news that the riots are going to break again, so you must come with me now."

Looking into Bhola's innocent, fear-stricken eyes, my own suddenly mist with emotion. I swallow hard over the lump forming in my throat from recalling the irony of my life. Ronjit uncle, his wife Mrinalini, daughters Ratna and Madhavi, and their children, all of whom I considered family, for whom I worked tirelessly all of my growing years, have not enquired about my survival, in spite of the ferocity of the riots. But this little boy, in whose house I have spent only a few months, has come to my rescue, to take me home with him, worried about my safety. To Ronjit uncle and his family I realized desolately, I was perhaps just a poor relative who fed off them. My earnest love for them, every kindness of theirs that I repaid with my time and services, the two resources at my disposal in the absence of money, is taken for granted. It is as if I were the servant's daughter, who in spite of not being employed is duty-bound, due to the handouts she receives.

    Shuvashree Chowdhury

To prevent Bhola from seeing my tear-filled eyes, I look over his head, as it will be difficult to explain to him their state. I notice his father's jeep parked outside, the driver looking at me eagerly, hoping to resume the driving lessons he had started with me, on my return.

"I cannot come with you now Bhola, my exams are very near," I say tenderly, bending low to look into Bhola's eyes, after the mist in mine has cleared. "Don't worry, I will be fine and I will visit very soon."

Grudgingly he agrees to go home without me, after I promise I will go to see him on completion of my exams. I walk him to the jeep, waiving him goodbye as the jeep rolls out. Viewing the receding vehicle till it is out of sight, I feel grateful for his having come; it proves I am still wanted and loved, not having overstayed my welcome in their house.

After the extended stay in their house, Bhola's being granted the sanction to come and fetch me in his father's official jeep, means his parents still care for my well-being and safety. God frequently reassures me I am not alone in the world, that he is with me every step of the way, however uphill. With these signals, of his ceaseless love for me, God ensures I will never lose my faith in him lifelong. After my final exams for a Bachelor of Physical Education degree, I visit Farouk uncle and his family. I thank them wholeheartedly for all they have done for me. I know, no amount of words is enough to repay my debts to their kindness, but words are all I have now to express my gratitude. Then I go to Vishnuganj, knowing Sudeep has returned home from the detention camp. He is wrapping up his work, so he can leave for Calcutta to join Kalpana and Swapnil.

Having a permanent guardian back in my life is comforting to say the least. Sudeep promptly organises the documents required for my departure from East Pakistan on a Pakistani passport. With the volatile situation after the riots, it is best I leave right away. He rides with me to the airport, ensuring I am leaving for good. I do not know now, but I will not return till I'm nearing my seventieth year. It is not that the opportunity to return will not present itself before that. Perhaps my lack of keenness to walk backward in life's journey, wherein every step of the past entrenched in my memory, will be embroiled with my subservience, toil and tears will prevent me.

On my arrival in Calcutta, Kalpana comes to the airport to receive me. I am overjoyed to see her, after the uncertainties of never seeing her or anyone for that matter. Surviving the riots has taught me among other things to value life, it being so transitory, and to cherish those dear to me. Kalpana signals to me with both hands forming a square from beyond the arrival lounge grille, indicating that my prospectus for admission to the Master's Degree course has arrived. I had sent my application by post from Vishnuganj, so as not to waste any time in my stride towards a career, not sure my degrees from East Pakistan will qualify for a good job in India. I will perhaps be granted a provisional admission till I submit my Bachelor's Degree. So Sudeep has promised to collect my certificate before leaving East Pakistan and bring it along with him.

On the taxi ride home, Kalpana encourages me to continue my studies at any cost, promising to finance me even if it ever comes to having to sell her jewellery. My success is of utmost importance to her. Though she did not have the opportunity to achieve much personally, her marriage to an affluent man is her success. The best settling of scores between Baba and us will be when we as daughters do better in life than his sons from his second marriage, after deserting us. I will soon be leaving for the college at Gwalior, after submitting my Pakistani passport and acquiring an Indian one. Although going with the strength of my own conviction, I will be fortified by the guardianship of Kalpana and Sudeep. In life's journey, I feel like a trapeze artiste, taking a giant leap of faith, knowing someone will grab my hands in time, preventing me from falling.

Chapter 7

My Younger Sister Neelima

It is a cold January morning in the year 2006, when Neelima, my younger sister last visits me in Calcutta, now renamed Kolkata. As she climbs the stairs to the second floor of my house, I notice the apple of her weather-beaten, wrinkled cheeks are almost as pink as her attire. It is but natural, coming from the cold of where she still lives, in our childhood home at Barpeta in Assam. She is wearing a pink and white floral-printed georgette sari and a pink sweater. The pink scarf securely tied at her neck, covering her head and ears, pulled low over her forehead, also seems normal due to the biting cold wind outside. She looks up at me standing atop the staircase, smiling broadly, her oriental eyes as radiant as always crinkling deep on the sides. Once level with me on the landing, she hugs me warmly. I hold on to her for a few brief seconds. Her two grown sons, ascending on her heels, bend to touch my feet one at a time. I place my right hand over their heads in blessing.

Though surprised by her unannounced visit, I am very pleased to see Neelima. The last time she was here was a year back, for my husband's shradh or last rites. She had stayed a week then. Neelima is the only direct blood relative I have left other than my two daughters, since Ma, Baba and Kalpana are no more. Even Sudeep and Ronjit uncle are long gone now. Kalpana's son Swapnil visits me sometimes, when in need of money. My housekeeper brings into the living room steaming cups of tea and slices of fruit cake. Leisurely reclining on the sofa, over tea, I chat with Neelima and her sons, catching up on their lives. One of the boys is now a doctor, having followed in his grandfather's footsteps. The other runs a medicine shop, also like Baba, that does brisk business due to his brother's patients. Neelima's six children have all completed their graduation by now. Her husband continues to run his retail store in fruits, vegetables, groceries and essentials, in the main market area.

All our lives Neelima and I had our differences, due mainly to my insistence on her continuing her studies while she was disinclined to as a child. She would complain to Ma, who blindly supported her. It is only much later in life that Neelima learnt to value education. But by then it was too late, having struggled lifelong from the lack of it. Perhaps now she appreciates my persistence for her to pursue education. As I observe her now, Neelima seems much mellowed as compared to her last visit after my husband's death. In spite of the warm and brilliant smile she flashes me, I sense something amiss. My perception could perhaps have been accentuated by her sudden visit, considering it is a two-day train journey from her home to mine. I fear she is in some kind of trouble, probably needing financial help or maybe her husband is unwell. Unable to hold my curiosity over her unexpected visit, I decide to ask her sons.

"So Vikram, you are here on work, I presume?" I ask of the doctor cheerfully, trying to ensure he does not think I mind their coming.

He remains silent, while Neelima and the other son Ashok look at me simultaneously, breaking off their muted conversation. An abrupt silence ensues, wherein the two boys look at their mother, while Neelima turns towards me, her face a sudden mask moulded from fear. I am immediately sorry for having asked, as knowing how sensitive Neelima is; she might think I mind her coming. This is a strain, the thin thread of our relationship that was just starting to strengthen, could perhaps have done well without. Though never good on tact, I try changing the topic, in a desperate bid to salvage the situation, asking,

"How are Choto-ma and her sons?"

"They are all well," Neelima replies, composed by now; then in a small voice matter-of-factly she adds, "I have been detected with cervical cancer, Mej-di (Middle-sister)."

I am at a loss for words, hers taking the wind out of my sail, as a sudden gust of wind from a boat in a hurricane. I stare at Neelima shocked, a sudden spurt of pain in my chest. My sight slowly moves up, and then rests on her head. The implication of it

 Shuvashree Chowdhury

being wrapped so securely in the pink scarf strikes me brusquely now.

"I have been undergoing chemotherapy, Didi," Neelima blurts, following the course of my gaze, adding, "and have little hair left, but the doctor says I need not worry, once I finish the therapy, it will grow back again as before."

I look at Neelima, envisioning her with her earlier thick, long hair up to the waist, swallowing hard to remove the constriction in my chest.

"So how long have you known of the cancer?" I ask sadly, recalling the hardships she has suffered all her life due to financial constraints. It is so unfair, that now when the burden has eased, with her children working and established she has the biggest impediment of her life to contend with.

"I learnt of it a year back, when I came to Kolkata for Jamai-babu's shradh" Neelima replies, "since then, I have been coming to Kolkata every few months for the treatment at the cancer hospital at Thakurpukur. Vikram usually accompanies me, as being a doctor he understands the situation and can monitor my condition when we return home."

"Why didn't you tell me earlier, Neelima?" I ask disappointedly. "You have been coming to Kolkata regularly, yet didn't visit me before? I might have perhaps helped in some way, if nothing else, at least visited you in hospital."

"Mej-di, I didn't want to agonize you" Neelima replies, looking into my eyes earnestly, "after Jamai-babu's death, it is hard on you already, and you don't keep very well yourself. On my last visit, I learnt from your younger daughter of your hypertension and high blood sugar levels. Moreover, I must admit I was embarrassed of my illness, too proud to let you know, hoping it would cure soon."

I silently look into her eyes to gauge the fire in her soul, to decipher whether she has the strength left in her to combat the killer disease. I fervently hope she does, as I can distinctly see in her eyes the desire to live.

* * *

That evening in 1948, when Kalpana and I left our childhood home along with Ronjit uncle, Neelima had become Ma's emotional anchor. She remained forever clinging to Ma's pallu (sari's edge), while Ma clung to her desperately like a person drowning would even to a straw, in drawing mental strength from the sliver of hope it provides. Baba continued his life with his new bride, oblivious to Ma and Neelima's existence in the house. With me and Kalpana gone, having lost the strength of those on her side, Ma lived like a pathetic loser in the game of life, too weak to even leave the court. In the months after our leaving, extending to over a year, Neelima did not go to school. As it is she hated school and this situation wherein Ma did not want to let her out of sight even for a moment served her well. She was happy to help Ma with the cooking and chores, for their household of two.

Soon Baba's new bride gave birth to a male child and in the ensuing delight it was as if he forgot his first wife's existence, and the girl who was his daughter. He did not give Ma any money and she was too proud to ask, already burdened with living in his house under the circumstances. Luckily, her portion of the house had a small patch of land adjacent to it. On part of it Ma grew vegetables; on the rest, she sowed seeds for fruit trees like mango, banana, guava, jack fruit and coconut. These were in time to yield good fruit. Some of the produce she and Neelima consumed, but most she sold in the local market; through a man she paid in kind to do so. With the earnings from her husband's land, the only right she still exercised in marriage to him, Ma purchased rice, pulses, cooking oil, spices, and tiny fish, as they were cheaper. With the little kerosene she bought, she lit the only lantern she possessed, on occasion; to illuminate her life in the darkness after its literal sunset.

Luckily Ma had the high regard of the neighbours that was rightfully due to the wife of their kind and efficient doctor. They were stringent however, in according his second wife the same, stemming from their opinion that she had deviously entrapped the good doctor. Ma needed little for herself, wearing a plain cotton sari with an underskirt and laced blouse in summer, wrapping a thick dark shawl in winter. Of these she already had a few sets, from the good old days when she had a real husband, not a man she merely referred to as one. She now took extra care of her clothes, rarely washing them, so they would last longer. Ma seldom wore

                    Shuvashree Chowdhury

the two pairs of leather slippers she owned, saving them for when she might travel, perhaps to Mihirpur, intending on making them last her lifetime. In any case she never used soap but chickpea flour to bathe, using shikakai to wash her hair and applying coconut or mustard oil before or after. She even found a suitable time to use the common bathroom, so as not to come across her husband's now valid wife.

Neelima followed Ma in the tacit household conventions, leading a Spartan life, though poorer in education than even Ma, who had at least passed the sixth-standard. Ma did not consider Neelima's formal education of any significance. In truth, even if she thought Neelima's education was necessary, she could not afford to send her to school, with her limited finances. By not having sent her with us to school at Mihirpur, Ma denied Neelima access to a better life through education. Soon there were other children in the house, with Baba's younger bride giving birth to one child after another in succession, to a total of six. With his swelling paternity of male children, Baba became more engrossed in his new world. Ma, the custodian of his earlier life till usurped from the position, continued to view his world as hers, from a distance.

Baba's second wife and children had everything they needed and a lot more. While Ma and Neelima, the equally rightful but deprived beneficiaries of Baba's flourish, struggled for their very sustenance. Ma bit by bit sold all her jewellery to supplement the meagre income from her garden produce, rather than ask Baba for money. It was after a year of Kalpana and my joining school in Mihirpur that Ma and Neelima came there for the Durga Puja. After the five day celebrations, followed by Lakshmi Puja in a week, and immersion of the idol the next day, Ma was to customarily visit her maternal home. Before she left, Ronjit uncle was able to convince her to admit Neelima to school. Unable to disregard Ronjit uncle's request, in spite of her wishes to the contrary, she agreed to leave Neelima in school with us.

After a month long visit of her family, when Ma returned to Mihirpur, she saw Neelima in school-uniform, amongst children her age. She instantly knew that Neelima belonged there, rather than in the life of hardship with her in Assam. Ma realized with

Neelima gone, she would have to find another foothold in the loose sands of her derelict marriage, in order to stay ashore at her husband's home. She would have to learn to swim against the strong current of her husband's present life threatening to throw her emotionally into sea. So reining her flailing emotions, Ma decided to return home alone. Though after her leaving, it was Neelima who felt misplaced. She had been a quiet and morose child from the start, now she withdrew completely, into a shell. Kalpana and I tried to coax her out, spending as much time we could with her of the little we had to call our own, but she remained stubbornly rooted inside her cocoon.

However, in spite of her reticence, Neelima managed to do well in the annual exams year after year. Starting from the second standard when admitted to school, she reached the eighth standard effortlessly. Every time Ma came to Mihirpur, which was a couple of times in the years Neelima was at school, she would beg to return with her. With a flood of heart-wrenching tears, she threatened to wash away Ma's resolve in keeping her there. Neelima complained to Ma about my scolding her to study or participate in extracurricular activities. She referred to my scolding as being mean and nasty, citing it as primary reason for her wanting to go back home. But Kalpana and I always intervened, sending Ma away; determined that our younger sister also benefit from all the opportunities we were getting. We knew Ma could not afford to educate Neelima back home, while here she did not have to pay anything for any of us.

Ma often reprimanded me in support of Neelima when she complained, for pushing her to do things she did not wish or like to do. It would frustrate me to see Ma's attitude, fearing Neelima was going to turn out as helpless and dependent as her, if lacking the education and ability to be financially independent. But in spite of my dogged perseverance, Neelima ultimately dropped out of school while in the eighth standard. This was after the Durga Puja, before her eighth standard annual exams. She managed to convince Ma to take her back home, while I was away at school in Darjeeling to learn English. Ma returned home with Neelima, glad to have her back, certain an eighth-standard education was more than she would require in life. Neelima, given similar

     Shuvashree Chowdhury

opportunities as Kalpana and me, threw it all up in being the mistress of her whims, thereby choosing her destiny of lifelong struggle.

Neelima returned to doing nothing of consequence except assisting Ma with the day-to-day chores, which Ma was used to managing on her own anyway. The difference now was that she had become used to the disciplined routine of boarding school. She started getting restless, finding it difficult to pass the innumerable purposeless hours stretching into days, months and years before her. Neelima soon began going out of the house frequently, to the local bazaar or to neighbour's houses, on some pretext or the other. In the course of these outings, she became friends with a boy from the neighbourhood named Ramesh. He was a few years older than her, had never been to school, and helped his father in retailing fruits and vegetables at their shop in the local market area.

She first met Ramesh on a visit to his father's shop, where Neelima sometimes went to sell the produce of Ma's garden. When Ramesh's father was not in the shop, the opportunity for them to talk arose. Their initial stilted conversations in time grew into long heartfelt chats. Soon they became close. Neelima found his ignorance and simplicity very endearing. Ramesh was enthralled by stories of her years at boarding school, her husky voice, her sparkling eyes and dimpled smile. Neelima by now was a pretty young woman with a radiant complexion. She had narrow oriental eyes that ended in slits, a shapely nose, high cheek bones, slender lips and a longish face with a broad forehead. Though closely resembling Ma, Neelima was not as beautiful as Ma was in her youth. Perhaps the lack of proper diet and a good life that Ma had enjoyed in her early years had something to do with it. Now Neelima regularly draped a sari, having outgrown her frocks, plaiting her long hair in two.

Neelima, however, was not impressed with Ramesh's plain looks, his plump face, huge black eyes and curly hair, but enjoyed the undivided attention he paid her. Their meetings slowly increased in frequency and duration. Ma, happy to have Neelima back and someone to share her life with, did not grudge the long time Neelima started spending outdoors. Neelima often returned late into the evening, by which time Ma would light the kerosene oil lanterns she now lit regularly, herself. It was when Neelima had not returned an entire night, that Ma brusquely awoke to the whereabouts of her daughter. One cold winter evening, she had been waiting as usual for Neelima to return, before they had dinner together. Wrapped in a quilt, Ma sat waiting on the mattress she and Neelima slept on, in the absence of a real bed. Their portion of the house had no furniture, while Baba and his other family lived amidst their comfort. Ma did not realize when she dozed off into a deep sleep.

It was with the sunlight on her face the next morning, that Ma sat up with a jolt. The lantern by her side had burnt out the oil she recalled filling its metal base to the brim with. Looking around, not seeing Neelima, concluding she had not returned all night, Ma dashed outside, frantic with worry. Strolling into the neighbourhood, she asked everyone she encountered, whether they had seen Neelima. They replied that they had not. It was then that she came across a group of women huddled together, basking in the sunlight, knitting, chatting and chewing beetle-leaf with mouths spurting the red residue intermittently.

"I saw Neelima yesterday" one women blurted in response to Ma's query, while another added, "She was talking and giggling with the fruit seller Ramesh."

"With Ramesh? You mean Gobindo's son Ramesh?" Ma asked perplexed, and then added reflectively, "Yes, Neelima takes fruits from our garden to them, to sell. But that would be last evening, she has not returned home all night."

Ma abruptly dashed off to Gobindo's shop with long, purposeful strides. She had walked out of the house barefeet, braving the chilly wind without a shawl, in her haste and nervousness. Gobindo had barely opened his shop, and was lighting incense-sticks in front of numerous idols of different Gods, arranged on a makeshift shelf made of a plank of raw wood.

"Gobindo, where is Ramesh?" Ma asked anxiously, panting for breath from the brisk walk in the cold. With the worst possible thoughts rushing to mind, even to the extent of Neelima eloping, she added, "Neelima has not returned home since last evening. Bimola and Pushpa say they saw her talking to your son Ramesh

     Shuvashree Chowdhury

yesterday; perhaps he will have a clue as to where she might be."

"Ramesh has gone to the Rother mela at the adjacent town of Tara Bari, with his friends." Gobindo replied matter-of-factly, and then added rapidly, "Didi, perhaps Neelima has gone with him. They are expected back today."

"Gone with him?" Ma blurted, enraged, "What do you mean by gone with him? How can she go off with Ramesh, without even telling me?" Then with a new insight, glaring at Gobindo menacingly, she shrieked, "Oh my God! Now I get it. You father and son planned this, didn't you? If my daughter is defamed, no one will marry her. So she will have to marry Ramesh. Isn't that your plan?"

Then abruptly turning around in a huff, not wanting to press on with the discussion, wherein more people could learn of Neelima going off to the mela with a young boy overnight, Ma marched back home. With no option but to wait for Neelima's return, she agonizingly went about her regular work. Her anger propelling exaggerated movements, she even absent-mindedly toyed with the idea of discussing the matter with Baba, but finally decided against it. Late in the afternoon, after Ma had cleaned the house several times with nothing else to occupy her, since she had no appetite and so need to cook, Neelima arrived.

"Where have you been?" Ma asked sharply, as soon as she laid eyes on Neelima walking in through the door, "and with whom did you spend the night?"

Neelima looked down sheepishly, but did not respond. She knew no explanation would be good enough on the face of Ma's temper, so it was best to remain silent, till she cooled down. As Neelima walked further into the room looking downwards, she heard footsteps in the doorway. Turning in the direction of the sound, she saw four women, all of whom she recognized as neighbours, entering the room, leaving their shoes by the doorway. Ma looked at the women in alarm, recognizing them as Bimola, Pushpa, Sabita and Lopa. They were the ones huddled together, chewing beetle-leaf and chatting in the sun. She instantly regretted having asked them about Neelima's whereabouts when out looking for her, but more for telling them that Neelima had not returned home the entire night.

"Good to see Neelima is back," Pushpa the hefty, dark woman said tauntingly, facing Ma. "We all were so worried about her. Times are awful and one can never know what may befall a young and beautiful girl like her."

"Yes, thank God she has returned safely," Ma replied, trying to sound as nonchalant as possible, brushing aside Pushpa's inferences.

"But where did you disappear, my child?" Bimola mockingly chided, turning towards Neelima. "You should have informed your mother, she was so frantic with worry, out searching for you."

Neelima did not respond, but continued looking at the floor. On the face of her silence, Lopa blurted, "We heard that you went to the mela at Tara Bari, with Ramesh the fruit seller, is that true?"

Neelima, taken aback, looked at Ma to gauge her reaction to the statement.

"Yes, I went with his friends," she replied crisply, after composing herself from the suddenness of the query, "I didn't go alone with him. We were five of us."

"That is alright, my dear, but a young and unmarried girl, staying out with a boy all night!" Bimola continued, in a voice dripping with fake concern. "You know how people will talk when they hear of it, don't you?"

"Is anyone going to believe you went to the mela with a hot blooded young man and he did not even touch you?" Sabita added caustically. "The neighbours are already spitting on your name Neelima, you have defamed your own, as well as your family's name."

Then, turning to Ma, she nastily concluded, "You should have controlled your daughter's urges earlier, in going to meet Ramesh daily."

Having poured all the venom they could, so characteristic of neighbours in small towns, the four women left as abruptly as they had come.

Neelima, trying to placate a by-now hysterical Ma, forcefully said, "Believe me Ma, nothing happened, Ramesh did not even touch me. We were never alone; his friends were with us throughout. In fact we stayed the night at his aunt's house."

"Go tell this story to the world Neelima, and see if anyone

     Shuvashree Chowdhury

believes you. Try convincing our neighbours," Ma raged.

With tears streaming down her cheeks, in a choked voice she added frantically, "But how could you just go off like that Neelima, without even telling me?" Then breaking into a sob, Ma concluded, "How do I face people now? What is a lone woman without a husband and above that an irresponsible daughter, to do?"

"Ma, please forgive me," Neelima replied, intensely regretting her impulsive decision to go with the boys without considering the repercussions on Ma and herself. "When I went to the shop last evening, Ramesh's group was leaving for Tara Bari. In my excitement to visit the mela, I went along with them without sparing a thought to what you would go through."

Slowly composing herself, reconciling to this situation just as she had every one before, Ma wiped her eyes with her pallu. She realized she had no alternative now but to get Neelima married to Ramesh, though he was far from a fit groom for her. She decided she had to speak to Gobindo immediately. Gobindo did not mind, giving his blessings for the nuptials readily. He would have one son less to worry about now. His small shop would be inherited by all his six sons one day, so not much any of them would get from it. He knew that as the daughter of the respected doctor and his virtuous first wife, Neelima was of a good lineage. In addition, she was educated unlike his son, which would be good for their children. Hence Neelima wed Ramesh in a simple ceremony at the local temple. It was best this way, since neither Ma nor Gobindo could afford a lavish celebration. Baba was obviously not part of the wedding and made no contribution, either financially or by his presence. I doubt by now he even remembered or considered Neelima to be his daughter anymore.

Ramesh worked all day at his father's shop, but his share was meagre and he could not afford to take care of himself and his wife with it. Moreover there was not sufficient room at home for him to take his bride to, as the house was small. All the brothers shared a common bedroom and outdoor bathroom. Therefore Ramesh moved in with Ma and Neelima. It suited all of them very well. Ma would not have to live alone, but soon be part of a large family Neelima was about to endow her with. Neelima could take care of Ma as she aged, till her death. Ramesh, through his wife, would inherit what was Ma's, which even if split between Kalpana, Neelima and me, was more than he could get from his own parents. Neelima, far from gaining materially in marriage, except for more responsibility, started her new life on the edifice of her pre-marital one. Continuing to live in her own home, with the combined earnings of Ma and Ramesh, also not needing to adjust to her in-laws, for a while married life was indeed comfortable for Neelima.

It was in giving birth to one child after another in short succession, to a count of six, that Neelima started feeling the financial crunch. The idea of family planning was something as alien to her as it had been to our parents. Children were a gift from God, she believed, so she would gladly receive one every other year, till God could no longer give her any more. The little knowledge of biology she imbibed at school did not encompass birth-control and its methods. No one in the neighbourhood even considered, let alone practised any form of it, so her ignorance remained. Soon it became difficult for her to keep up with buying provisions like milk, cereals, clothes, shoes and woollens for her burgeoning family. Most of the produce from Ma's garden began to be consumed by the family, leaving little to sell; even while her husband's earning remained as before. Ramesh, being illiterate, could consider doing nothing other than trading in fruits and vegetables like his forefathers, after having produced one child after another like them.

After Neelima left school, neither she nor Ma ever returned to Mihirpur. Periodically Kalpana and I received letters from Neelima, which earlier Ma would get someone in the village to write for her. It is through these letters that we kept abreast with the latest happenings in Neelima and Ma's lives, though Neelima omitted unsavoury details, such as the incidents leading to her marriage. Neelima had practically studied as little as Ma, but stayed in touch with literacy throughout life, from helping her children with school work and studies. Ma, however, had totally forgotten the use of the written word from disuse, since her marriage. This aspect of Ma's personality often made me wonder whether Baba was justified in abandoning her for a literate wife, considering he was much educated. What I could not comprehend, however, was

                    Shuvashree Chowdhury

how could an educated man neglect his duties like Baba had?

After dropping out of school herself, unlike Ma, Neelima developed a new-found respect for education. Her realizing its worth, even though late, improved her plight from educating her children. Perhaps following the course my life had taken, as compared to hers without education, also married to someone illiterate, had opened Neelima's mind to its immense necessity. She was determined that all her children would be educated well. This decision was wholeheartedly supported by God too. In time for her children's education, a Catholic missionary school opened its gates nearby, which luckily she could afford. Neelima could speak English, having learnt it at school, so was able to communicate with the nuns. The Sisters, taking to her immense enthusiasm to educate her children in an English medium school, promptly admitted her two elder children, followed by the rest in coming years.

Though educating the children meant curtailing other expenditures, even to the extent of her food, Neelima gladly did it. When hunger pangs did not desert her after a frugal meal of rice, boiled potato, salt and lemon juice, she made do with a mug-full of water instead. Luckily for Neelima, Ramesh was in tune with her drive to educate the children at any cost. He was restricted in life due to a lack of education himself, so he valued it over everything. He increased the quantum of his trade, no longer in collaboration with his brothers and father, setting out on his own, working day and night to increase his earnings. Often Ramesh travelled out of town, going those extra miles to procure and supply his commodities, ensuring he was transacting in the finest quality and best possible prices.

On her part, Neelima spent every waking minute, often curtailing her sleep, to bring up her children well. She cooked, cleaned, stitched their clothes, and taught them as best she could. Ma's life was full too. What she missed in bringing up her own children, either due to having lost them to death or to her husband's desertion, she more than compensated for by taking care of the grandchildren. By this time Kalpana and I were married, had children and were settled in our respective lives. In addition to the money I sent Ma regularly ever since I started working and the clothes for Durga Puja, I made it a point to add to the parcel a sari for Neelima and a set of a shirt and trouser material for Ramesh. The money I sent Ma also enabled her to visit Kalpana and me more often in Calcutta now, at least every other year. On these visits, Ma always brought along one of Neelima's children, which often was Vikram, now the doctor. It was perhaps that she was much attached to them, or so they could get an exposure to a city and a better life.

Once the elder children were grown, Neelima's life eased considerably. They were able to help with the younger ones - feeding, bathing, teaching and escorting them to and from school. The few years at the school in Mihirpur had broadened Neelima's horizons and thinking. It had taught her, in addition to valuing a formal education even though much later, to bring up her daughters to run efficient households and be good wives and mothers, simultaneous to working outside the house. Whenever Ma visited, Kalpana and I would send our children's outgrown clothes for Neelima's children, to help her. Neelima continued to write to us sporadically; but gradually her letters to me developed a sarcastic, touchy undertone. She complained about the quality of the clothes I sent for her or her children; about how the money I sent Ma was not enough. In time, every letter she wrote to me was full of complaints and bitterness, distressing me immensely.

Ma, too, on her visits would bring up issues Neelima had in her letters. This further upset me, resulting in my relationship with Neelima reaching an all time low. I stopped sending Neelima and Ramesh new clothes for Durga Puja or my children's clothes, though continuing to send Ma as usual. After the birth of my second child, I asked Ma to come live with me in Delhi where I worked then, for a few months. It was hard for me to manage two young children, along with a career and household, in spite of hiring an ayah. At the time my husband lived in Calcutta and I in Delhi. We travelled to either city during my vacations. Ma agreed, returning home to Assam, saying she would come back to Calcutta in time to accompany me to Delhi, but did not return. Ma's turning her back on me, when I needed her support the most, upset me a great deal, but I continued to send her money every month nevertheless.

I never held against Ma what happened to our childhood,

                    Shuvashree Chowdhury

always sensitive to her limitations. But when she did not come to Delhi with me for the short period that I requested her to, choosing instead to return and live with Neelima, I found it impossible to forgive her. I had always known Neelima was her favourite and never grudged her that, but duty and responsibility in my mind is above all else. Ma's partiality, of always choosing one daughter over others, would make me conscious to never repeat the same with my two daughters. I would always mindfully ensure to treat them alike. It was only much later, after Neelima's children were all grown and had completed their college education that Neelima and my relationship slowly revived. It started with her visiting me along with a son and daughter in 2001, after Ma had passed away, spending a few days with me and my family of her own accord.

It was then, that I learnt of Neelima's son Vikram having qualified as a doctor, after an internship in Delhi, while the other two sons ran a medicine shop. Her eldest daughter married an established businessman, the second one taught at the convent school near their house, while the youngest took private tuitions for children at home in batches, making good money. Neelima's efforts had paid off and her children now were well settled. I felt proud of her success in raising her children well in the given circumstances. Neelima and Ramesh no longer had to worry about money, leading a fairly comfortable life. When Ma passed away in 1998, Neelima telephoned me to give me the news, but since my husband was ill, having just had a cardiac bypass surgery, I was unable to go to Barpeta for the funeral. Moreover, it would not have been possible to wait for the cremation in order for me to reach. After the short flight from Kolkata to Guwahati in Assam, it is a long rail or bus ride to Barpeta.

I conducted Ma's shradh or last rites in Kolkata, through a priest at the local Kali temple. I had done the same at the Delhi Kali-bari after learning of Baba's death in the year 1973, the same year my second daughter was born. Perhaps Ma's not leaving Baba's home even after his passing, to live with me in Delhi, was due to her grief over the finality in loss of the man she loved lifelong, even though from a distance, and not due to Neelima. However, I could never forgive her for it. It was after Ma's death, with Baba, Kalpana and Sudeep all long gone, that Neelima found the urge to really connect with me, the only living member of her family. By now, Kalpana's son Swapnil having been kicked around by the spiked feet of time since his parent's death, had also started visiting me for financial aid. Neelima's difficult circumstances had perhaps made her bitter; jealous that my life was far secure in comparison. But now with her life having eased considerably, she opened up to me.

I wish I had been more supportive of Neelima and Swapnil, instead of shunning them when circumstances made them harsh and cynical towards me. Neelima was able to take charge of her life midway, as a pilot taking over steadfastly in the cockpit in turbulent weather, thereby navigating to a brighter future. Swapnil however, in trying to do likewise, since unequipped, crashlanded into a murky life. Perhaps if I had been more supportive and patient with both of them, I could have helped in guiding the aircraft of their lives, as if brandishing neon lights from the tarmac, bringing them to a safe halt after unsteady landings. It is the unwavering forgiveness and acceptance by loved ones in difficult times, added to one's fortitude, that decides how skilfully one will navigate life's boat through troubled waters, into a peaceful, calm and secure lake. Ma's steady support of Neelima lifelong, perhaps did just that.

* * *

It is six months since Neelima's last visit, when I learnt of her being diagnosed with cervical cancer. I have barely woken in the morning, when my bedside telephone rings. I grab the receiver in order to stop the loud ringing. It is Neelima's son Vikram on the line.

"Ma is no more," he says softly into the phone, on hearing my drowsy voice at the other end. "She gave up early this morning, in her sleep."

The tears involuntarily spring to my sleepy eyes, the sudden lump in my throat is so big, that by the time I try to swallow in order to reply, Vikram disconnects. I am still holding the telephone receiver, when the images of Neelima as a child leap to mind. The first picture is that of her holding my hand outside the bamboo-fence of our childhood home, the day Kalpana and I were leaving for school with Ronjit uncle. She looks so sad, continuing to hold my hand, till I get into the jeep. I distinctly recall the heart-rending look in her eyes, as the jeep drove away, and she strained her neck to hold on to my gaze.

My heart feels much heavier now, than it did in leaving her clutching Ma's hand when I was eight. I sit down on my bed, my thoughts winging back to her. The images come to mind, as if in an automatic slide-show, sequentially. When I come to the ones in which Neelima is complaining about me to Ma in school, I desperately wish I had another chance to show her how much I loved her, to let her know all I wanted was for her to do well and be happy in life. I am so sorry she misunderstood my dogged persistence for bossiness. However, with the thought that in her last few visits, we had somewhat made our peace, I feel better. It wrenches my heart to think of how in spite of her desire to live, Neelima's body must have lost the strength to fight the cancer anymore. She had neglected herself lifelong, leading an undernourished existence due to financial stringency, unlike Kalpana and me who were well fed since school.

Neelima was diagnosed with cancer only at a very advanced stage. With surgery or radiotherapy no longer possible to arrest it by then, the only option left had been chemotherapy. Neelima, as always overlooking her own health, had ignored symptoms like her loss of appetite, immense weight loss, constant fatigue, shooting pelvic pain, back pain and leg pain, for long. In fact she had attributed all these signs to aging, not telling anyone, so as not to direct any undue attention towards herself and away from her husband and children.

She even tried to cover up the heavy erratic bleeding she had, thinking it might be a menopausal phenomenon. It was when her youngest daughter noticed the thick blood on the back of her sari one day, that she drew Vikram, the doctor's attention to it. It was after much probing, that he learnt of her other symptoms, insisting on taking her immediately to an oncologist in Kolkata.

The pap smear test, followed by a biopsy of her cervix recommended by the consultant at the cancer hospital, had confirmed what Vikram suspected. Neelima had lived with a number of risk factors leading to cervical cancer in women, like stress and stress-related disorders, dietary factors, multiple pregnancies and unprotected sex. Vital vitamins in a nourishing diet, like Vitamins A, C, E; folic acid, carotenoids and antioxidants can reduce the impact of these risk factors. But in Neelima's case, her neglect of her personal diet had not made that possible. A lot of women like her tend to neglect their diet, health and personal needs, so their children and families prosper, ultimately paying a huge price. They do not realize that with mental, emotional and physical health, they remain sources of strength to their families far longer. Neelima had struggled to make ends meet for her family, always sacrificing her own needs for them, to finally meet this gruesome end.

          Shuvashree Chowdhury

Chapter 8

Crossing the Border

After coming to Calcutta subsequent to the riots in East Pakistan in 1964, I intended to spend the rest of my life in India; sure my life in Pakistan is over for good. I had applied to an advertisement in The Statesman from Vishnuganj and have been called for admission to a post-graduate course in a nationalized college in Gwalior. Boarding the Toofan Express at Howrah station, I get off at Agra Fort, while the train carries on to Agra Cantonment. Throughout the journey, I gaze out of the window, at the scenery rushing by, pondering over my life which has similarly breezed past. As I look outside in anticipation of what is approaching en route, I look in eagerness to what lies ahead in life. From Agra Fort station, I take a train coming from the south of India, to reach Gwalior.

I am standing on the platform at Gwalior station, looking around expectantly, when a grey-haired, full-faced man, wearing steel-rimmed spectacles low on his nose, approaches me.

"Are you coming from Calcutta?" he asks anxiously, in a gracious voice. After I nod, he introduces himself. "I am Subir and you must be Maya," he smiles, "Kalpana would have told you about me."

"Yes, she has," I promptly reply, "thank you for coming to meet me."

"Don't thank me, Maya," he says pleasantly, "how could I not have come, when a brave girl from my hometown can come to a distant land all by herself, in pursuit of further education?" I smile graciously, as he adds, "I am so proud of you, Sister. My mother and wife will be very pleased to meet you too, to be able to talk to you in Bengali."

Then picking up my suitcase and holdall in either hand, he

begins to walk, as I fall in step beside him. Outside the station, hearing Subir-da (elder brother) speaking fluently in Hindi, not understanding a word, I am immensely relieved he is with me.

After quick negotiations, we take a horse-drawn Tonga, the popular form of transportation here, to Naya Bazaar where they live. On the way, I make a mental note to learn Hindi soon, so as to get by on my own in a Hindi speaking land. On reaching Subir-da's house, I am warmly greeted by Pishima (Aunty), his mother, and wife Aruna, a Bengali from Delhi. It is about 5pm now. After a quick bath, over cups of cardamom tea and samosas, I tell Pishima, Aruna and Subir-da, of the latest happenings at Vishnuganj, Dacca and Calcutta. They listen attentively, their expressions wavering between nostalgia and fear when they hear about the current rioting. The family had left East Bengal years ago, when Subir-da's father, who is now no more, had come to work for the then state of Gwalior. Subir-da, an excellent photographer, runs a photo studio very successfully at the local market.

After a traditional Bengali meal of fish curry and rice, followed by a good night's sleep, Subir-da accompanies me to the college, to meet the principal. At the college office, I encounter Mr Pathak, the administrative officer with longish curly hair and an elongated nose, dressed smartly in a business suit. He takes an instant liking to me, perhaps since his wife is also a Bengali, whose roots are in the district of Khulna in East Bengal. I show him the prospectus I have received via post in response to my application for admission. Mr Pathak takes me inside to meet the principal in his office, while Subir-da waits outside, on the sofa. The principal, Mr Abraham, is very pleased to meet me. He is impressed at my immense enthusiasm and dynamism, considering I have come alone, from such a distance. On learning of my Pakistani citizenship, of not having my Bachelor in Physical Education degree yet, only the Bachelor of Arts degree, he asks Mr Pathak to guide me on the provisional admission formalities.

I return to Subir-da's house along with him, after preliminary enquiries with Mr Pathak, staying there for another four days. During the time, I come to meet Mr Pathak daily, to fill out various forms and understand what I need to do back in Calcutta,

     Shuvashree Chowdhury

before being admitted to the college. I telephone Sudeep, who is still in Vishnuganj wrapping up his work, before he can join Kalpana and Swapnil for good. He reassures me he will collect my results from Dacca before leaving East Pakistan. I therefore now thoroughly enjoy my stay at Subir-da's house. The family is very warm and kind towards me. They show me around Gwalior, a town in Madhya Pradesh known for its grand hill-top fort containing elaborate palaces, water tanks and temples, founded by the Rajput prince Suraj Sen in the 900s. The oldest buildings in the fort are a pair of elaborately carved Hindu temples and giant Jain figurines, sculpted out of the hillside from the 600s.

Mr Pathak takes me on a guided tour of the large campus of the college on one of my visits, as well as introduces me to a few teachers and senior students. I am enamoured by the vastness and impressive facilities at the college, including an indoor swimming pool and well constructed courts for basketball, tennis, gymnastics and other sport, as much as by the charm and history of Gwalior. By the time I go back to Calcutta, I am eagerly looking forward to return. The homely presence of Subir-da's family in an unknown land, also strengthens my resolve, to traverse the distance from my hometowns in the east to the northwest. By now, I can speak a little Hindi, mentally correlating its similarity with Bengali.

On returning to Calcutta, I have a lot of paperwork and documentation to take care of, in acquiring an Indian citizenship, without which admission to the college will not be possible. I am required to take an oath, after submitting my Pakistani passport, for which I take the help of a lawyer friend of Sudeep's. In the meantime, having received my Bachelor's degree and marksheet, Sudeep sends me by registered post. He will come to India only a few months later. On completion of all formalities, equipped with relevant documents, in a relaxed frame of mind, I take the train back to Gwalior. I join the Master's degree course in July 1964 as a resident student. In the two years that I pursue the course, I frequently visit Subir-da's family. During the vacations I return to Calcutta, staying with Kalpana.

On completion of the course, I am awarded the degree in 1966. I then apply for the position of lecturer in the same college, in response to a post-vacancy advice on the notice board. I am one among the four short-listed candidates, but it is a woman from Delhi who finally gets the much coveted position. I, therefore, return to Calcutta, lucky to get a temporary appointment for three months at a government college there. On receipt of my first salary, I hand it over in totality to Kalpana. Though very pleased at the gesture, she suggests I send it to Ma, as she is more in need of the money. But knowing Kalpana, it is perhaps so Ma can flaunt my employment and first earnings to Baba, his other wife and their sons. Starting from my very first pay, I will continue to send Ma money every month till her death.

Before the three months of my temporary employment are out, I am contacted by my college in Gwalior. Mr Pathak tells me the woman who was appointed to the position I had applied for, is unable to take it up. She needs to return to her hometown in Delhi for personal reasons. I am to therefore be offered the post, if I wish, having qualified in the second place. Therefore, in 1966, on a regular and permanent appointment in the position of lecturer, I join my college in Gwalior. This gives me immense satisfaction, knowing my position in the world is now secure. After two years, I move to Delhi, to take up employment at a college in the north campus of Delhi University. I clinch this job as lecturer, on selection through a series of interviews, from amongst a number of competing candidates. This further increases my sense of self-reliance and wellbeing. It is during my stint in Delhi that I get married.

* * *

It is seven in the evening when my sister Kalpana is standing at the roadside window of her husband's office in Calcutta. She is peering outside from behind the curtain, so as not to be noticed. Sudeep is luckily out of town on business, so she does not have to explain what she is doing there, hiding behind his office curtains. Along with her, is her accomplice Shuklal, the owner of the neighbourhood laundry. The man they are patiently waiting for, goes past this window, about the same time every evening, on his way to the local cigarette shop. Shuklal wants to show this man to Kalpana, as a prospective groom for me, having known him for a while, as a regular client. Shuklal's laundry washes the man's clothes, just as it does all of Kalpana's silk sarees and Sudeep's tailored suits.

Ever since I started working, Kalpana has been obsessing over my marriage. As my guardian, she feels it is her duty to find me a bridegroom soon, as I am now above twenty-eight years of age. She has told friends, relatives and neighbours of her urgent quest for a suitable groom for me. After considering several pictures, also having met a few men in person, she has not yet found an appropriate match. Shuklal's pitch for this man, stems from his awareness of Kalpana's quest, not following any direct communication from her in the regard, or any ulterior motive. As a matter of fact, he has not yet discussed with the proposed groom, before playing match-maker on his account. It is Shuklal's simplicity and goodness that propel his desire to unite two young people he knows, who though eligible, are not yet married.

"Kalpana-di, see, there he goes," Shuklal abruptly points outside, to a tall man walking past with long strides. Then excitedly, in his usual stammer, he proudly adds, "Tell me, isn't he handsome? With such a regal bearing, he can well pass for a prince."

As soon as Kalpana sees the man, she is spontaneously impressed with his height and dashing good looks, like that of a film star. She decides right away that this is the perfect man to be her sister's husband. In Kalpana's opinion, I am the most eligible bride for any man, as in addition to my being good-looking, I am educationally well qualified and earn as well. She does not regard my swarthy complexion a drawback; as I am also capable of running a household efficiently. Kalpana mentally seals my fate with this man, even before knowing who he is or what his social credentials are.

"Shuklal, I like him and am sure my sister will too," Kalpana says eagerly, and then adds, "Maya has left the choice of groom to me entirely; so please bring this man to see me, soon."

Elated at receiving a go-ahead from Kalpana, Shuklal promptly rushes off. He now has the arduous task of broaching the idea of marriage to the potential bridegroom. He had been waiting for Kalpana to approve of him before doing so. Shuklal is a middle-aged, fleshy-faced man, whose mouth does not shut totally over his over-sized teeth. With large purposeful strides he presently heads down the road, to meet my prospective groom. He is the proprietor of a printing press. After shutting the press after the day's work, he has gone on his regular stroll, passing Kalpana's house. He will shortly return, as he lives in the attic above his press, with a boy to cook, clean and keep his single-room home.

Shuklal waits for him outside the rolled-down collapsible gate. He does not have to wait long for the beneficiary of his benign disposition to arrive. The man soon returns puffing a cigarette, a regular day-end ritual. Shuklal's eager briefing on his proposed marriage is met with an outright turndown; this in spite of his communicating objectively, choosing the appropriate words through his stammer. The reason is not the man's lack of interest in me as a bride, but his disinclination to get married just as yet. He feels his business is not as flourished as he would like, so he will not be able to provide a stable and secure marital existence to any woman yet. This is quite converse of Neelima's husband's jumping into marriage, like a man unable to swim jumping into sea to save another. However, Shuklal is not about to give up on advocating God's will and creating my destiny.

After much persistence, Shuklal is able to convince the man to visit Kalpana, if only to have a cup of tea with her. In a week's time, Shuklal brings him to Kalpana's house. Sudeep is away again, gone to drop their son Swapnil to school in Dehradun. Kalpana does not want him around for the initial meeting. Barely has the man walked in, his head bent in passing through the low doorway with his imposing height, when Kalpana is certain he is the perfect match for me. Up close, the man is more handsome, with his sharp features, large magnetic eyes and wavy hair, adding to the tall, broad shouldered, athletic physique. As he puts his hands together in a nomoshkar - bowing slightly, with a shy charming smile, which Kalpana reciprocates, she mentally places me beside him.

She visualizes us making a good-looking couple. To her, that is perhaps adequate, confident as she is of my capability to adjust to every situation. I am independent and by now also earning well, which she feels will override any problems I might encounter in my marriage. Ma's personality or the lack of it, inability to take

     Shuvashree Chowdhury

control of her marriage and life, in spite of Baba being a good man in general, has made the biggest impression in both Kalpana's and my mind. But Kalpana is assured such a situation will never arise in my case.

"Kalpana-di, this is Nayan Saha," Shuklal introduces his companion to Kalpana. Then, after the three of them are seated on the sofa in Sudeep's office, he adds, "And Nayan, this is Kalpana-di, the elder sister of the bride, currently working in Delhi, as I mentioned."

Nayan nods respectfully at Kalpana and then softly states, "Didi, I have not decided on marriage yet. I have come to meet you on Shuklal's insistence, since he gave you his word on bringing me."

"So, what do you do Nayan?" Kalpana asks, ignoring his admittance as if unheard; certain she will convince him on matrimony shortly.

"I own a printing press down the road, with a few machines, run by over a dozen machine men, compositors and administrative staff" Nayan replies, "I just about get by, investing most of my earnings into the business. Hopefully in a few more years my business will be established, and then I can settle down, but not as yet."

"There is never a perfect time for marriage, Nayan," Kalpana replies, smiling. "There is no limit to ambition either, which actually is a good thing, you know, it drives a man," then abruptly, in a teasing but firm tone, she blurts, "Tell me Nayan, will you marry my sister?"

Nayan is taken aback by the abruptness, but more by the vehemence of her suggestion, in spite of stating his dissent earlier. He remains silent, seeking a polite but firm way to turn down the proposal.

"Don't worry, you won't have to provide for my sister, Maya works and earns pretty well at that." Kalpana teasingly persists, on the face of Nayan's silence. "She is very independent and will not be a burden on you; rather she can partner you in your ventures, to achieve the success you dream of."

Shuklal till then silently witnessing the proceeding interrupts, "Maya-di is also very beautiful, Nayan." Then, turning towards

Kalpana, he adds, "Kalpana-di, why don't you show Nayan her photograph?"

Kalpana promptly gets up, goes inside to fetch my photograph. A housemaid comes in with plates of fish-fry, cutlets and sweetmeats, on a tray. She sets the plates down on the table, in front of the guests.

After another maid has placed a loaded tray of Kalpana's favourite bone-china tea-set, with the delicate white, pink and gold floral designs on the table, Kalpana walks in. Handing over my photograph, taken in a studio at Karol Bagh in Delhi, to Nayan, Kalpana sits down. She steals sidelong glances at Nayan viewing the picture, before proceeding to pour the golden-brown Darjeeling tea liquor into a stainless-steel strainer she places into a cup. After topping with milk, and adding two spoonful of sugar and stirring the tea, she hands the cup to Nayan. She follows with a similar cup for Shukhlal, then for herself. All the while, her attention is riveted on Nayan's reaction to my picture.

"So, will you marry my sister?" Kalpana asks Nayan grinning mischievously, certain he has liked my picture, gauging from his expression.

"Didi, but you will have to ask your sister, whether she likes me," Nayan replies shyly, no longer protesting the idea of marriage. "A woman like her will have more expectations from a husband than I have to offer. I am neither rich nor educationally well qualified."

"Don't worry on that account, she will certainly like you," Kalpana replies resolutely. "Moreover, she has left the choice of groom to me."

After a few moments of silence, Nayan says in a regretful tone, "I have only completed my Intermediate exams, while your sister has a post-graduate degree. I have never been to college, while she teaches at one." Then he adds briskly, "I opted out of college to work and support myself after coming from Dacca during the riots."

"What about your family, will they have any objections?" Kalpana asks, ignoring his revelations, to Nayan's utter surprise. "I could speak with them, in order to finalize the match and the wedding."

"My parents are no more," Nayan replies solemnly. "My father

Shuvashree Chowdhury

passed away when I was six years old. My mother brought up three of her sons with a lot of difficulty after that. Having come to Calcutta with me, she passed away a few years ago. Mother lived with her sister, while I was setting up my business with the little gold she had given me. She divided what little was left of the immense amount she once had as a zamindar's wife, after having sold most to bring us up, after father's death. My two elder brothers had plotted to take away all remaining material possessions from our house, before we left East Bengal, when mother took the decision to divide and give each of us a share. My brothers, much older than me, are both married and have grown children now, but are still as worthless, living off past riches."

"I'm very sorry to hear about your parents, Nayan," Kalpana says tenderly, before adding, "Now I am even further convinced of your being the best match for my sister, since you are a self-made man."

After Nayan and Shuklal leave that evening, Kalpana telephones me excitedly.

"Maya, I have found the perfect match for you. His name is Nayan and he is very handsome. I'm sure you're going to like him."

"Didi, is being handsome the only criterion for your choice?" I ask cautiously, not putting it past her in it being so, adding, "What are his educational qualifications, what does he do, what about his family?"

"He runs a printing press down the road from our house," Kalpana replies proudly, almost as if she is his sister as well.

"What about qualifications, Didi?" I press on, "how far has he studied?"

"He has completed his eleventh standard, but had to opt out of college," Kalpana replies, adding nonchalantly, "But Maya, that is not relevant, as he is self-employed and runs a successful business."

"Not relevant?" I retort, "Are you crazy, Didi? Whatever do you mean by it is not relevant?" Then irritated at her attitude, I firmly finish, "Of course it is important, I am the one getting married here, and to me it is very significant. I wish you would understand that."

"Maya, what is Ronjit uncle's educational qualification?" Kalpana abruptly asks, in a mellow tone, adding purposefully, "doesn't he run a very successful business without much formal education, funding so many charitable institutions from its earnings? Remember, what both of us are today, is due to a less educated man, not our well qualified father. Education is no doubt a prelude to success, while talent and intelligence are its props; but without the right attitude, vision, willpower, hard work and perseverance, they are useless."

Kalpana's reasoning rendering me speechless, I reply, "Ok then Didi, send me his picture, you have obviously made up your mind about him."

Kalpana's choice in my groom, added to her views, makes me doubt her satisfaction in marriage to a highly educated man. When Sudeep on his return learns of Kalpana's choice of groom for me, he is aghast.

"Kalpana, education may not be the only mark of a good man," Sudeep says dismissively, "but the bride being so much more qualified than the groom is going to be a clear cause for mental differences between them. It will ultimately cause a serious rift."

"A person's business success and resultant confidence can substitute the self-assurance a high level of formal education generates," Kalpana argues, "making him secure about his place in the world, allowing him to stand up to anyone with abundant education." Then abruptly she adds, smilingly, "Isn't our marriage a case in point? I'm a school dropout like Ma, but I'm not a frog in a well, so not intimidated by you."

In a couple of weeks, I am sent Nayan's picture by post. There is no scope of my disliking him from his photograph. He is a good-looking man, with a touch of simplicity and shyness in his smile, adding to his charm. I agree to the match and our engagement is planned for a few months later, for when I am next expected in Calcutta, during the Dussehra holidays. I am surprised at myself - for all my independence to agree to get married to a man I have not met or even spoken to yet. But that is the faith I have in Kalpana, as blind as it may seem, knowing she has only my best interests in mind. I had always secretly wished to marry an army officer, for their core values, discipline and personality, perhaps influenced

          Shuvashree Chowdhury

by Ronjit uncle's army background; but I have never voiced my preference to Kalpana or anyone.

My wedding is more or less fixed in my absence. However, in spite of her high-handed concern, open-minded as Kalpana is, she has left provision for Nayan and me to change our minds, in case we do not like each other on meeting. A few months back, Kalpana had also tried to match-make me with a widower with two children. She had liked the man, but I turned him down, wanting my own children, not to be a step-mother to any. Now that the day of the wedding and my arrival is drawing close, Kalpana telephones me often, on one or other preparatory grounds. She and Sudeep are planning, financing and organizing the entire event, as well as my trousseau. But I will be paying for my wedding jewellery, purchased by Kalpana, from my savings of the last eight years of working.

After my arrival in Calcutta in October, I meet Nayan for the first time, at Kalpana's house. Sudeep and she leave us alone, after the initial introductions, over cups of Kalpana's well-made Darjeeling tea. Having already reconciled to each other's bio-data, aware of as much as is required to be disclosed in an arranged marriage, we like each other in person. We confer our acceptance to Kalpana's matchmaking, by announcing we would like to take a walk to Nayan's printing press, much to her delight and Sudeep's consternation. Nayan would like me to see the place that truly defines him and which will provide our marital livelihood. There I am introduced to his staff, waiting after their day's work, to know of the confirmation of their beloved master's betrothal and to meet their future mistress.

In the next few days that I am in Calcutta, I meet Nayan's close friends and relatives. In the absence of a real guardian, he takes me to meet his best friend since childhood, a man named Satyen, who is still unmarried and works at the State Bank of India. He wholeheartedly consents to our match, himself remaining a bachelor and close to us lifelong. Nayan's other friends approve of me too and are very happy for him. The relatives are eagerly waiting to organize the Bou Bhat or the customary reception by the groom's family. It is to be organized at the home of relatives in Park Circus, as Nayan does not have any real family in Calcutta. The cost of the wedding trousseau and the celebrations by the groom's side are to be borne by Nayan alone. His brothers, who live in the suburban towns of Bardhaman and Rishra, might perhaps attend the wedding with their families, but as guests. Nayan's only contact with them now is through their sons, who visit him when in need of money for their education, their sister's weddings or other exigencies.

After the short vacation and informal engagement to Nayan, I return to my work in Delhi, certain that Kalpana has indeed found me a good man. I interpret this by the way Nayan's workers, friends and even distant relatives love and respect him; rather than by his charming manners and soft-spoken disposition. Being well read and aware of current happenings in the world makes him a good conversationalist. He is also a thorough gentleman, with pleasing manners. Each time we went out to meet someone, he would pick and drop me from Kamala's doorsteps in a taxi. Nayan does not have a house or car yet, but plans on acquiring both sometime after we are married. I have not told him yet but will in time, of my aspiration for my own home, having been displaced from my childhood one.

I next return to Calcutta by the first week of December, during my college's winter vacations. By now preparations for the wedding are well under way and Ma has come too. Baba has obviously not been invited, just as he had not been for Kalpana's wedding. Ma continues to live in a portion of Baba's house. Though the difference now is that it is legally hers. The year before, I had travelled to Barpeta in Assam on Sudeep's initiation, to meet Baba. It would be the last time I saw him before his death in 1973. During the visit, I got him to legally write in Ma's name the portion of the house she and Neelima's family live in, which is a little over one fourth of the whole. Ma is a rightful beneficiary to Baba's property; but without his legally transferring part of it to her, if he passed away, she might live under threat of being evacuated by his second wife and her children.

On the 11th of December 1969, draped in a shocking pink zari embroidered Benarasi sari, wearing make-up for the only time in my life, I marry Nayan. I am amply adorned in gold jewellery bought with my personal savings, in keeping with Sudeep and Kalpana's social and economic status. Wearing a

          Shuvashree Chowdhury

mukut (ceremonial headgear made from shola, a soft reed) with floral designs etched out of sandalwood paste on my forehead and cheeks, I am the quintessential Bengali bride. I wear a demure look, in observance of the customary demeanour for a bride to be. Nayan looks no less than a Bengali film actor, dressed in a raw-silk crushed dhoti and kurta, with real gold buttons, and Kolhapuri jootis or shoes. I have a conventional Bengali wedding. The Sampradan or being given-away-as-a-bride, is done by an elderly uncle. It is followed by the seven pheras (walking around the sacred fire); the garland exchange or mala-bodol and then the sindur (vermilion smearing) ceremony.

The wedding ceremony is followed by a full course, sit-down Bengali mahabhoj or feast, for the large number of guests. This is on the first floor of a three-storey rented house, while the ceremony had been conducted on the second floor. It is convenient to have wedding functions at houses specially let out for the purpose, to prevent the chaotic condition they leave one's home with in their aftermath. The house on Beadon Street has been abundantly decorated with fresh flowers like marigolds, red roses and white tuberoses, available in plenty in winter, in Calcutta. The outside is well highlighted with multi-coloured tiny lights. Even the white ambassador car that fetched the groom to the venue has been prettily decorated with a variety of flowers. A coloured butterfly, a sign of prosperity, made of flowers, is pasted upright at the edge of the car's bonnet, for good luck.

At night, after all the guests leave, Nayan and I stay on at the wedding house along with Kalpana, Sudeep and a few close relatives and friends. We barely sleep, engaging in a number of games, customarily organized for the just-married couple to break the ice between themselves and the bride's family. There is plenty of singing, dancing and general bonhomie, among the people who have stayed on. It is now that we open up the gifts received. They include sewing machines, crockery, clothes-irons, bed-linen and a large number of saris. We take a brief nap towards the early hours of the morning, then bathe and change into fresh clothing. After breakfast, followed by a short ceremony called the bashi-biye or out-of-date-wedding, is my bidai or farewell ceremony.

Nayan and I leave for his relative's house in Park Circus,

escorted by them. On reaching and completion of the initial welcome ceremony, we are customarily separated for the night, referred to as the Kaal Ratri. Though having mythical origins, this custom could well be for the couple to get a refreshing sleep and prepare for the final ceremony the next day. The Bou Bhat is a ritual where the bride symbolically cooks and serves a meal to members of her husband's family, followed by a banquet. I wear a golden coloured Benarasi sari, personally chosen by Nayan for the occasion. Standing alongside him, I greet his rather large number of guests and receive their blessings. After all the invitees leave, is our Phool Sojja wherein we are adorned with flowers and left alone in a bedroom. The four-poster bed has been ornately decorated and strewn with flowers, to create a romantic ambience and mood, for us to consummate our marriage.

The next day, now truly married, after the vast array of rituals and festivities, we move into the apartment we have rented, to start our life together. It is at Sovabazar in north Calcutta, pretty close to the river and not far from Kalpana's rented house at Amherst Street. Kalpana had order-made basic furniture – a double-bed with mattress, two side-tables, a dressing table and a wardrobe, all customarily given by the bride's family. These have already been delivered to the two room flat by the time we arrive, along with our personal belongings in a few suitcases. Thereby, with a few pots and pans for the kitchen, basic furniture, our clothes and personal effects, along with the variety of wedding gifts to help us get started, I set out on my marital journey.

* * *

After our wedding, I spend a few weeks at the newly rented apartment in Sovabazar with Nayan. I then return to my lecturer's job at Delhi University, continuing to live alone in the apartment in Rajendra Nagar near my college. For the next few years, Nayan and I manage a long-distance marriage successfully. I come to Calcutta for the summer and winter vacations, while he spends the Durga Puja holidays, the only time of year when his printing press is shut, with me in Delhi. Before the completion of two years of marriage, we become the proud parents of a baby girl, followed by another one shortly. Through both my pregnancies, I continue

     Shuvashree Chowdhury

to work in Delhi, coming home to Calcutta by train on maternity leave, before the birth. At the end of the official maternity-leave of three months, I return to join work in Delhi, along with the tiny babies.

These are trying times for me, managing a job, as well as two small children on my own. I request Ma to come with me to Delhi, but she turns her back on me, not showing up from Assam the day of my departure from Calcutta. Though I take a nanny from Calcutta, I am not sure if I can trust her to leave the children alone with her, while I go to work. With our current financial situation and Nayan needing to regularly invest in his business at this stage, leaving my job is not an option. I struggle on, hoping to see a better and easier life in a couple of years. Moreover, every time the idea of quitting my job comes to mind, I see the fearsome ghost of my mother's existence. In about six years of being married, I decide to move to Calcutta, realizing my children are growing up barely knowing their father.

After the non-existence of a father most of my life, I cannot allow the situation to be repeated with my girls. Luckily, in lieu of my long and dedicated service, my college grants me an extended leave-without-pay, wherein my job remains assured on return. With the security of still having a job in Delhi, I come to Calcutta and look out for another. I find a suitable opening as a lecturer at a college in Calcutta, though having to settle for a substantial salary cut. I agree to curtail my remuneration, in the greater cause of living together with my husband and children as a family. This is something I have sorely missed after a point in my childhood. It is only after the girls are beyond the sixth and seventh grades in school that I enrol for a MPhil degree at my college in Gwalior, attending classes there only during the vacations.

After being awarded the MPhil degree, which now also enhances my salary, I buy a plot of land at Salt Lake in Calcutta, with money I have saved over the years. I then shift my focus from qualifications and career, to building my own house. Nayan, elder to me by six years, understands my need to do so, as he was able to relate to my continuing my education even after marriage. He agrees to the registration of the land in my name alone, as well as complete legal ownership of the house. Nayan has allowed me to save my entire income over the years, with us spending only out of his. However, at the time that I start construction of my dream home, I realize my money is not sufficient. So I take a loan from Nayan, conscientiously repaying him monthly, out of my salary. By the time our daughters complete their schooling, we have a lovely three-storey home of our own.

After moving into our new home and furnishing it to my satisfaction, I again turn my attention to my academic qualifications. It is after I have been awarded my PhD degree, dedicating my thesis to Ronjit uncle, that I feel fulfilled in my mission to acquire the highest qualification in my field of work. I am shortly designated as professor, going on to become the principal of my college. By now our daughters have completed their college education and are working in their chosen fields, for which I am very proud. I am in no hurry for them to marry and have children, knowing that will happen in due course. It is around my fiftieth birthday, after a lifetime of struggle, that I feel content in achieving all I set out to in my career, and in fulfilling my dream of a home and family, from which I can never be displaced.

I am, indeed fortunate, to have a self-assured, empathetic and supportive husband in Nayan. He had no qualms in my following my ambition for higher degrees, in spite of not being educationally highly qualified himself. All through the time I pursued my goal, enrolling at my college again in Gwalior during vacations, to complete my thesis or curriculum, Nayan managed home and children, in addition to his own work. He was never insecure of my legal ownership of joint assets, always happy to allow me to take the lead.

In spite of physically traversing the geographical border between East Pakistan and India in 1964, to begin a new life, getting married was truly the real crossing of the border for me. It was not the finishing line in life's marathon race, as it tends to become for a lot of women, but the commencement of the final laps when I accelerated to make a winning finish.

                    Shuvashree Chowdhury

Chapter 9

The Death of My Hero

While at college in Dacca, on a visit to Mihirpur for the vacations, I am introduced by Ronjit uncle to a pretty young girl, with curly brown hair, large hazel eyes, honey coloured complexion and a radiant smile.

"Maya, this is Rupali," he says, "she is visiting from Calcutta, and will be staying at the guesthouse for a few weeks. Please show her around and see that she is comfortable."

I nod, smiling warmly at Rupali, while she smiles back shyly. Liking her instantly, I take her with me on my usual visit of the hospital and the dispensary. Later I show her around the school and hostel. In the coming days, over our interactions, we become close and exchange notes on our respective lives. Rupali tells me about her school in Darjeeling and of life with her family in Calcutta. On my part, I tell her about my schooling in Mihirpur followed by college in Dacca.

After we get to know each other, our discussions shift to Rupali's curiosity on Ronjit uncle. She wants to know everything about him and quizzes me on his family and life. It is not uncommon for guests to want to know more about the man behind all the charitable work here, so I fill her in on as much as I am aware. Since I love Ronjit uncle's family as my own, talking about them is a pleasure. It is later in the course of our friendship, a few days before her return; that I learn in disbelief that Rupali is Ronjit uncle's real daughter.

"You are the only person outside our family who knows of this," she adds ingenuously, after the startling disclosure. "I like you, Maya, and know I can trust your not mentioning it to anyone else."

I merely nod, stumped by her revelation. She has a sister and brother I learn, who are in school with her in Darjeeling. Their mother lives in Calcutta and father Ronjit uncle visits them in school, as well as at home in Calcutta. Rupali even shows me a family-picture of the five of them, taken at their home in Calcutta, to my utter bewilderment.

At first I think this story is a figment of her imagination. But on seeing the perfect family-picture, I gauge there is truth in her revelations. But how can this possibly be, I think desperately? All my life I have known Ronjit uncle's family in Mihirpur. He seemed pretty content or so I believed. Moreover, Rupali is as old as his grandchildren from his daughters, through his wife Mrinalini. But ironically, whether or not a man is satisfied in his marriage has no bearing on his likelihood of straying. Rupali does not realize it, but her disclosure is as hard hitting on me as it would be on Ronjit uncle's real daughters. I hold him in such high regard, possibly more than his own children and grandchildren.

Since my father's abandoning us, it was Ronjit uncle who gave us a new lease of life. I had since then, mentally placed him on a pedestal corresponding to God. He is my hero, my ideal man who can do no wrong. Now learning of his fallibility rattles me to the very core. My delusion of Ronjit uncle as different from my father, snatched from me so brutally, is excruciating. I try to squash my unrest by telling myself that in spite of his waivered interests late in life, Ronjit uncle, unlike Baba, has provided well for both his families. He has kept the families apart, not letting the existence of one come in the way of the happiness and well-being of the other. I remember him reprimanding my father for bringing his second wife home. Ronjit uncle had been of the opinion that she should be kept separately, her presence not allowed to mar the peace and well-being of the family. I realize now, that ironically he was preaching what he would soon practice.

My estimation of Ronjit uncle shattered, I can no longer look upon him as my ideal man. But I do not tell anyone of his undisclosed other family. After all, though imperfect, he is still my hero, the man who saved me, gave me a new life. Perhaps it is Ronjit uncle's fall from grace in my view which will enable me to defy him, opting for a life of my own, on completion of my graduation. After Rupali's departure and my return to college, my curiosity over her mother

     Shuvashree Chowdhury

is piqued. I am keen to meet the woman who created such a deep impact on Ronjit uncle, into conduct so contradictory to my belief of his values. Soon, on a trip to Calcutta along with Ronjit uncle's first family for my summer vacations, the opportunity presents itself. To my amazement, Ronjit uncle himself takes me to Rupali's house, to meet her family, as she is now my friend. Though oblivious of my awareness of his relationship with them, perhaps a part of him wants to find in me a bridge between both his families.

In spite of my prolonged consternation, on meeting Rupali's mother Sumitra Banerjee, a reputed actor, I am awestruck by her beauty and poise. I had been mentally prepared to hate or at best be immune towards her, like I was to my father's second wife, but such is not the case. I fall in love with her instantly, after she smiles affectionately, taking me on as a daughter right away. I am now able to envision how difficult it would be for Ronjit uncle or any man to resist Sumitra with her aura, once he has had the good fortune to meet her. Perhaps it is Ronjit uncle's managing of this weakness of his life, if I may call it as his only significant one, by giving due respect to both his families, that allows me to forgive him. I can no longer put him back on the pedestal as God, but I find him a place I reserve for God's chosen ones.

After meeting Sumitra, her two daughters Rupali and Sonali, as well as son Debashish, I look upon them as extended family. Sumitra also has two other children from a previous marriage, who are well settled now and live away. Perhaps it is my great love and regard for Ronjit uncle that makes me love him along with his weaknesses. Someday, my husband, children, even Ronjit uncle's granddaughters, will tease me for my blind eye towards his faults. But in the face of his prominence and magnanimity, my unfathomable gratitude, I will defend him to everyone, lifelong. Sumitra has long stopped acting, but I now become her ardent admirer, visiting her of my own accord whenever I am in Calcutta. I hope to feel guilty for liking her so much, as Ronjit uncle's first family is so kind to me, but I am unable to find it in my heart to do so. At times, the chemistry between two people makes them powerless to resist each other, as between Sumitra and me. This must also be the case with her and Ronjit uncle, I rationalize in his defence.

Sumitra dresses as a conventional Bengali married-woman, wearing the symbols of marriage like the sindur, shakha and paula, so I presume she and Ronjit uncle are married. He has bought her a house, takes care of her and their three children financially and emotionally, as any good husband and father would. I suppose, then, his keeping his two families apart is better than together and unhappy like my father, who neglected his responsibility to one completely. But then isn't life paradoxical, and I a hypocrite? Since I am no longer the child who was a victim of bigamy, but a detached mature woman, I choose to be non-judgemental about my hero. Or it is my deep rooted sense of gratefulness to Ronjit uncle, for my now secure place in the world, that in returning his immeasurable favours I forgive him.

A regular visitor to Sumitra's house now, I also attend her elder daughter, my friend Rupali's wedding, escorting Ronjit uncle to it. He is in a hurry to leave after the ceremony, but I insist on having dinner, to allow him to spend more time at the function. A father's presence at his daughter's wedding makes her special day more so, though I will not have my father at mine. Ronjit uncle is still unaware of my knowing of his second family, and I prefer it this way. I hold him in such high regard, that I cannot allow his sight to stoop in looking at me, out of unease, or risking his avoiding me. However I am very curious to know how Sumitra and he met. On a visit to her place one day, I hesitantly ask her about it. As fond of me as Sumitra is, she relives her clandestine happiness with me, filling me in on details she cannot share with her own children or anyone else.

* * *

The first time they meet is in the lavishly decorated lobby of a renowned luxury hotel in the heart of Calcutta on Chowringhee Road. Sumitra has arrived early for their lunch appointment, having read of his punctuality and discipline in magazine articles. Though staying at the same hotel, he has told her he will be going out, to return in time for lunch with her at one o'clock. Sumitra quickly visits the washroom by the poolside, checking whether her make-up, hair, and the pleats of her aqua-blue-georgette embroidered sari are in place. On returning to the foyer, she sits on

     Shuvashree Chowdhury

a sofa facing the main doorway, so she can see him come through it. She is certain of recognizing him from pictures of his she has seen in newspapers. Every time the door swings open, a liveried guard holding it for a guest after a bow; she looks in its direction expectantly.

Sumitra is slightly nervous about the meeting, not quite sure why he wants to meet her. She distracts herself, looking at the twinkling lights of the chandeliers illuminating the place with their tender light. At first he had sent her a hand-written letter, about how he had loved her performance in her latest movie and would like to meet the real person behind the sterling performance. As a successful actor, she receives fan-mail regularly, each of which she reads in reassurance of her continuance to rule as a star. But this particular letter was different, in that it was written on an official letter-head paper and was crisp and businesslike. He wrote that he would like to talk to her telephonically and then meet her if she did not mind. Sumitra knew of him, even held him in high regard from the media reports of his charitable works; so she replied to him giving her telephone number.

Staring at the streaks of light emanating from the prisms of a chandelier now, Sumitra wonders if he wants to offer her a role in a movie he might be producing. She does not know of him being in the film-production business, but then people diversify all the time, she thinks. After another swing of the door, she looks in its direction to notice a man of average height, and regal bearing, wearing a black sweatshirt and brown jacket over olive-green trousers, walk with brisk confident strides in her direction. She instantly recognizes him as none other than Ronjit Roychowdhury. Sumitra stands up, and he offers her his hand to shake. She instantly feels the power of his persona through the firmness of his grip. The next thing she notices is his eyes, which are mesmeric. They seem to be fiercely drawing her into them, even while radiating warmth. Sumitra feels awestruck in his presence, as if caught in the current of his individuality.

It seems as if they are standing in a magnetic field, inexplicably drawn to each other, finding it difficult to break away from the other's gaze. Surreal forces acting between them seem to be pulling them together. Though they have never met before, it is as if they have known each other for long. Slowly they walk to one of the restaurants of the hotel, initiated by his guiding her in the direction with a nudge on the back of her shoulders. The captain of the restaurant smiles warmly at the doorway, ushering them to a cosy table for two. They sit down, after a waiter pulls out their chairs with a bow. Ronjit uncle again looks deep into Sumitra's wide, almond-shaped eyes, as though trying to reach into her soul, his own clear and calm as a still lake.

"I knew I was going to like you more in person," he says, smiling.

Sumitra smiles back shyly, as he continues holding her gaze intently. Then he shifts his attention to the menu card the waiter is holding up in front of him. He orders a bottle of beer, asking her what she would like. After a moment's hesitation, she decides on a glass of beer. The waiter leaves, to promptly return with a bottle and two glasses, and then pours the bubbly liquid into their respective glasses. A few sips of the chilled beer seem to soothe Sumitra's flustered nerves, as she sinks back comfortably on her cushioned chair. Ronjit uncle asks her about her work, which further puts her at ease, as that is familiar territory. As passionate about her work as she is, Sumitra happily tells him about her current roles and movies. Then she speaks of the characters she has played, as well as those she hopes to play in the future.

Sumitra soon tells Ronjit uncle about the death of her husband, feeling secure in talking to him, and on being a single working mother to two school-going children.

Ronjit uncle on his part shares with her stories of his days with the British army and experiences of the World War II. Sumitra listens attentively, enthralled by his exposure. He also tells her about his various businesses, with details of the charitable works they fund. He is as passionate about his work as her, but Sumitra finds hers paling in significance as compared to his philanthropic work, which makes such a difference to the world. She has read of it, but hearing the details now she is further in awe of him. After two bottles of beer shared between them, without accompanying snacks or appetizers, they each order portions of grilled fish with sautéed vegetables and bread-rolls. Both are disciplined about their diet and lifestyle. She for the obvious reason of maintaining

                    Shuvashree Chowdhury

her weight and attractiveness for an acting career that demands it, now that she is nearing forty years; he to remain fit and active, that he has just crossed sixty.

Having exchanged letters and spoken telephonically has not prepared them for the way they get along in person – like fuel and fire. Sumitra intermittently feels shy, unable to control the racing of her heart, powerless to harness its acceleration from a trot to a steady gallop. Ronjit uncle is like a stallion, raging to go, waiting for her to loosen the reins. Horses are incidentally one among his passions in life. He goes riding on his favourite mare he calls Rani, every morning.

"You know something, Sumitra," he says conspiratorially, bending towards her over the table, "as soon as I met you, I felt my blood gush, just as it is every time I see a horse." Sumitra bursts out laughing at the comparison, then composing herself, says softly, "I'm really flattered Ronjit, considering horses are your first and childhood love, as you mentioned earlier."

"Well, that's the truth lady," he replies nonchalantly, still looking intently into her eyes, "I don't know how better to describe how I feel."

After lunch, as they stroll along the corridor towards the hotel's lobby, Sumitra realizes she does not want to part with him yet. There seems a bizarre connection between them. She does not want to break this spell, but realizes how unreasonable the idea is. After all, he is going back home to Vishnuganj the next morning. He checked into this hotel, in spite of a house in Calcutta, for a meeting with a foreign client who is staying here this evening. They are at the end of the corridor near the elevator, when abruptly Ronjit uncle turns to face her.

"Sumitra, don't go yet," he says firmly, looking earnestly into her eyes, "come upstairs, I'd like to show you what I do, its' all in a folder for a presentation I will be making to my client this evening."

Surprised at the request, but compelled by her own urge to stay, she finds herself silently nodding in agreement, following him into the lift.

In his suite, sitting on the sofa in the living-area, she flips through the pages of the folder detailing his businesses and charitable organizations. Ronjit uncle is seated close to her, leaning back comfortably on the sofa. Sumitra is acutely conscious of him watching her. She turns to glance at him sideways, when unable to resist, he slowly runs his fingers through her long flowing hair. Then encouraged by her silence, her not stopping him, he continues with firmer strokes.

"Don't worry Sumitra," he says, noticing her uptight position, her firmly upheld head, sensing her dilemma, "things are not always in our control. Leave the steering of your life to God. He has a route chalked out for each one of us; we are mere rear-seat riders."

Sumitra tries to relax, but the tension within her only grows. By now fiercely drawn to him both mentally and physically, she nestles closer to him and involuntarily places her head on his shoulder.

Ronjit uncle encircles the back of her shoulders with his right arm, continuing to cradle her head on his right shoulder. After a few brief moments when she lifts her head, she finds him watching her curiously. As their gazes meet, seeing the flaming desire in his light brown eyes, unable to control her own yearning, she tilts towards him, and their lips touch in a flash. Then without much ado they are locked in a passionate kiss. Their kiss is electrifying, sending shock waves through their body and mind, as they continue to kiss breathlessly. Taken aback by their reckless passion, but with no power to restrain themselves, they get up slowly, arm in arm they walk towards the bedroom. Sumitra has been lonely for a very long time. As attracted as she feels to this man, she cannot hold herself any longer. The age difference between them, his grey hair and the deep lines on his face, are overshadowed by his lean, toned and athletic form. But in reality, it is his mind that has ignited hers; the physical longing is a manifestation of that mental attraction she feels.

Sumitra is willing to throw caution to the wind, in allowing him to make love to her, even if it is only this one time, never to see him again. Ronjit uncle is surprised at his own longing, brought on by his immense fondness for this woman with large, innocent, dreamy eyes and a voluptuous, shapely mouth. She has a radiant youthful face, and the most endearing smile he has ever seen, which caught his attention while watching her perform on

    Shuvashree Chowdhury

screen, compelling him to meet her. In bed in each other's arms, now stripped to their skin, with her soft and supple body against his lean, muscular frame, he feels blessed for this rush of passion in the dusk of his life. He kisses and caresses her tenderly all over, as she reaches out to his fingers and mouth hungrily, craving for more, and more.

At his age, his love making is like a calm sea softly caressing the shore; while hers is a wild and rough ocean violently crashing on the coast, desperately trying to break its reserve to be one with it. Inside her, he can feel the pulsating heat like a volcano about to erupt and in moments he feels his own explosion, struggling to catch his breath to feel her simultaneous rhythmic one. Still clinging to each other in the aftermath of their lovemaking, breathing heavily, shocked at their passion and its fierce zenith, neither has an iota of guilt or remorse. It feels so natural for them to be in each other's arms.

"My darling, sweetheart, you are so beautiful," Ronjit uncle almost croons, choking with emotion, as he hugs her tenderly from behind, lying as she is on her side with her back to him.

His endearing tone and words touch a tender spot in her heart. She turns around to kiss him in reciprocation, at first tenderly and then passionately.

In moments they are hungry for each other again. But this time, Sumitra takes the lead, by now having overcome her shyness completely, wanting to please him. He lies back, watching her affectionately, delighting in her adept manoeuvres as she works on him, then when he is ready she adroitly climbs over him. After making love slowly and deliberately a second time, exhausted but content, they lie in each other's arms quietly lost in their own thoughts. Then slowly they tear themselves apart, to take a steaming shower together in the large, well-equipped bathroom. Sumitra briskly rolls up her long hair into a shower cap, so as not to wet her loose curls, stepping under the shower with him. After they lather, giggling like children they cling together under the shower, then dry one another with a single towel.

Standing on the bedside rug, Sumitra looks in amusement at the disarrayed bedclothes and grins at her co-conspirator. As she drapes back her aqua-blue sari in front of the dresser, Sumitra smiles at her reflection in the mirror. She feels elated, and madly in love with this man who was a stranger even till this afternoon. Ronjit uncle quickly dresses, then comes and puts an arm around her waist cosily. Looking at her reflection in the mirror glowing pink and fresh like a baby's, more beautiful now than ever, he asks her to join him with his client for dinner that evening. She spontaneously nods in agreement, as there is nothing else she would rather do. On her way out, she gives him a quick hug at the door, avoiding kissing for fear of her inability to leave. As Sumitra walks through the foyer, people are looking at her, recognizing her, but she is living in the past couple of hours.

That evening, Sumitra arrives dressed in a black georgette sari, with floral patterns embroidered in soft pastel shades. When Ronjit uncle answers the door-bell of his suite dressed in a black silk shirt and trousers, he cannot take his eyes off hers, now highlighted with kohl and brightened wide with mascara. Slowly he shifts his gaze to the familiar smile on her luscious lips in light pink lip-gloss. He feels his heart skip a few beats, as he opens the door wide to let her in, the whiff of her perfume pervading his senses. The guest, a German, is already seated inside, a glass of whisky on the rocks placed before him on the table. On seeing her, the man named Reimund Schmidt gets up, offering her his hand to shake which she does firmly. Ronjit uncle introduces them to each other, her as a close friend and Reimund as a business associate.

After they are all settled comfortably, when offered by the butler in attendance, Sumitra opts for a glass of red wine, avoiding the snacks served with it. The conversation between the men is mostly business for a while. Sumitra listens intently, again marvelling at Ronjit uncle's personality and wit. She is stupefied by his baritone and businesslike conduct, so different from the casual, warm and cosy tone and manner of the afternoon. The men wrap up their business shortly, and then Sumitra joins them in discussing the political and social changes in India and Pakistan, post-independence and after Partition. They also discuss music and latest film trends in Bengal and Sumitra is amazed at Ronjit uncle's awareness. He has an excellent sense of humour, too, she notes, coming across in his witty remarks.

   Shuvashree Chowdhury

Sumitra is glad to have returned this evening, to see Ronjit uncle's multi-faceted personality, making her fall more in love with him. The full-course dinner with soup and desserts, is of both Continental and Indian cuisine. After cups of coffee each, in washing down the sumptuous meal, the guest Reimund and the butler leave. Sumitra and Ronjit uncle, happy to be on their own again, snuggle up close on the sofa, cosy in each other's presence.

"I am fascinated to see the varying sides of your personality, all in a day," Sumitra says, smiling warmly into his eyes, and then she lightly places a hand on his arm, adding "the warm, mushy, romantic man of the afternoon, turning into a tough, steely businessman in the evening; followed by the charming, humorous host over dinner."

"Thank you ma'am," Ronjit uncle replies, laughing, with a mock bow. "I set out to impress you, glad you noticed. The steely businessman earns the money the compassionate one can put to charitable use."

Sumitra, giving in to a sudden urge, hugs him, with a swift peck on the cheek. Then unable to resist, they kiss passionately for long. After breaking away, on gazing into each other's eyes, they find themselves drawn into an obsessive kiss all over again, finding it impossible to tear apart. It is Sumitra who steals out of his embrace, then gets up to leave, as Ronjit uncle follows her quietly to the door. He requests her to stay the night, but Sumitra refuses, she has to go home. They hug for a few brief moments; then again kiss fervently, wondering at this deep connection between two people who have just met. Sumitra walks out of the door quietly, exercising all her will power. Any words now might break the magic spell they have spent the day in. As she walks down the corridor, Sumitra wonders if they will ever meet again, but even if not, she is happy to have had today.

On the way home in a taxi, with the cool February breeze on her cheek, Sumitra is surprised at her sudden wish to be pregnant with Ronjit uncle's child. It will be an honour to have his child, she thinks, one who will be a token of their deep love - even if it lasted only for a day. She can then keep a part of Ronjit uncle with her for life. She assumes forlornly that they might never meet again, but the possibility of bearing his child makes her smile. As for Ronjit uncle, watching her saunter away down the corridor, he had felt a part of him walk away. He decided then that he will not let that happen, not let her get away from him. On his next visit to Calcutta, he telephones Sumitra and they meet again, then repeatedly, feeling powerless against the strong tide drawing them together, into building a family of their own.

* * *

Ronjit uncle banished me from his life, after I chose to take the decision of my life in my own hands. This was after I graduated with a Bachelor of Arts degree, during which time I learnt of and met Sumitra. After my amputation from his life, through the riots of 1964 to leaving East Pakistan, then taking on Indian citizenship to study and work in Gwalior, I was not in touch with him or anyone from his immediate family. This ended my newfound friendship with Sumitra abruptly. Both Ronjit uncles' families seemed to forget my very existence, since he chose to forget me. It was from my sister Kalpana that I continued to be informed of Ronjit uncle and of his first family. Kalpana never mentioned Sumitra and I never asked, not sure if she or anyone for that matter, knew of her at all.

It was a year after I started working, then employed in Delhi in the year 1968, that I was reunited with Ronjit uncle. I was in Calcutta for the summer vacations, staying with Kalpana as usual, when I learnt that Ronjit uncle was in Calcutta and critically ill. Squashing my pride, allowing my deep regard and gratitude for him supersede the hurt caused by his cutting me off completely, I decided to visit him along with Kalpana. Perhaps what also propelled my decision to meet him was that I was now well employed. I had proved, as I had set out to, that I could survive without him and successfully so. However in truth, all the time that I was trying to prove myself to him in addition to Baba, I never forgot that my ability in attempting to do so was possible only because of what he had made of me.

On meeting Ronjit uncle, standing at his bedside, I was touched to see how happy and proud he was to learn of my achievements, wanting to know every minute detail. His wife Mrinalini asked

     Shuvashree Chowdhury

if I would like to stay for a few days, to help her nurse him back to health. I promptly agreed, telephoning my college in Delhi to extend my leave. There would never be a better opportunity to repay a little of what they had done for me. It is during the weeks while I nursed him, that I was finally able to tell Ronjit uncle the real reasons for my decision to choose a career without his permission. He understood my need to do something of my own, rather than continue to live on charity all my life. After he was well, I returned to Delhi, having myself recovered from the trauma of his misunderstanding me for so long.

On his return to Vishnuganj, Ronjit uncle wrote me some heart-wrenching letters. I have reread them several times since. He wrote how grateful he was for my deep regard for him; that he was sorry he had misunderstood my far-sightedness for ingratitude. He agreed, it would indeed be difficult for me to work under his family after him, as they might see me as a threat to their inheritance and authority. In another letter, he wrote that he was glad that as a daughter, even though not in blood, I have inherited his fortitude and tenacity. That he now realises, what I did - go away to make a life of my own - was out of genuine reverence for him. The lines, about him seeing my face when sitting in prayer to Ma Durga, made me weep. My eyes mist when I read the letters even today, as I do sometimes. His words of adulation make all my life's struggles seem worthwhile.

* * *

After Partition of British India in August 1947, two new states were formed. One was the secular state of India and the other the Islamic one of Pakistan, made of two culturally and geographically separate areas to the east and west of India. The western zone was officially termed West Pakistan and the eastern one called East Bengal. It later came to be known as East Pakistan, which is the current day Bangladesh. Though there was not much difference in the population of the two zones, political power came to be concentrated in West Pakistan. This led to many grievances, with the perception that East Pakistan was being exploited. In March 1971, the rising political and cultural discontentment in East

Pakistan was met by a fierce suppressive force from the ruling elite of West Pakistan.

This brutal crackdown by the West Pakistani forces led to East Pakistan declaring its independence and the beginning of a civil war. It resulted in the cessation of East Pakistan, to form the independent nation of Bangladesh. This war led to a vast number of refugees flooding the eastern part of India. Faced with a rising humanitarian and economic crisis, India started organizing and aiding the Bangladeshi resistance army, known as the Mukti Bahini or the Liberation Army. The Mukti Bahini was made up of Bengali military, paramilitary and civilians, using guerrilla warfare tactics to fight the West Pakistan army. The war broke out in March, 1971. The Bangladesh Liberation War was an armed conflict between East Pakistan aided by India, versus West Pakistan.

The army units directed by West Pakistan launched a military operation in East Pakistan. It was directed against Bengali civilians, students, intellectuals and armed personnel, who were demanding the separation of the East from the West of Pakistan. India aided the Mukti Bahini by providing economic, military and diplomatic support, leading Pakistan to launch an attack on the western border of India, thereby starting the Indo-Pakistan War of 1971. In December 1971, the Indian army and the Mukti Bahini defeated the West Pakistani forces deployed in the east. The surrender resulted in the largest number of prisoners of war since World War II. During this war, there were widespread killings and violation of human rights and atrocities by the Pakistani Army.

The intellectual community was murdered on the instruction of the Pakistani army who picked up physicians, professors, writers and engineers, in and around Dacca. They murdered and left the bodies in mass graves. There are many such mass graves in Bangladesh and many more are discovered continually. Many women were tortured, raped and killed during this war, giving rise to a large number of war babies. The Pakistani Army also kept numerous Bengali women as sex-slaves inside Dacca cantonment, mostly captured from Dacca University and private homes. There was also violence perpetrated by the Bengali

     Shuvashree Chowdhury

nationalists against non-Bengali minorities like the Biharis. A large number of people fled East Pakistan to seek refuge in India during the time.

It was the first week of May 1971, at the peak of the killings of noted civilians and intellectuals during the Bangladesh Liberation War. Late one evening, a Pakistan Army jeep loaded with soldiers arrived at Ronjit uncle's office-cum-residential premises at Vishnuganj in East Pakistan. After a loud knock on the main door of his office where he also slept on most days, Ronjit uncle came out. The armed soldiers, with guns pointing in every direction, asked him to get into the jeep. Under the circumstances, not wanting them to know there were other family members inside, including women and children, he complied with their wishes. He left in his night-suit and robe, without informing anyone that he was leaving. However the next day he returned home, after a night with members of the Pakistani Army.

Two days later, the Pakistani army, with the obvious help of their local collaborators, once again abducted Ronjit uncle from his residence. This time on the way out at gun-point, he called out softly to his younger son Romit, who was working late with him in the office, to say he was leaving. Little did he know that this leave-taking would cost him dear? The armed soldiers directed his son to get into the jeep as well, leaving behind his young bride and a year-old son. Luckily no other members of the family, above all the women, stepped out then, or who knows what might have been done to them. After the night of their leaving home, no one ever saw Ronjit uncle or his son Romit again. They were officially declared missing, though presumably murdered shortly after their abduction.

However, there is no evidence to date of their murder, as the bodies were never found. Their surviving widows continued to dress as married women for the next twelve years, as is the Hindu custom, in the hope their husbands may return someday. I was lecturer at a college in Delhi University, married by then and pregnant with my first child. I read of Ronjit uncle's abduction along with two other men of repute, in an international newspaper at the college library. The news in bold letters, making me intuitively certain Ronjit uncle had been killed, brought tears spurting out of my eyes. I called the Red Cross Society in Delhi to verify the news, but could get no further information. It was alone in my room that evening, with vivid images of my life with Ronjit uncle since leaving my childhood home that I bitterly wept for the death of my hero.

                    Shuvashree Chowdhury

Chapter 10

My Daughters

It is a chilly January evening in the year 1977, when Nayan and I walk through the convent gates, with our two daughters. The elder, Sanjana, is five years old and the younger, Dipanjana, over three. Sister Louisa, who has been expecting us, approaches and offers us her hand to shake. Sanjana briskly pulls her hand out of mine and thrusts it into the nun's, keenly falling in step beside her. The rest of us follow, leisurely strolling over the sprawling grass field. Sanjana is soon engaged in conversation, in responding to Sister's queries. She narrates that we are in Darjeeling on vacation, it is two days since our arrival and she loves the place already. Our convent visit, is part of our sight-seeing list, she adds. We stop briefly, admiring the pretty chapel with the high steeple and grotto, encircled by a divine garden.

As we cross the grey school buildings and assembly hall, separated by neat flower-hedges from the play-field, nostalgia sweeps over me. This is the school where Ronjit uncle had sent me to learn English, after my stint at his school in Mihirpur. Everything is much the same since my time, though many of the nuns are different now. I point out particulars in the campus to Nayan, briskly recalling my life here. Sister Louisa, just transferred here, shows us inside the classrooms, junior dormitory, dressing-room and refectory. Sanjana has so many questions, as she skips along cheerfully, at ease with the nun in the navy blue habit. Her questions come faster than Sister can reply. Dipanjana walks along quietly, looking around, concentrating on her bar of Five-Star chocolate.

After the guided tour, we pass by the concrete basket-ball court, adjacent to the junior dormitory. It is dotted with girls in light pink and green sweat-shirts, engaged in a swift game vociferously cheered.

"One, two, three, four, who are we for?" the huge crowd bellows in unison. "Five, six, seven, eight, whom do we appreciate?"

This is followed by the names of the two Houses yelled simultaneously, competing with each other in pitch and volume. Sanjana, and Dipanjana by now having consumed the entire bar of chocolate, are both delighted by the excitement, rooted to the ground fascinated. Sister Louisa, watching them indulgently with a smile, bends low, puts her arm around Sanjana's shoulder.

"Come now, darling" she almost croons, "say goodbye to mummy, daddy and your sister, they will come again tomorrow."

Sanjana looks up at Sr. Louisa blankly, and then turns to Nayan questioningly - why would we want to leave so soon? Is Sister not coming back to the hotel with us? Sanjana however, overlooks Nayan's lack of response and sad face. By now she feels close to Sister Louisa, trusting her in her five year old's innocence. She feels privileged to stay and watch the match, assuming it is what she is staying back for. Clutching Sr. Louisa's hand, she smugly turns to wave us goodbye, in the belief we will come to fetch her the next day. I look at her tenderly, my heart wrenching at the treachery in leaving her here without warning. But I am proud of her independence in agreeing to stay on with a complete stranger. Sanjana has no inkling that she is going to be here for a long time to come. The formalities of her admission to the boarding school have been completed and Dipanjana is to join her the following year. The scheme is to let Sanjana adjust to the new place, the nuns, her classmates, and then tell her she is here to stay.

It was after my moving to Calcutta from Delhi, the year before, that I had toyed with the idea of a boarding school education for my girls. But I was not sure how the expenses would work out, whether Nayan and I could afford it. I decided on admitting Sanjana for a year to begin with, on a trial basis. A boarding school education was, however, not a mutual decision, but mine alone. Nayan was much against sending the girls away, but as in most situations, I was finally able to have my way with him. On the one hand, I obviously desire to bring up our daughters from home, personally monitoring every stage of their growth. But more than

                    Shuvashree Chowdhury

that, I want them to develop into resilient and self-reliant women, prepared to face any exigency in their lives. Also, having studied at this girls' school for two years, it was an aspiration I long nurtured, to educate my daughters here.

After our leaving, once the basket-ball match is over, the girls proceed to the study hall. Sr. Louisa takes Sanjana along with her to the chapel for her regular evening prayers, and then walks her to the refectory. By now, the other girls are seated in silence, eating, awaiting the bell that will allow them to start talking. Sanjana looks around her eagerly. Over a hundred girls are at about ten tables, seated class-wise. Sr. Louisa guides Sanjana to the table allotted to girls of Class I. There she is introduced to eight girls, who appraise her curiously, before she sits down. After a supper of chicken soup, bread and vegetable curry, ending with a bread pudding, Sanjana rises to the bell with the other girls. She tries to burble the prayers she does not know, along with them.

Sr. Louisa then leads Sanjana by hand to the dressing room, where she changes into night clothes - a pair of black and red checked woollen night-suit under a red kimono. She is helped by a lady named Philomena wearing a white floral printed frock and pink cardigan. Then in queue with the rest of the girls below Class V, she goes upstairs to the junior dormitory. Prayers are said kneeling beside their beds, and Sanjana is tucked into hers, under a thick quilt. She promptly falls asleep, tired from the activity and excitement of the day. The morning after, she is awakened by the ringing of a brass hand-bell, followed by Sister Louisa's soothing voice in her ear.

"Wake up Sanjana, we have to get ready for school," she says softly.

Sanjana opens her eyes and swiftly jumps out of bed. The other girls are kneeling beside their beds, so she rapidly does the same.

After prayers, everyone comes downstairs in a queue. In the dressing room, Sanjana brushes her teeth and washes her face, with new toiletries provided by Philomena. Little does she know I have alredy supplied everything as enlisted by the school. Sanjana is then dressed in a sea-blue woollen dress, with colourful boats knitted at the base, and a multicoloured woollen belt with two pompoms' attached to either ends. She promptly recognizes it as the one I had been knitting for a while, but does not question its getting here. Children can at times be so perceptive, yet miss glaring telltale signs, like I had on the day I left my childhood home in Assam. After putting on her navy-blue socks and black shoes, Philomena ties Sanjana's shoulder length hair in two ponytails. Sr. Louisa then escorts her to the refectory, as the others have left.

After breakfast, of slices of white bread with cottage-cheese and milk, Sanjana joins the girls in the study hall. There she flips the pages of a rhyme book, going over many she has learnt in her previous school, as well as those I have taught her. This is followed by the school assembly at the auditorium to the left of the main gate, where movies are also screened for students. Sister Blaize then takes Sanjana by the hand to her classroom. There she hands her a school-bag, that contains a few books, notebooks, and a pencil-box with pencils, erasers and ruler. Sanjana takes the bag graciously, mentally noting to return it before she leaves, not knowing it is hers. She spends the day merrily, assuming this jaunt here will be over by day-end. She looks forward to sharing her experiences with me and Nayan, but more so with her sister. Dipanjana will be extremely jealous, hearing the minute details of her escapade, she muses.

At 3pm, after the bell, all students swarm out of the class rooms into the corridor, dashing into the field, headed out of the main-gate. Sanjana follows them, not knowing what else to do. None of the teachers or nuns notices her, to stop her going out. She has not figured out the difference between boarders and day-scholars yet. Let alone knowing who the boarders in her class are, for her to accompany them to the hostel. As she saunters out of the gate, having left her bag, Sanjana is sure we will be among the parents waiting outside. She looks around, scanning every face. In her quest for us, lost amidst the sea of adult legs, she walks further and further beyond the main-gate. But there is no sign of our smiling, sincere faces, as is vivid in her mind. She stops walking, and turns in every direction searchingly, hoping to spot us. But to her dismay we are not there.

As she resumes walking wandering further away, a fear starts to arise from the pit of her stomach. It slowly creeps up to her chest, and then reaches her throat, strangling her. She feels desperately

                    Shuvashree Chowdhury

lost. The world seems too large, imposing and frightening, as if about to devour her. She abruptly remembers Sister Louisa, frantically turning back to go and find her. But Sanjana has turned all around, and with people looming large over her head, the gate is no longer visible. She has no idea how far she has wandered. In sheer panic now, she is unable to recall the faces she set out to look for. We her family have receded into nonexistence. She feels as though sinking down a precipice, into a dreadful, deadly sea. Tears spring to her eyes, and roll down her cheeks in abandon.

Sanjana, unable to withstand the large boulder of fear and loneliness, is about to collapse, her head stooped low, when Sister Louisa bends down and grabs her into her arms.

"My child, my poor little child, however did you get here?" she almost whispers in Sanjana's ears. "I was looking for you everywhere."

Sanjana does not respond, seemingly not recognizing Sister Louisa. She remains as if transfixed to the ground, her eyes wearing a lost look. Sister Louisa shakes her hard, before Sanjana, as if coming out of a trance, slowly shows signs of recognizing her. By now her tears have dried, though her eyes wear a sad, hurt look.

"I'm looking for my Mummy and Daddy," she mutters blankly, again looking downwards. "I want to go home."

"I'm so sorry darling, but they won't be coming now," Sr. Louisa replies softly. "They have returned to Calcutta. You will be staying with us at the boarding and will go home in the next vacation."

Sanjana stares at Sr. Louisa in disbelief. How could we abandon her like this? She had wanted to stay here one night. Did it deserve such a severe punishment? But she does not respond, swallowing hard the feeling of abandonment. In her tender heart and mind, she is lost in the world. Sanjana takes Sister Louisa's hand proffered to her, and walks back through the gate in stony silence. The subsequent evening, after school hours, during the games time, Sister Louisa escorts Sanjana through the garden into the parlour where Nayan, Dipanjana and I are sitting on the sofa. We have not left Darjeeling, even having visited here the evening before. It was Sr. Louisa's idea for us not to meet Sanjana, so she can settle down knowing we have left.

On entering the parlour, Sanjana's eyes meeting mine, are cold and steely. My heart lurches. I feel as though I had floated my child on a raft into sea, and she has returned to shore hating me. Was I testing her resilience and destiny, in surviving the perils at sea, in returning to me strong and invincible? Sanjana is an extremely sensitive child. Wishing to gear her for the tough world, have I unintentionally created her lifelong resistance towards me? Will she silently, stubbornly, oppose me throughout life? As I walk up to her now, gathering her in my arms, she dislodges herself promptly. Nayan looks at me menacingly, as if to say I deserve it for taking this rather cruel way of dealing with his good-natured, trusting, compliant girl. Dipanjana holds Sanjana's hand, but she withdraws, looking away.

I notice Nayan's eyes well up with tears, as he places his hand over Sanjana's head. He gingerly strokes her hair, testing her reaction. Surprisingly, she does not flinch from his touch. In her heart she knows he is innocent, that he would never knowingly subject her to the horror of last evening. In spite of my efforts in pacifying Sanjana, she remains cold and stiff. Sister Louisa tries to justify to Sanjana the reason for her being admitted to boarding school. She tells her that we her parents love her, and so want her to grow up into a fine young lady. But Sanjana remains unforgiving of me. She apparently reconciles to the idea of her new life at the boarding school, in silence.

"I think we should have prepared the child, I'm afraid she hasn't taken it well," Sister Louisa says, holding my hand. Then noticing my pained look, she adds, "But don't worry, she is young and will bounce back."

The fear, hurt, and abandonment Sanjana felt cannot be reversed now. They will form the basis of her shy and withdrawn psyche for a very long time, without her actually recalling this childhood trauma. A child at four to five years is unconsciously imbibing, assimilating circumstances and experiences, to create lasting impressions. Sanjana will remain very introverted and timid, especially till her fifth or sixth standard. Sister Angelina will then suggest I take her home, allow her to attend a day-school, so as to develop her personality.

"The child is timid and is not blooming in boarding school,

 Shuvashree Chowdhury

amidst so many children. She requires special attention," she will then say.

But in my bid to make my daughters tough, driven by my paranoia for vulnerability due to my own childhood experiences, I will not concede.

It is after a whole year that Sanjana will come home for the winter vacations. In the shorter vacations till then, we visit Darjeeling and Sanjana comes and stays with us at the hotel. These are really memorable family-times for us, spent in the heavenly beauty of Darjeeling, in the lap of the Himalayas. We go on drives amidst the mountains, hitchhike at times, roam the Mall road shopping, and even see a few movies at theatres. Sanjana seems adjusted to life at boarding school, even though still shy and timid as Sister Louisa recounts. But when with us, she seems happy and enjoys herself. She plays with Dipanjana in the hotel's garden and comes out of her usual introversion. It is on one such vacation that Sister Louisa recommends we transfer Sanjana to a school close to home. It is from her I learn this school has a parallel branch close to Calcutta.

My mind is immediately made up on getting Sanjana transferred there. It seems like the perfect way out of my dilemma of sending the girls to boarding school. They will continue to have a robust convent upbringing, yet we can visit often and monitor their progress. Moreover, once Dipanjana joins, both the girls will be able to come home frequently, even on long weekends or short vacations. Nayan is very happy with the arrangement. One for the obvious reason of being closer to the girls, being able to spend more time with them, but also for the difficulty he has in visiting Darjeeling shutting his printing press for long. I go to fetch Sanjana from school for the winter vacations. Her holdall and trunk atop the white Ambassador taxi we are riding, I discover she cannot speak a word of Bengali. In the last year she has only communicated in English, as was the compulsion in school. So by now she is very fluent in the language, as compared to when admitted, for which I am happy. I know she will rapidly pick up Bengali again, as it is after all her mother tongue.

As the train chugs out of the Siliguri station, after the long taxi ride from Darjeeling, I feel a twinge of guilt. Sanjana has no idea she is not coming back here. I have chosen not to tell her till she joins the new school, knowing she loves Darjeeling and how averse she is to change. I will continue to manipulate her lifelong, with all good intention every time, much to her exasperation, especially in later years. She is hence a stubborn child, but fortunately will grow out of the severity over the years. As a grown woman, this very obstinacy to my admiration, will translate into her doggedness in life.

Sanjana will however defy me lifelong, usually unconsciously, little recalling the origin of this attitude. On my part, I will be more pushy and assertive in combating her stubbornness. At times even slapping or beating her, more than I will Dipanjana, who is actually the naughtier one. It will reach a point when amongst her other rebellions, Sanjana will insist on learning to cycle and swim by herself, resisting me, pushing me away when I try to teach her. How I wish today I had handled her differently. Children need to be weaned into changes in life and circumstances to avoid trauma. Even unintended psychological assaults can create insecurity and rebellion in a child, perhaps for life. There were so many subtleties of good parenting I was unacquainted with in bringing up my children, in spite of every conceivable effort on my part to be the best mother possible.

* * *

The new school is over an hour's drive from Calcutta, in the former French colony of Chandannagar, on the banks of the river Hooghly. The headmistress, an Irish nun named Sister Helena, suggests I admit Dipanjana as well, even though she is underage. This works out well, as Dipanjana by now feels her elder sister is always the privileged one. This outlook will to an extent remain with her for life, without any actual basis. Strange are the subtleties of the impressionable child's mind that picks up cues and interprets them in involuntary ways. Perhaps these anomalies in their perception stem from my insufficient communication with my children. Like most parents of my generation, I never find the need to justify my well intentioned decisions to them. It will only be much later, when they are grown, that I will realize the need for timely and relevant communication, in good parenting.

     Shuvashree Chowdhury

Childhood experiences, especially those with parents and siblings, form the basis of a person's individuality and attitude. Therefore, a child's tender mind is like putty in the parent's hands. It is to be shaped cautiously, watchful of external factors that may cause misshape. Luckily for me, in spite of my few minor erroneous dealings, my daughters will grow up to be fine, strong and steady women. They will one day value my judgements and decisions, even though they do not now. Sanjana hates boarding school, while Dipanjana does not want to come home, preferring to be in the company of her friends, rather than in my controlling presence. But both my daughters, as grown women, will accept it is their boarding school exposure that shaped their independent, resilient, dynamic, and capable personalities at work and in their personal lives.

During the years that our daughters are at boarding school, it is the first Sunday of every month that Nayan and I love the most. These Visiting Sundays are the only day in the month when boarders are allowed to meet and spend quality time with us parents and family. These Sundays will play a significant part of the memory of my daughters growing years, in spite of the rest of the days spent engagingly in the company of friends, schoolmates and nuns. Life has a way of straining the good times through a sieve, preserving it to conscious memory. Just as it has a way of disallowing one to reach out to the unpleasant memories as easily and frequently. Visiting Sundays, like every other day, is time bound for the boarders. The visiting hours, between 1pm and 5pm, never seem long enough.

Unlike other Sundays, these mornings pass like a breeze for the girls. Their routine jobs of changing bed-linen, giving clothes for washing, keeping uniforms and clothes ready for the coming week, over, it is time for lunch. Anticipation sets wings to their feet, making them expedite otherwise mundane tasks. But their appetite takes a beating in excitement. Though Sunday lunches are of a special menu, most girls barely eat on the visiting ones. The reason being, we parents bring their favourite home cooked dishes when we come to visit them. For me, these mornings are spent cooking, then setting all the dishes into a multi-layered hotcase. I also pack into a basket two portions each of tucks -

biscuits, hot-grams, chips, powder-milk, marmalades and pickles, for the month ahead, bought the day before.

The hot-case and basket, along with a mat for us all to sit on, I shove into the rear of our olive coloured Ambassador car, before we set out. I never forget to take a water-carrier, plates, napkins and cutlery either. Every Visiting Sunday is for us a picnic on the river strand, running alongside the school. We sit facing the quiet and majestic flow of the river the girls see the sun rising over, from their dormitory on the first floor. As they step out of the formidable schoolgate, it is again this river that is first visible, through the large trees lining its banks. On reaching their school, Nayan and I wait in either of the two parlours flanking the school's entrance, after signing the visitor's slip. The girls are waiting eagerly in the study hall, for the ayahs they term Didi, to call their names aloud from the visitor's slips.

On hearing their names, the girls pick up their empty tuck boxes, bringing them along for us parents to fill. When older, they fill the boxes themselves in the refectory, after we leave. Sanjana and Dipanjana usually walk into the parlour together. They briskly hug Nayan and me, after identifying us amongst other waiting and eager parents. Both girls, then pulling us by hand, urge us to step out of the gate immediately. The outside denotes freedom to them, even if for a few hours. Now they can be themselves, away from the hourly bells and constant vigilance of the nuns that regulate their every waking minute. The girls skip alongside Nayan and me, rapidly trying to update us on their lives since our last meeting. Though they write letters to us every Sunday, they cannot be free, as the letters are read by the Sisters before dispatching. All letters they receive is also read by the Sisters.

Walking along the strand to the car, we pass groups of people sitting on either side of the road, in varied sized picnic groups. The school's Sunday uniform - aqua-blue pleated skirts and white shirts, worn by one or more in each group, identify them as boarders. The children eat hungrily, as the parents look on indulgently, listening to their simultaneous chatter.

"What have you brought for us, Ma?" the girls always ask en route to our car, to retrieve the basket in the rear after greeting the driver.

                    Shuvashree Chowdhury

We find a shady, vacant spot, under one of the several trees lining the river. I spread the straw mat on the moist green grass, before we take off our shoes, to sit facing the river. Tiny fishing boats are bobbing about, and steam-launches packed with commuters are spurting water, leaving a brief trail as they cross the river noisily.

I love watching the boatmen sway back and forth rowing. It reminds me of the river in Mihirpur and my boating escapades as a schoolgirl. The images seem pretty remote now, like from another lifetime. I have not returned there since leaving in 1964, and will not till a long time yet, that too only on a brief visit. It must be my childhood association and yearning for the river that brings me to its banks repeatedly, even though to a different one. Those the boatmen are ferrying now are expectantly looking ahead at the approaching bank, to their destination. They are overlooking the vast expanse of water and sky, impatient with their present situation, not relishing the moment like I am. Close to the shore in the water, little and large fish play. At times we can spot a snake or two, shooting up from the water.

My girls are terrified of snakes, unlike me, who has grown up with them almost as pets in my childhood home in Assam. But the presence of their Ma and Baba make them feel safe and secure now. They know with us around, no harm can come upon them. It is so disparate from my own childhood, when it was my parents who brought upon me the most damage. Those, on whom God bestowed the responsibility of my upkeep, ironically pushed me unprepared into the hightide of an abandoned adolescence. By now Sanjana and Dipanjana are relishing the mutton-curry and fried-rice I have served them. They have put the cutlery aside, bored of its constant and compulsory usage at the refectory, preferring to eat with their hands.

On the opposite bank of the river is the industrial belt. The jute, paper, rayon and other factories' huge chimneys sporadically emanate clouds of thick black smoke up in the sky. But they fail to take away the beauty and serenity of the place. Like the soot from my early life's burns fail to take away the loveliness of my current life, as I sit contentedly in this picturesque location, with my husband and children. The river is lined by huge banyan, mango, guava, and other unidentifiable trees, some bending low to allow their branches and leaves to kiss the water. Sitting under trees here, one has to be careful of bird-droppings. There are varied birds - parrots, mynahs, crows and pigeons in abundance. Their chirping merges harmoniously with the sound of the launches plying to and from the jetty.

The well-built concrete strand, beyond which we are sitting close to the water's grassy edge, runs for quite a distance, maybe a mile or two. Beside the school are other well-constructed buildings, belonging to the French era – identifiable by the balustrades and French windows. After the girls have eaten their fill, finishing with sweetmeats Nayan brings them in abundance, as his share of treating his daughters, we go for boat or launch rides across the river. The girls enjoy these immensely, bending to touch and play with the clear water mid-stream. Nayan and I usually have a quick cup of tea each, across the river, from a tea-stall. On our return, we all go to the local market on two cycle-rickshaws. The girls can supplement their month's supplies we bring from Calcutta, with their personal choice of things.

We return from the market by 5pm, to wait outside the boarder's side school-gate. If the girls miss going in on time, the gates will close. One has to then draw the attention of the nun on duty, and spoil a perfect afternoon with the ensuing reprimands for indiscipline. Since I am a stickler for discipline since my own school days, I do not make the slightest compromise when it comes to my daughters. The nuns at this school too have become fond of me. Perhaps it is due to my being a lecturer at a teacher's training college now, and on the same wavelength as them on discipline. I make it a point to follow all the rules unlike some parents, constantly urging my daughters to do the same. I always bring them back from home on the designated day and well before the due time, with all requisite supplies as per the lists.

A brass hand-bell will be rung outside the gate, to announce the end of our time with our children on Visiting Sunday. Till then, the girls gorge on street-fare including ice-creams along with their friends, from hawkers crowding the strand by now. It seems like they will never eat again. Their stomachs are rather elastic, considering they have already eaten two lunches. It will be a month before they experience the outside without a nun monitoring them

      Shuvashree Chowdhury

- as during their weekend walks, or have the freedom that comes with one's family. My daughters, to my satisfaction, in getting on with their lives through college, then career, marriage and parenting, will imbibe the self-discipline propagated in school. They will then, fortunately, also not forget the love, security and care Nayan and I provide, even if demonstrated on a day in the month, other than on vacations.

It is the quality of time together that creates lasting impressions and a strong bond between parents and children. In addition to the Visiting Sundays, Nayan and I never miss any parent-teacher's day, sports or concert days, ensuring we are part of their growth and progress always. We wait till the girls are well inside the school premises, in case they turn around, before leaving after every visit. On vacations, however short, we never fail to take them home.

It was during the major floods of 1978 that Dipanjana, only five years then, is diagnosed with jaundice. The Sisters telephone me at home in Calcutta, to break the news. It is simultaneously announced on the radio, there is no television yet, that high tides in the river Hooghly will keep its adjacent areas submerged. Some areas of West Bengal are already 18 feet below water, as the monsoon continues beyond the usual season. I set out for the school braving the flood, walking intermittently between bus rides. Taking the car is not a wise decision and the local trains are defunct by now. After great difficulty, I arrive only by night. I cannot take Dipanjana home due to the late hour and the incessant rain, and flood. But seeing her pacifies my overwrought nerves, sick with worry that I was since learning of her illness. Her smile makes the wearisome daylong trip worthwhile.

I return home past midnight, to find Nayan anxiously parading outside, awaiting my return. I again come back to the school after a couple of days, when the flood situation improves, to take Dipanjana home. I take leave from work, till she is able to return to school and regular life. Though I have sent my girls to boarding school, I never allow them to feel neglected, or sense we are emotionally ever absent. On every birthday, Nayan and I make it a point to visit them. We take new dresses, chocolates, sweets, cakes and goodies, for the birthday party at the refectory with their classmates. Nayan buys everything personally, spoiling his daughters as best he can on these occasions, as much as on vacations. I never object to his over-indulgences, as they balance my steady strictness with them.

* * *

On completion of their schooling, I plan on my daughters attending college from home in Calcutta. So we can now live truly as a family, after the years of mere vacations together. But to my surprise, Dipanjana, now in her eleventh standard, shows a keen interest in going to college at Delhi University. She manages to impress upon an unwilling Sanjana, who has just completed her twelfth standard, to proceed to Delhi. Initially I try to dissuade them, disappointed they do not want to stay home with me and Nayan. But having wished for them to be independent, strong and decisive women, sending them to boarding school at such tender ages to achieve the same, I cannot complain now. Thus I relent, escorting them to Delhi myself; decidedly to admit Sanjana to the college I had worked in for long.

I know Sanjana will be safe in the hostel here. The warden is a friend, and many teachers of the all-ladies college, are since my time. Also, Dipanjana will join her shortly, and then the girls will have each other to look out for. Sanjana, having the required grades for her desired course of study, is admitted to the college and hostel on completion of formalities. A close friend, a lecturer who lives in the teacher's quarters on the college campus with her family, is registered as her local guardian. Another friend, who lives nearby, is registered as the second local guardian. Satisfied with the absolute security of my daughters, in my view, knowing they will be in familiar surroundings, amongst people I trust, I return to Calcutta with them. When it is time for her college session, Nayan comes along with me to reach Sanjana. Both he and Sanjana detest her going away, but are compelled by my decision.

At the hostel, Sanjana is to share a room with two other girls. It is a fairly large, airy room, with two windows, three beds, cupboards and study tables each. After we leave, Sanjana grudgingly tries settling into her room, unpacking her suitcases. She is desolate at being back in another hostel, further away from

                    Shuvashree Chowdhury

home this time. It is all because of Dipanjana's stupid, heady enthusiasm, she ruminates, followed by my assertive stance. As she sits down quietly on her bed, a wave of frustration washes over her at my constantly pushing her, making decisions for her against her wishes. One of Sanjana's roommates is already in the room by now, having come in before her. This girl is from Jamshedpur, she will soon learn. But neither speaks yet, engrossed in their personal melancholy of having left home.

On her school-leaving character certificate, from which I am quoting verbatim, the Headmistress commented, "Sanjana is a quiet girl, reserved and refined in her ways. She is intelligent and capable. Her work is always neat and commendable. She writes and speaks fluently and participated in all school competitions. She was a first class Girl Guide and a good Athlete. Sanjana has received many prizes during her school career. Her moral character is good."

By these words, Sister Rosaline aptly defined the woman they created, of the five year old child I handed over in all earnestness to them. This woman, Sanjana, inheriting her father's good looks - his large intense eyes, charming smile, luminous complexion, and his athletic frame and height, has turned out to be rather striking.

It is after her third roommate, whose father is a senior army officer, arrives, that the three women start to interact. This girl is vivacious and congenial. Perhaps more so from her varied exposures in accompanying her father to all his postings. Together the three of them go down for dinner. It is at the dining-hall that they come head on with the senior students and caught unawares, mentally unprepared, encounter mass ragging. After dinner, all the first year students, referred to as freshers, are made to assemble in the lawn in front of the dining-hall. The second and third year girls standing facing them, size up each of the new students. Then the freshers are made to introduce themselves, thanking the seniors who interrupt each one making personal digs, addressing them as Ma'am.

Many of the freshers are nick-named, based on their introductions and the assessment of their individuality. Sanjana coming across as arrogant, perhaps due to her reserve, also since she is dressed trendily, is named "Ms Calcutta." Most other girls are from small towns, mainly of Bihar or Uttar Pradesh. Both my girls, unlike me who still has a penchant for simplicity, have turned out to be fashion conscious, wearing chic attire, hairstyles, and even makeup, much to my disapproval. The code of conduct and dressing for the months of ragging is now informed to them, with firm warnings against non-adherence. All freshers are to wear mismatched salwar suits, oil their hair, tie it in three braids – yes three, and wear a bindi at all times. They are to also go out dressed this way. Every evening after dinner, the freshers are asked to sing, dance, read or enact erotic passages from novels, climb a tree, make love to a tree, bark or whimper like a dog, whatever takes the fancy of the seniors then.

By the time Dipanjana joins the following year, having obtained above the high grades required for admission, ragging is more absurd. She is at times sent with her classmates to the nearby Kamala Nagar market, to fetch a broom and bucket, dressed in the mismatched salwar suits, with the three braids of oiled hair. They are not allowed on their feet anything other than bathroom slippers, that too only the Bata Hawaii chappals. Even when they step outside their college, they are to address every senior of Delhi University as Sir or Madam, wishing them the time of day. Once few girls including Dipanjana are sent out on the University streets with a bowl in hand, to beg at bus stops the way common beggars do. The ragging at the college for day-scholars lasts about a week, but at the hostel it continues for months.

The freshers abhor being ragged to begin with, but in time drop their resistance, and enjoy themselves. In fact they get smarter day by day. For example, Sanjana, who always hated oiling her hair, would water her hair under a tap every few hours, to get the desired oiled look, during her ragging period. One evening, the water having evaporated due to the immense Delhi summer heat, a whole bottle of oil was poured on her head after dinner, kneeling in front of everyone. The more rules were imposed, the smarter the girls got in breaking them, till detected. Dipanjana and her roommates, every morning, took out three salwar suits. They then wore three pieces - including a dupatta which was compulsory, from each of the different sets. So when going out, they could

    Shuvashree Chowdhury

interchange amongst themselves into matching sets and easily change back before returning to the hostel.

Initially, the freshers feel self-conscious in their ragging attire, but soon realize that irrespective of what one wears, ones individuality comes through in the way one carries oneself. Dipanjana, by now, is a slim, tall and gorgeous woman, with sharp facial features like mine, black mysterious eyes, a dusky complexion, and thick, long, lustrous hair. Whenever she passes groups of male students along with her classmates, they walk with their head held high, irrespective of how they are dressed and look. If the men laugh, they confidently laugh along, wishing them 'good evening Sir,' and they reply, 'good evening Freshers.' At times, when stopped by other college seniors, asked to sing or dance right there, they sportingly oblige. If not, they will be made to serve ridiculous penalties. Anyone in the north campus of Delhi University rags a fresher, irrespective of college or gender.

A few freshers, who refused ragging in the previous years, were ostracized by everyone in the hostel. They were not included in group activities, or invited to socials, or allowed to participate in hostel events. Therefore, the current freshers do not risk non-participation in ragging. Some of the things new students are made to do in addition to the regular singing, dancing and mono acting is to demonstrate their awareness on sexuality, men-women relationships, alcohol and drugs. Those who blush or giggle are made to go through the discussions at length, till they hold a nonchalant expression. In the four months of ragging, innocent schoolgirls lacking exposure and awareness are hauled into confident, well informed women. My daughters are smarter and more resilient, as compared to some girls with a sheltered childhood by protective families, so manage well.

Those freshers who are apparently shy, or in the case of Dipanjana bold and self-assured, are ragged the most, with the view to increasing or puncturing their confidence. It is thus getting unbearable for Dipanjana to undergo this constant bullying day in and day out, for months on end. So, one day, her group of six girls decides to defy the dress code, in having an early dinner at a Chinese restaurant in Kamala Nagar. The hostel gates shut by 7.30pm so they have to be back by then. They interchange amongst themselves, into matching salwar suits, in a clothes store's trialroom, on the pretext of buying. Then they wear the good shoes they have carried along. They have not oiled their hair that day, repeatedly wetting it with water all day. So they open up their by now dry, three plaits, then apply makeup including lipstick and eye-liner.

On entering the plush restaurant, ushered in by the manager himself, they are glad they look well turned out. After a sumptuous meal, they step outside, content and smug in their deftness in executing their plan. They are headed to another store's trial-room to turn back into their Cinderella of the cinders look. When to their horror, they come across a group of second-year students of their college.

"Why, it's you freshers dressed up like this?" one Senior blurts, after a few moments of deliberation, unsure it really is them.

"We were not allowed inside the restaurant, in the ragging attire," Dipanjana rapidly justifies. "So we had to go and change."

"Ah! But you still had to eat Chinese, hmmm …?" another senior states mockingly, then adds menacingly, "Now since you all look so pretty, let's do something really different today, shall we?"

"Sure, why not?" Dipanjana replies, naive about the extent to which the seniors might go, in humiliating them. "It sounds like fun. In any case we are bored of the same gimmickry every day."

"Well then, let's see … let's spice up your lives, shall we?" the senior replies sharply. "Perhaps get you all boyfriends. In any case, you won't find any by yourselves, in the dreary ragging attire. But dressed prettily as you all are now, it should be easy."

Dipanjana and her group are now alarmed. They interpret trouble brewing, from the senior's stern expressions and tone.

"We are sorry, we really are," one of the freshers blurts anxiously.

"No, no, don't be. There's nothing to worry about, really," the senior replies matter-of-factly. Then nastily grinding her words, adds: "After all, you girls are so smart, aren't you?" She abruptly turns towards Dipanjana, announcing, "now come on, you smarty, go up to that group there and propose to the guy in the black Benetton T-shirt."

 Shuvashree Chowdhury

The rest of her group looks at Dipanjana aghast. What is she going to do now? How they wish they were in their ragging attire, so this drama could be pulled off in the guise of ragging. But then, if they had been, this situation might not have arisen. Dipanjana will make an idiot of herself now as the young men will have no idea her behaviour is a part of ragging. Knowing of the meanness of these very seniors, Dipanjana realizes there is no way out. She must think and act fast. So taking a deep breath, holding her head high, she walks to the group of six men, after one look at her group for moral support. She looks in the direction of the tall, athletic, handsome man, in the black T-Shirt she is instructed to 'propose' to. He looks back at her quizzically, as she approaches, since her gaze is steadfastly on him.

"Excuse me … look, I'm being ragged." Dipanjana begins abruptly, still holding the black T-Shirt man's gaze, then adds, "my seniors are watching me from there," she points to them watching her amusedly, then mumbles: "I've been asked to 'propose' to you."

"Oh! Well, well … let's see!" one of the other men exclaims, after registering the abrupt intrusion to their conversation, sizing her up. Then another adds, grinning, "in that case you had better do it well."

Dipanjana flinches, looking downwards, as the men simultaneously size her up, laughing in unison. She promptly determines she is not going to allow them or the seniors to belittle her spirit.

So looking the man in the black T-shirt once again in the eye, she nonchalantly and dramatically says as if enacting lines in a play, "I love you Sir. I fell in love with you, since the moment I set my eyes on you. Will you be so kind as to marry me?"

The man proposed to, is at first shocked, then acutely embarrassed.

"It's ok, Fresher, now you may go," he mutters considerately, adding "that was truly a brave act. I'm sure your seniors will be satisfied."

But one of his friends, who are in the mood for more amusement, looking at the others in the group, says, "So let's get them married here, shall we? All we need is some agarbatti (incense sticks) for them to take the pheras' (rounds around the sacred fire)."

The rest of the group bursts into peals of laughter. Dipanjana laughs along trying to hide her discomfiture, though blushing red.

"I must get going now" she blurts, starting to walk back to her group, with the collective male laughter resounding in the background.

After her, the rest of Dipanjana's group are also made to 'propose' to other men randomly, in the Archies card shop nearby and inside a men's hostel they cut across on their walk back with the seniors. By the time Dipanjana and her friends walk through their college main gate, the humiliation well behind them now, they laugh heartily at the silly joke. They discuss the reactions of all the men amusedly.

It is just before they walk through the hostel's gate, that a woman approaches them saying, "Dipanjana, your local guardian wants to meet you immediately. She is in her quarters, waiting for you."

Dipanjana is in no mood to go now, but somewhat alarmed at the urgent message, she promptly goes. Mrs Verma's apartment in the teachers quarters, is in the building alongside their hostel, on the second floor.

Opening the door wide for Dipanjana to step inside, Mrs Verma impatiently says, "How could you disgrace yourselves and the college, Dipanjana, by proposing to guys all over the marketplace?"

Dipanjana shocked that the incidents of the evening have reached her already, replies in exasperation, "But Aunty, what could we do? We were being ragged. You know how the seniors react if we don't comply."

"I know, and so I've complained to the warden about your seniors," is Mrs Verma's stern response. "This ragging thing is getting too much, I say. It has to be stopped before someone is seriously hurt."

Dipanjana guesses any of Mrs Verma's four grown children might have reported the matter to her. After all, the Kamala Nagar market is a buzzing place in the evenings, where students of all the north campus colleges of Delhi University, congregate. Mrs Verma did exactly what I would have, on learning of the girls publically demeaning theirs' as well as the college's reputation. Dipanjana is on the one hand pleased the seniors will be reprimanded, possibly

	Shuvashree Chowdhury

even punished, for putting them through such a humiliating public spectacle. But she is also worried they will make her life more difficult now, assuming she has complained about them to her local guardian. Walking into the hostel, on the corridor, Dipanjana finds the warden in conversation with two of the very seniors.

They give her a threatening look, as if to say, "You will pay for this, wait and watch."

But by now, Dipanjana is too tired to care. She unperturbedly walks up to her room on the first floor, to find her friends waiting for her.

As soon as she walks through the door, one of the girls says to her in an accusing tone, "The seniors told us we are henceforth boycotted by the rest of the hostel, for snitching."

Another adds, "In fact, they have been called by the warden; they threatened us before going to her."

"I know, I just passed them on my way up" Dipanjana replies, then impatiently adds, "I was with you all, all the time. How could I have complained to anyone?" Then in frustration mutters: "I cannot help that my local guardian lives here on the campus. Moreover, it's most awful for me, isn't it, as my parents are going to learn of this episode soon? Even if they don't, I have Sanjana to come and lecture me."

It takes a couple of days for Dipanjana's group to convince the seniors that they have not complained about them.

"We were so sporting in executing what you asked us to," Dipanjana pleads. "Then why would we complain? Just think about it."

Sanjana, on learning of her sister's escapade, done with reprimanding her, asks the concerned seniors to back off as enough is enough. Though usually quiet and reserved, Sanjana can be very assertive when provoked or threatened. Her normally high patience level can turn into abrupt impatience, when unduly challenged. In this case, her protective instinct towards her younger sister rises in protest. However things go back to normal thereafter. In another month, ragging ceases, with the grand induction party at the dining hall. After that, things fall comfortably into a routine. Both Sanjana and

Dipanjana are in their college's basket-ball team, as they were of their schools. The college has robust sports facilities. It participates in all inter-college matches, since the time I was secretary of the Delhi University Women's Sports Committee, including forty-five colleges.

Every morning, both my girls are ready and on the playfield by 5.30am. Accustomed to waking early, they do not have much difficulty in doing so even in the severe Delhi winters. After several rounds of jogging on the large playfield, followed by warm-up exercises on the basket-ball court, their team of ten is ready for rigorous practice with their coach, starting with layups. On the playfield, the college's athletics, hockey, cricket, volleyball and other teams are in training too. After a quick breakfast following this, the girls get ready and hurry to their classes. Most evenings, they go out with their friends, often to the Kamala Nagar market. They return in time for dinner, to study or chat in their rooms till bed time.

At the time of Dipanjana's leaving school, the headmistress's comments on her character certificate were - "Dipanjana has been studying in our school since 1978. She has grown up to be a fine young lady with commendable qualities. As the captain of Malachite House she worked hard and did her best. She was very good on the sports field and received many prizes in school, and at the sub-divisional and district level. Special mention should be made of her ability in drawing and essay writing. Morally she is good."

The individualistic remarks on all students passing out are a validation of how they have turned out. These certificates, though somehow never required for college admissions or job appointments, will give me an immense sense of pride, lifelong. They will confirm Nayan and my efforts in bringing up our girls well, providing a justification to our sacrifices, in sending them to boarding school at a very young age.

Though it was their schooling that lay the foundation to my daughter's resilient personalities, it is their three years in college that tested its veracity, in readiness for their life thereafter. By the time they graduate, they are more confident, openminded and sporting. They have learnt through ragging, not to take themselves

 Shuvashree Chowdhury

too seriously, to be able to laugh at themselves with humility. These lessons they will carry into their future professional and personal lives.

After the ragging period, the entire hostel, be it the first year students or the third, have become very close. After all, they have seen each other without pretences, coping with stress together. Ragging can lay the foundation for strong friendships which may last a lifetime. However, the practice of ragging, like with most things when in excess, can also turn lethal. When students lose perspective - venting their frustrations, jealousies and insecurities in the name of ragging, as often happens, it becomes a menacing social evil. Since authorities find it difficult to regulate the extent of its practice, they are forced to ban it. In my daughter's lives, however, ragging, extra-curricular activities, fests and socials, have been lessons well learnt.

On graduating, returning to Calcutta, Sanjana is in a hurry to start working. She does not have much faith on mere academic qualifications as the means to success. She wants to do something different, rather than follow the regular beaten tracks. However, on my insistence, she completes a postgraduation course, even though in a subject not of my choice, Public Relations. She takes up a job thereafter, with a reputed organization. I see her metamorphose into a successful career woman, making me and Nayan very proud. Dipanjana stays on in Delhi for another few years, to study further. Then she returns to Calcutta to start her career with a renowned organization. By this time, Nayan is getting impatient about their marriage, looking forward to grandchildren which some of his friends already have.

But I am not disconcerted about my daughters not being married yet, even beyond thirty years, let alone not having children. I know all that will come in time, pleased with their present focus on their careers. I feel secure that whether they continue to work lifelong or not, they have honed their skills as successful professionals, to be able to do so. Since college, they have had their share of boyfriends and relationships, some of them men whom I have met. I never interfere in their choice of men or decisions to marry them, knowing my girls are capable of making the right choices. Nayan is against their close interactions with men outside of marriage. But I have no qualms in my daughters going through failed relationships, to make up their minds on who they want to marry. In my view, marriage is for keeps, so partners should be wisely considered before one takes the plunge. Today, I am proud of both my sons-inlaw, as I am of my daughters.

Chapter 11

An Everlasting Presence

"Wake up, Baba" she says repeatedly, shaking her father's arm.

It is 8.30am and well past his normal waking hour. Our elder daughter Sanjana is ready for work and as usual, before leaving the house, has gone to see her father. I am reading the newspaper over a cup of tea, at the dining table of our home in Kolkata, having woken up late myself. Nayan had been awake through the night, unable to sleep, dozing off only at dawn. I have not woken him for his much needed regular morning walk, escorted by a servant, allowing him to sleep late. Walking into our bedroom, Sanjana is surprised to find Nayan snoring loudly. He seldom does. She shakes his arms compellingly to wake him up, or he will be very upset to find her gone when he awakens, now that he is home all day.

Nayan opens his eyes, looks into hers for a few brief moments, before dozing off again. It seems as if he is trying hard to awaken, but failing. On shaking his arm yet again, with apparent effort he opens his eyes wide, only to involuntarily shut them. After that, in spite of her shoving and calling out to him, Nayan does not open his eyes. Sanjana is very alarmed. Nayan, now seventy-one years of age, has a recurring heart condition, having undergone a bypass surgery five years ago. He had also suffered a cerebral stroke two years back, leaving him partially paralyzed. It is through regular and sustained physiotherapy and walks, that he has recovered somewhat. But the residual limp, asymmetry of his face, slight slurring of speech and frail left arm have made Nayan a chronic depressive. A handsome man with a stately bearing, he cannot come to terms with this sudden distortion of his appearance and posture.

Since after the stroke, Nayan has no desire to go out in public or meet anyone at home. But Sanjana has been persistent. She forcibly takes him out to restaurants, even though he curses and sulks through the meals. She compels him to go for movies to multiplexes, forcing him out of the car into a wheelchair she organizes through the manager. Nayan would not have a haircut or even shave his beard after the stroke. Dipanjana did the needful then, catching him unawares at the dining-table, whilst fooling around with him. After her leaving, I hired a barber from a local saloon to come home. I took Nayan to a psychiatrist repeatedly, but after he refused to go any longer, I arranged for one to come home, till he curtly asked her to leave. In spite of every conceivable effort to get him out of the oppressive whirlpool of depression devouring him, we have been incapable of hauling him out of it.

After warning me that there might be something wrong, the way Nayan is unable to wake up; Sanjana calls his cardiologist from her mobile-phone. I do not perceive anything amiss, since knowing he has slept very late. So I continue to read the newspaper calmly, over a second cup of tea.

"The symptoms you mention are not unusual," the cardiologist tells Sanjana, "so there is nothing to worry about really. Nayan has perhaps taken a higher dose of sleeping pills than usual. I would advise you to get a general physician to check on him, just to be certain he is alright."

"I gave him only one sleeping pill as usual last night," I reply, when Sanjana quizzes me after ending her conversation with the doctor.

As she dials the local physician's number, Sanjana has a premonition of something serious having happened to Nayan.

While the doctor is on his way, Sanjana abruptly asks, "Ma, where have you kept the rest of Baba's sleeping-pills?"

She suddenly panics, assuming Nayan has popped in a large number of the pills himself, being unable to sleep.

"That is not possible, Sanjana," I assure her, "as I keep them locked, ever since Nayan has been randomly speaking of wanting to die."

Nayan lately insists he does not want to live a useless existence, unable to go to work at the printing press or lead an active regular

     Shuvashree Chowdhury

life. Sanjana, far from pacified by the cardiologist's words or mine, is fretting, while I continue to remain unruffled. Perhaps the reason for my calmness is that in the last seven years of Nayan being sporadically sick, since his first heartattack, I have worried so much, I have become immune to worrying without real cause.

Lately, Nayan is unable to sleep most nights, sitting up in bed at odd hours. It is but natural, since he sleeps through the day, from high doses of assorted medications. Even last night, he had sat up in bed at two o'clock, talking aloud to himself.

On waking me with the noise of his speaking, he had abruptly said, "Maya you must perform Sanjana's Sampradaan at her wedding, since I will not be around to do so myself."

I rebuked him as one would a child, to go back to sleep, saying we could talk in the morning. Working all day at household chores and nursing Nayan, in addition to managing his printing press now, I need the sleep of which I barely get a few uninterrupted hours. Since his stroke and my retirement as principal of my college, I manage his business, of which I admittedly know little, with his guidance.

In the last several years of Nayan's recurring illnesses, I am in a state of constant fatigue from sleep deprivation. I awaken several times at night, either to help Nayan use the toilet or to drink water. There is an ayah to take care of him when I go out, which is only on work. I prefer not to keep an ayah during the time I am at home, lest Nayan should feel neglected in any way. He has become very touchy lately. Moreover, I am now over sixty-five years and added to that, the constant anxiety over Nayan's physical and now also mental health have taken their toll on me. Perhaps these factors have caused the dulling of my reactions, considering I have not yet thought of the plausibility of something being seriously wrong with Nayan, serenely sipping my tea. Or perhaps it is my self-preservation mechanism working to protect me from the upcoming turmoil. Sanjana, with a sense of foreboding, is sitting at Nayan's bedside, awaiting the doctor, after informing her office of her delay in coming to work.

On arrival, the doctor first checks Nayan's pulse, lifting his eyelids to check his eyes, which he can no longer open himself. On the doctor's advice, Sanjana promptly calls an ambulance to rush Nayan to hospital. It is shortly at the main-gate of our house. A friend of Sanjana's named Rahul, whom she telephoned, has arrived on hearing of Nayan's condition. Sanjana decides on going to a prominent hospital, where another friend is in charge of administration, so Nayan can get the best possible care. After the doctor leaves, it is only when the attendants are carrying Nayan down in a stretcher that I awaken from my trance, suddenly becoming alert. As usual, overtaken by my need to take charge, I rush downstairs and into the ambulance along with Nayan. By the time Sanjana comes down, much to her annoyance I have left with the ambulance.

Sanjana frequently chides me on my compulsive impatience, obstinacy, and need to be in command of every situation.

"Ma, why can't you just act your age?" she asks me exasperatedly, time and time again, "and let us take decisions to handle issues? We are grown now and more aware of current situations than you."

But old habits die hard and mine will go with me to my death. I have by now reached the nearest hospital, a heart-care unit in our locality. In my opinion, it is safer to get medical-aid at the earliest, rather than reach a better facility late. I rush to the reception, where a sleepy looking man is on duty from the night before, to complete the registration formalities. The attendants carry the stretcher bearing Nayan inside. Even before Sanjana, driven in by Rahul, reaches the hospital, Nayan is admitted and in the Intensive Care Unit.

The preliminary checks confirm Nayan's heightened blood pressure and sugar levels. Only a resident medical officer is on duty now.

"This case is too complicated for me to handle on my own," he says. "I suggest you take him to a bigger hospital. A CT-scan of the head is required urgently considering his medical history, to ascertain whether his current condition is a cerebral stroke or a heart attack. This will help determine the appropriate medication to be administered. We have no provision for a CT scan, as this is only a preliminary heartcare centre."

Sanjana gives me a disparaging look, before dialling her friend who is the administrative head of a reputed hospital.

    Shuvashree Chowdhury

"Aneesha, please send me an ambulance with a paramedic and a cardiologist urgently," she says, after briskly narrating the circumstance of her request and location.

In little time the ambulance arrives. But we learn we have to wait for Nayan's blood-pressure and sugar levels to stabilize, before we can move him safely. I go home escorted by Rahul, to pack a bag for Nayan's hospital stay. Sanjana waits outside the Intensive Care Unit. Abruptly the young medical officer rushes out of the ICU, his face ashen. He approaches Sanjana awkwardly.

"Please call whoever you need to call," he stutters; then noticing her blank expression, he adds, "Please hurry, he has little time left."

Shaken by his harried tone, but not sure what he means, Sanjana mumbles, "Mother has gone home to get father's stuff. I've also called a senior doctor I know. He should be here any time now."

After the medical officer returns to the ICU, there is a sudden flurry of activity inside, nurses rushing about. With guidance from a senior doctor telephonically, the medical officer administers a defibulator to revive the normal rhythm of Nayan's failing heart. Sanjana sits down on the staircase outside the ICU, stumped. Part of her mind is in denial, part fighting to come to terms with the implication of Nayan's heart suddenly failing. She feels frustrated, then livid, at her inability to do anything. Her father is probably dying inside due to the incapacity of a dimwit doctor, when we can afford the best for him.

Overwhelmed by the conflicting emotions flitting through her, Sanjana feels hot tears streaming down her face uninhibited. There are people around watching, she notices, but she does not care. She is angry at the world, at her own helplessness, but most of all at me, for coming in haste to this hospital. A nurse comes out and calls Sanjana into the ICU. With tears blinding her, she follows the nurse to her father's bedside, relieved to see him still breathing heavily. She looks up at Nayan's heart-line on the monitor. It reads a straight line, but its implication is lost on her. By now Rahul and I have returned with Nayan's bag. Sanjana directs us to his bedside. I notice Nayan's heart-monitor reading and register its inference immediately. But to my surprise I am unruffled. The medical officer tells us to wait downstairs at the reception. He will give us the final verdict in a few hours.

Sanjana squeezes her father's hand, then giving him a sweeping look, walks downstairs. She goes to the small Ganesha temple at the reception, praying fervently for her father to survive. He has to give her away as a bride in a few months. After all, her wedding has been his biggest dream, intensifying since her graduation. I come down to the reception along with Rahul, wearing a lost look, unsure how to respond to the gravest emotional impact of my life. Soon friends and relatives, on hearing the news from Rahul telephonically, have started to come by. Rahul by now has also informed my younger daughter Dipanjana, who is settled in Bangalore. She and her husband are expected by the evening flight. Rahul insists we have lunch, while waiting for the doctor to confirm Nayan's condition.

Sanjana, Rahul and I go home, to return to the hospital after a quick lunch. We are waiting at the reception, when another senior doctor on duty now, calls me upstairs to the ICU. Looking at me dispassionately, he announces that Nayan is no more. I impassively nod back, too wound up to react. I give him all relevant details to prepare Nayan's death certificate dated 5th of January, 2005, timed 1300 hrs. Nayan had departed of a massive heart failure while Rahul and I had gone home to fetch his bag that morning. Since it is customary to monitor for about four hours to declare a person legitimately dead, we had been made to wait till now. I had known Nayan was gone, when on my return I saw the straight line on his heart-monitor. It had seemed he was still breathing perhaps due to the ventilator or life support he was on. But I had let myself hope for a miracle.

The death certificate is handed to us after formalities, by about 4.30pm. Before Nayan's body is brought down to take home, a close friend of Sanjana's asks her to go home. She feels it is better for Sanjana to learn of her father's death in the privacy of our home.

"How can I go home now?" Sanjana retorts," it is visiting time, isn't it? I'm going up to see Baba. He is unconscious, but if he should wake up even for a minute, I want to be there to meet him."

Suddenly Nayan's close friend, more like his brother, decides the news of his death has to be broken to Sanjana here and now.

     Shuvashree Chowdhury

She has been in denial since the morning and it is detrimental to her.

"Your father will never wake up Sanjana. He has passed away," he states, without any prologue, "So go home now."

Sanjana gives him a glassy stare, while he looks back at her searchingly. The rest of us watch, anxious about Sanjana's reaction.

The words hit Sanjana like a physical blow. She noticeably winces. Looking through us all, she remains speechless for a while.

Then with their implication registering, she snaps: "But how can he just go like that? I've been waiting for him to awaken since morning. How can he go without telling me?"

The agonizing information disseminating through her senses like shrapnel, looking at me accusingly, she dashes outside. I am calm from the outside, though in my mind I am a whirlpool of flailing emotions, though the real impact of my loss is yet to hit me. But I know I have to be strong for my daughters, for the world. I find myself viewing the situation as an outsider, not like the death of my dearest husband, the man I loved for thirty-six years.

In reality, I am the one in denial here, not Sanjana. Unlike me, till moments back, she was still unaware of losing her father, not having comprehended the situation at the ICU this morning. Now walking outside, Sanjana brusquely gets behind the wheel of her car, in which we had driven here after lunch. Before anyone can stop her, she drives away angrily. She needs to be alone, disappointed in all of us as she is, mostly in me. I have betrayed her by not telling her of her father's passing earlier, allowing her to hope and pray for his recovery all day. But more so, she feels betrayed by God, for his taking her father away just before her wedding. As for Nayan, she is furious with him too. She never leaves for work without seeing him, whereas he has gone away forever, without telling her. She drives aimlessly for a while, the music on the car-stereo blaring, hoping for it to douse her rage and the din inside her head.

Once in charge of her emotions, after a tirade of angry tears, Sanjana drives back home sombrely, to prepare for her father's funeral. After all, she is my daughter, so she is not going to wallow in self-pity for long. By now Nayan's body has been brought home. She takes her responsibilities headon thereafter, asking his physiotherapist, who is present then for his regular sessions, to change him into new clothes. She hands over a new silk churidar-kurta set she had kept aside for Nayan to wear at her wedding in a few months. Then she organizes the flowers, wreaths, incense and all that is required for the funeral. She goes about it as though organizing a farewell party at short notice. Soon there is a deluge of people at home. Nayan was a popular man due to his congenial nature. Everyone says he looks handsome in the beige silk churidar-kurta, with the matching stole and jutis.

There is no crying and wailing like at some funeral gatherings, only a sombre mood. My face is a mask of absolute composure, as I go about meeting everyone as though invitees to my house. My younger daughter Dipanjana and her husband arrive from Bangalore before 10pm. Nayan and I have no son, so it is assumed that our son-in-law Arun will light his pyre. Our male neighbours, friends and relatives assume they will accompany Nayan's body to the crematorium, while my daughters and I will stay home. It is only when the flower bedecked Hindu Satkar Samiti vehicle with the glass-enclosed, wreath-covered body is about to leave our house front that I firmly announce that my daughters and I will be going to the crematorium as well. I also make it known that it is my elder daughter Sanjana who will ceremonially light her father's pyre and not my son-in-law Arun.

Everyone looks at me shocked, but my firm tone deters any disagreement. Nayan and I have brought up our daughters equal to any son we might have had, and the right to light our funeral pyres is theirs alone. Moreover, I rationalize there must be a reason why her father left us barely months before Sanjana's proposed wedding, without giving her away as a bride. Perhaps it is so she can light his pyre, as his son. According to Hindu rites, a married girl belongs to her husband's gotra or family-line, no longer her parents, so is not entitled to do so. My daughters and I follow Nayan's body in another car to the Nimtala Ghat crematorium in north Kolkata. On reaching, we stick together. As we stand in a queue for the cremation, we discover we are the only women there. Our male relatives, the friend Rahul and Dipanjana's husband Arun, all ask us to wait in the car, but we refuse. We want to be

                    Shuvashree Chowdhury

with Nayan till the very end. There is no way we are leaving him alone in a queue of the dead.

There are a number of bodies lying in line before us and soon others join the file after us. Sanjana holds her father's hand right up to the time it is his turn for the electric cremation. She ceaselessly looks at him, as if trying to register every part of him to memory, afraid she may forget what his face or hands looked like. Dipanjana is going in and out with her husband, perhaps tired and unwell after the long flight and emotional turmoil of the day. Though the men suggest using their contacts to help bypass the queue, we prefer to wait our turn which is after ten bodies. Sanjana insists on keeping Nayan with us for as long as possible, perhaps psychologically preparing herself to let go off him, after the suddenness of his death. She now acutely regrets missing dinner with him last night, attending to an overseas call from a friend at the time. Nayan and I had his last dinner by ourselves, discussing Sanjana's wedding.

The Hindu dead are customarily undressed and covered with only a single white sheath for cremation. But my daughters and I are reluctant to strip Nayan of his dignity even in death. We know how particular he was of his looks and attire. Even people at the crematorium are curious as to who the handsome, well dressed body in such expensive clothes belongs to. The priest does not have the heart to ask us to remove Nayan's clothes. He can see how important it is to us that he be cremated in all the finery, requesting us to only remove his shoes. When it is his turn, dressed as if attending Sanjana's wedding, in her choice of clothes she had bought for the occasion, Nayan is laid on the ground in front of the electric furnaces. A lit splinter is shoved into Sanjana's hand, after she has walked the customary three rounds around his body.

When asked to touch the lit splinter to her father's face, I see her noticeably shudder. In spite of my bringing up my girls to be strong women, I have not prepared her for this moment, which is perhaps the biggest test of a woman's inherent strength. She looks at me, as if to ask me how she can possibly put fire into his mouth. For in her mind, it is not his corpse in front of her, but her father whom she has known and loved lifelong. After a few moments of hesitation, fighting to control her quivering nerves, Sanjana takes the burning splinter close to his face, but involuntarily withdraws her hand. Nayan looks so alive and peaceful in death, she fears burning his soft skin, which by now is turning ashen. Arun and Rahul hold Sanjana's hand firmly from behind, shoving it to touch the fire to his face, as is customary.

After a quick brush of the fire to his mouth, she rapidly withdraws her hand, as if feeling the burn on her own skin. The priest nods sympathetically; already having made many concessions for us, he proceeds to complete the rest of the rites promptly. Sanjana looks on in a daze, seeming physically sick now. Nayan's body is placed inside one of the two electric burners, as we all stare on till he is visible, knowing it is the last we will ever see of his physical form. In a few minutes Sanjana is called down a short flight of stairs, below the furnaces. Before she realizes why she is there, a clay pot is thrust into her unsuspecting palms. Only when asked to walk with the pot to the adjacent river bank, does she realize the pot contains all that remains of her father now.

It is past midnight when all of us quietly follow Sanjana, who is walking in a stupor carrying the pot, to the river bank. As directed, she slowly bends and empties the pot into the fast-flowing river and then drops the pot too. As we watch the ashes scatter and mix with the strong current of the river water in high tide, the empty pot promptly sinking, we shut the lid on our aching emotions. We return home silently, as if in an emotional vacuum, escorted by the men. I walk into my bedroom and lie down for a few brief moments on Nayan's side of the bed, to feel him and smell him again. I can strongly feel his presence. The actual impact of my loss has not yet hit me so I cannot perceive him gone forever. I soon realize I have to pull myself together, be strong for my daughters and set an example.

They walk into my room and we hug each other, holding on for long, quietly sharing our loss, drawing solace from each other. None of us cries, as we are wound up from the events of the day. By now everyone who accompanied us to the crematorium has left. Arun my son-in-law has retired to bed, to leave us women by ourselves in our grief and loss. My daughters want to spend the night in my room, just so I am not alone. But I tell them I would rather be by myself. After they leave, I shut the door and lie back on Nayan's side of the bed. The events of the day come to mind

     Shuvashree Chowdhury

now, as if in a slide-show. I fervently wish I had woken up last night to chat with Nayan as he had wanted. He might have still lived, if I had not forced him into the sleep from which he was unable to awaken, I think wretchedly. I talk aloud to him now, promising to perform the Sampradaan or give Sanjana away as a bride myself at her wedding, as was his last wish.

It is late morning. I have not slept a wink yet, talking to Nayan. There was so much I had to tell him. It is easier to talk now, as he listens to me attentively without complaining of his illnesses. Lately he had been unable to concentrate on anything other than his ailments. But last night as we talked, he was relaxed and smiling, teasing me the way he always used to before, calling me malkin, referring to my being owner of our house. In the following days I feel as if I am sleepwalking, as I go about my routine household jobs. I meet the steady flow of people dropping in to bestow their condolences, though it hardly registers who is coming or going. In my mind, I am in constant dialogue with Nayan. I live along with him in my heart now, as I will lifelong; from where no one can separate us till my death.

I do not bathe my hair the following week, to prevent washing away the sindur. I allow it to fade naturally, gradually getting used to my image without it; having applied it daily for thirty-six years. My daughters prohibit my following any of the restrictions binding on Hindu widows, like wearing white or becoming a vegetarian. However we all abstain from regular food for the next 13 days of mourning. Sanjana resumes work in a few days. Dipanjana waits till after the shradh or final rites on the 13th day, to return to Bangalore. Sanjana and a family priest perform the shradh very elaborately - offering a bed, a mattress, even an umbrella, and whatever material possession is customarily offered to the departed soul to start a new after-life. Both daughters, in keeping with their father's penchant for celebrations, organize an elaborate communal feast in his memory, the day after the shradh. Our house is decorated with subtle coloured imported flowers and lights, and the best caterer is appointed, for a fitting farewell to Nayan.

After a year, on Nayan's first death anniversary, we customarily conduct his final rites over again. This time it is less elaborate than the shradh, but detailed nevertheless. In the coming summer, Sanjana marries the man of her choice. Considering my age, she organizes everything with help from her sister, brother-in-law, the groom and friends. On the wedding day, I play the role of her father to perform the Sampradaan or give-her-away, as well as play host to perfection. In Hindu society, a widowed mother rarely attends the wedding, let alone gives away her daughter as bride. It is the father, or in his absence the closest male relative, who gives the bride away. But Sanjana makes it clear to her groom and him in turn to his family, that there is not going to be a wedding in my absence, and that I will be playing her father's role.

Sanjana has been resolute as Nayan, that in his absence, I will take his place, not an uncle who had no role in her life to merit doing so. At the wedding, we miss Nayan profoundly. He had often dreamt and planned for it, as fathers do. It is with his eternal blessings and presence amidst us that Sanjana is wed. Nayan's soul can now rest in peace. Sanjana's living with me in the year after Nayan's death has helped start me off on life without him. In fact, the day after his passing, she had moved into his usual place beside mine at our eight seater dining table, even sleeping in our room at night. But after her wedding, Sanjana had to leave for her marital home in Delhi. It has been over seven years now. Both my daughters visit me regularly. They see to it I am not alone during festivals.

But in spite of all but me gone, our house doesn't seem empty. Often in the past, I would come home from work and Nayan and the girls would be out. I'd call and they wouldn't answer. Then the house seemed empty. But now the house never seems empty like that. Since Nayan is always away, he's never really away, never anywhere else but home with me. I can vividly see him walking about the house as before. We talk all the time, more than we ever did. I take his advice on everything, keeping him abreast of all the latest developments in our daughter's lives. Though living alone now, I'm never lonely. I live with Nayan's everlasting presence.

                    Shuvashree Chowdhury

9 789386 301994